BAD BOY MILLIONAIRE, THE TYCOON'S TAMING

CATHRYN FOX, LAUREN HAWKEYE

This e-book is licensed for your personal enjoyment only. This e-book may not be re-sold or given away to other people. If you would like to share this book with another person, please purchase an additional copy for each recipient. If you're reading this book and did not purchase it, or it was not purchased for your use only, then please return to your favorite e-book retailer and purchase your own copy. Thank you for respecting the hard work of this author.

ISBN: 978-1-928056-97-3

She's my best friend's kid sister, and I had long ago vowed to keep away. But when she asks me to help make her dream man jealous at her work's annual weekend getaway, I just about lose my Sh$%. She might think she's the ugly duckling, and maybe I teased her too much when she wore pig tails. But Fu%$ I had to do something to hide my real feelings, because she's the hottest girl I know. If some douchebag is too stupid to see the swan, she shouldn't be with him. No, she should be with a guy like me, one who would worship her, bring her to life beneath my hands...my mouth. But I'm a player with a reputation, and she's off limits. Yeah, keeping my hands to myself is what I need to do. Then again, they don't call me Bad Boy Millionaire, because I'm...you know...good.

BRAXTON

"**N**o. No way. Absolutely not. Not in a million fucking years."

I glare at sweet little Eliza Banks as she plants one hand on her hips and blinks up at me with big brown doe-eyes that could melt the paint off my Tesla. Flashing those long lashes might have other guys scrambling to give her anything she wants, but the approach is useless with me. It didn't work when we were kids, and it sure as hell isn't going to work now.

It's probably going to work.

"Come on, Braxton. Help a girl out, already."

I stare at my best friend's kid sister as we stand in the near empty parking lot, halfway between my office complex and my car. I can hardly believe what she's asking me to do, or how tempted I am to say yes. I'd left work tonight, beyond ready to relax this long weekend. The only things on my agenda are a few games of basketball with the guys, a midnight sail in the San Francisco Bay and a drink at my favorite Irish pub with my best bud, Derek—aka Eliza's brother—when he gets home Sunday. The last thing I expected was getting accosted by Eliza before I could reach my car. What she's asking me to do is so ludicrous, so asinine I'd have to be insane to agree. Which begs the question: why am I so goddamn close to saying yes. I must be out of my fucking mind.

Keep it together, Braxton.

Summoning all my willpower, a tactic born out of necessity after setting eyes on Eliza when we were teens and being warned to steer clear of her by her brother, I ask, "What part of *no* didn't you get, Lizard?"

She swats at a mosquito, annoyance flashing in her gorgeous eyes as she looks up at me. "Will you for God's sake stop calling me that? I'm not sixteen anymore."

I'm well aware of that. At sixteen she was a cute girl with freckles spilling from her nose to her cheeks, and I had a huge crush on her. But now, at twenty-six, she's all grown up, and sporting a sexy body full of lush curves and sweet valleys that I'd love to get my hands on...my mouth all over.

Fuck me.

But she was hands off when we were young, and she's hands off now. I made a vow to her brother—my goddamn best friend—never to touch her, and I don't break my promises. I can't blame Derek for not wanting a guy with a reputation like mine touching his kid sister. If I had a little sister, I wouldn't let Derek touch her either. That guy has reached out and touched more women than Hallmark. Yet I'm the one making the headlines. *San Francisco's Most Eligible Bachelor.* But fuck, how am I to say no to those seductive lips and pleading eyes. And when her fucking chest heaves from frustration...Christ.

"No," I say flatly, and grab a fistful of hair as I plot the fastest path to my car. The sooner I get away from her the better. I make a move to go, but she steps in front of me and digs her heels in.

"Braxxxx..." she pleads. The space between us sparks with tension, warning me to get the hell out of there before I do all the dirty things racing around inside my brain, things that would shock a nice girl like Eliza.

"Ask someone else." Fuck, my voice sounds like I've just eaten a bucket of gravel.

"It can't be anyone else." She moves closer and tugs on my lapels, clinging to me like I'm her lifeline. I watch the early evening sun light up the golden flecks in her eyes. Bad move. "It has to be you."

Shit, damn and hell! I'm this close to caving and being *one of those guys*.

Her knuckles brush my chest, and it takes every bit of strength I possess not to back her up, press her against the wall of my office tower and kiss the living fuck out of her. "Why, Eliza?" I grumble, losing patience, mostly with myself, as her scent fills my head. I take advantage of the situation and pull in a deep breath of her. Bad move number two. "Why does it have to be me?"

"Because you're smart, successful, a self-made millionaire and one of the hottest..." She freezes for a second, like she said too much, then continues with, "I mean you're not bad to look at."

I arch a brow. "Hottest?"

Her cheeks turn the prettiest shade of pink. I don't think I've seen her blush before. "Uh...hottest jobs," she explains.

Is that what she was really going to say? I don't think so, and let's be honest—it makes me feel way better than it should that she thinks I'm hot, but no way in hell will I let her know that—or take advantage of it. Instead, I say, "You think being CEO of New Tech Industries is a hot job?"

"Yeah, starting a tech company from your dorm room and turning into one of the world's most successful project management businesses is hot."

"Was that a compliment, Lizard?" I ask, purposely using her nickname to remind me this is my best friend's sister, and that she's never once complimented me over the years. She doesn't even like me, and I can't say as I blame her for that. "Trying to soften me up so I'll agree."

She lifts her chin. "No. Just stating a true fact."

"You've done all right too, you know," I step back a bit, putting enough space between us to get her scent out of my head. "Snatched up by Exact Inc. straight out of Stanford and now, as QA Engineer, you're advancing the 'art and science' of hiring for other businesses. I'm just sorry they got to you first." Her mouth drops open as she blinks up at me. "You might want to close your mouth, Eliza. Before you eat that fly buzzing around us."

"But...wait, what did you just say?"

"I'm always looking for top talent."

"You think..." She goes quiet for a second, glancing away. I can almost see the wheels turning behind her eyes, and then she frowns and shakes her head. "Wait, we're getting off track here. Will you do it, Brax?" she asks, steering us back onto the topic at hand. "Will you help your best friend's sister out?"

"Jesus, Eliza." I clench down on my jaw as a gust of wind whips through the parking lot, sending loose strands of chestnut hair across her face. I curl my fingers and resist the urge to tug them away. Or better yet, drag her to me.

She huffs out her annoyance. "For crying out loud, Brax, I'm not asking to marry you, or anything ridiculous like that."

Marrying me would be ridiculous?

"I just need you to pretend to be my..." she makes a frustrated gesture with her hands. "...significant other for a couple days. How hard could that be?"

Hard. Really fucking hard.

She glances upward and almost—not quite, but almost—rolls her eyes. "Just pretend you're really into me."

"Yeah, to get another guy to notice you." I shove my hands into my pockets, click my molars together. I don't think I like that. In fact, I know I don't. I'll worry about why that is later, but for now..."Do you have any idea how insane that sounds?"

She shrugs, and averts her eyes, but I catch that familiar sadness before she looks away. That sorrow takes me back in time, to when we were teens and she was always overlooked by all the guys. Jesus fucking Christ. Does she not have any idea that she was a swan then, and is a swan today? Any asshole who can't see that doesn't deserve her attention. No, she needs to be with a guy who will worship her, show her how beautiful she is, inside and out.

Of course, back in the day, I didn't help matters either. I was nice to her at first, worshiped the fucking ground she walked on really, and she took that as interest—rightfully so. One night, I was hanging at her place waiting for Derek to get home from soccer practice. She was at the table struggling with a math problem. Since I was always good in math, I sat down to help her. Our legs touched beneath the table, sparking enough electricity to light up the neighborhood in a blackout...for a week straight. She felt it every bit as much as I did, which was why she acted on impulse and leaned in and kissed me.

I laughed at her. The courage that must have taken for her to do that, and I fucking laughed at her, feeding into her belief that she was an ugly duckling. I was a stupid fucking kid, and I was crazy about her, yet I couldn't let anyone know it, especially her. So after that, I started calling her Lizard, and teasing her relentlessly. I needed her to hate me, otherwise I would have taken her to my bed and shown her just how much I wanted her.

"Brax," she says again, quietly. "This is important to me."

Every fucking bone inside my body softens. Yeah, okay, okay. I get it. I owe her one, but pretending to be her boyfriend, and not being able to exercise those boyfriend privileges is a special kind of torture reserved for Hell— exactly where I'll be going I agree to this ask for boyfriend privileges.

"Shouldn't you ask someone you don't hate?" I shoot back, a last-ditch effort.

"Probably, but you're perfect for the role."

I exhale a heavy breath. "What exactly is it that you want me to do?" I hold up a hand when her face lights up. "And that doesn't mean I'm agreeing to this."

Who the fuck am I kidding? It means I'm agreeing.

She folds her hands in front of herself, a smile turning up the corners of her perfect mouth, because yeah, she knows it means I'm agreeing, too. The pleasure on her face, the triumph dancing in her eyes, fucks me over. Goddammit, I love that look on her, can think of another, more pleasurable way, of putting it there.

"We just have to pretend. Maybe a few touches here and there. A kiss too, possibly." She crinkles her nose. "Although I'm not really sure it will come to that. At least I hope not."

"Me too."

Liar.

"We'll set rules and boundaries. You won't have to do anything you don't want to do. Hey, we can even write up a contract, to keep this deal professional."

"Professional boyfriend? You make it sound sordid."

"No, no. I didn't mean that."

Too bad.

"What did you mean?"

"Look, I just mean behind closed doors we can go back to hating each other. In front of everyone we pretend we're lovers. Then, after we get Jason to notice me, we can have a fight about something, and I'll break it off."

We stand there looking at each other for a long moment, a staring contest like when we were kids. She always won those, too. I used to cave just to get a grin from her. "Fine, Eliza, I'll do it, but that doesn't mean I'm going be happy about it."

She crinkles her nose. "You have to at least pretend to be happy about it if we want this to work."

"Is this guy worth it?" I ask. I'd actually like to punch him in the face for not noticing the amazing woman standing before me. Then again, there's a good chance I'll punch him in the face if he does.

Oh, yeah, this ruse is going to work out just fine.

"He is. I really like him."

"Does he know that?"

"No, we work on the same floor, but I'm not on his radar. He's a software engineer," she says, like that explains every-thing. "You know how those guys are?" she adds with a laugh.

"No, I don't."

"Always have their head down, lost is some code."

I arch one brow. "You do know I'm a software engineer too, right?"

"Yeah, right...I...uh, didn't mean that in a bad way."

"Is that another compliment?"

"Just stating a fact."

"You seem to be stating a lot of facts today." The sound of footsteps approaching gains my attention, and I nod to two employees headed to their cars. I wait until they're out of earshot before saying, "And you think if he sees you with me, he'll finally notice you?"

"What I think is, if I show up at my boss's estate for our annual team building weekend..." She pokes me in the chest and waggles her brows. Jesus, I wish she'd quit touching me all ready. "...with *San Francisco's Most Eligible Bachelor* at my side, and he's acting like he's totally into me, well, that's going to get a lot of heads bobbing."

Especially the one between my legs.

"I'll make it worth your while," she says, and my cock stands up to hear more. The little bastard has his own ideas on what he'd like her to do. "I don't expect you to do this without getting something in return."

"Tit for tat, huh?" She has one hundred percent of my attention now. "And what exactly do you plan to give me in return?"

"What do you give a millionaire who has everything?" She taps her chin, and purses her lips.

My head spins with possible scenarios.

"Wait, I know." Her eyes go wide. "How about I get you a date with Valerie? You remember Valerie, don't you?"

Que the screeching breaks as my lecherous imagination skids to a halt. "Your best friend, Valerie?" I say dryly. Why wouldn't I remember her? The two were practically joined at the hip growing up, and now both work in different departments at Exact Inc.

"You two seem to really hit it off at Becca's wedding last month." She nudges me. Enough with the touches, for Christ's sake. "You couldn't keep your eyes off her."

A sound catches in my throat, and I feign a cough. It wasn't Valerie I was staring at, it was Eliza, looking gorgeous, elegant and poised as she stood up for her friend in a curve-hugging, bridesmaid dress. I'd never seen her look more stunning.

"I can get my own dates."

"Well that's true." She crinkles her nose again. "What do you want then?" Before I can answer, and possibly get slapped, her phone pings. "How about you think about it, and let me know later." She fishes her phone from her purse. "It's

Valerie. You sure you don't want that date? She'll be at the retreat this weekend. I can talk to her about it."

"I'm sure."

"Okay, I have to take this." She slides her fingers across the phone, and says, "I'll text you the directions to my boss's place. We can meet there later tonight. He's expecting everyone around nine."

I step into her, and her breath catches as my eyes lock on hers, holding her captive. "I'll pick you up, Eliza. What kind of boyfriend do you think I am, anyway?"

"I...uh...just didn't want to put you out."

I cup her elbow, drag her to me. "Oh, you're putting me out. Let's make that perfectly clear. You're putting me out big time. But if I'm going to pretend that we're a couple for the weekend, you can't expect me to treat you any differently than I would a real girlfriend."

She laughs, but it has a nervous undertone. "I know what you do with your girlfriends. The whole world does. Your antics make newspaper headlines."

I dip my head, lock eyes with her. "Good, then we're on the same page."

ELIZA

"This was a mistake. A huge mistake, Valerie," I say into my phone as I pace inside my condo. I grab the TV remote and flick on the news to drown out the quiet of the place. After growing up in a house with a noisy, rambunctious brother, then living in a Stanford dorm with two other roommates, I thought I'd enjoy the solitude more than I actually do. Sometimes though, it's kind of lonely living here by myself. I can't imagine what it's like for Braxton to be in that big mansion all alone. Then again, he does have a different girl every night to keep him company. Not that I care. He can do whatever he wants.

"Why are you so nervous, anyway?" Valerie asks. "It's just Braxton. You've known him forever."

"I shouldn't have asked him." Of all people, I shouldn't have asked *him*. "I didn't think this through. You should have stopped me."

"Stopped you?" Her snort comes through the phone. "Come on, Eliza. No one can stop you when you put your mind to something."

I toy with the gold hoop in my ear. "Well, you could have at least tried."

She laughs and it reverberates through me. "I didn't even know what you were up to. I'm not a mind reader, you know."

I shake my head. Truthfully, my best friend isn't to blame for this. Two hours ago, I single-handedly lit a fuse that could only blow up in my face. Goddammit, you'd think I'd have learned that impulsive decisions based on gut feelings only lead to trouble— and a whole lot of embarrassment.

"I know," I say and pinch the bridge of my nose. "I'm sorry. Of course, this isn't your fault. It's just another one of my stupid spontaneous decisions."

"What brought it on, anyway?"

"I was driving past Braxton's office complex earlier tonight, saw him in the parking lot, and the idea hit like a bolt of lightning." If only that bolt had killed me! "At the moment, it seemed brilliant, and it actually was, right up until he said he was going to treat me the way he treats his real girlfriends."

"Ummm, lucky you," Valerie whispers, her voice all breathy, her words dreamlike.

I nearly swallow my tongue. "Lucky me? Are you serious?" I pace to my bedroom, grab my bathing suit from my dresser and toss it into my overnight bag. It's a cute pink bikini with a frilly edge. Valerie said it looked great on me but I'm not so sure. I'm used to one-piece suits that don't show a lot of skin. It's not that I'm self-conscious...well, okay maybe I am a little —a hold-over from my youth. I used to be heavier when I was younger, and wasn't comfortable wearing a two-piece except to lay out in the sun on my back deck, alone. Then again, I was never really *alone*. My brother and his best friend were always around. Not that they paid me a lick of attention.

I turn, catch my reflection in my floor to ceiling mirror, and examine my body. I'd shed my work clothes the second I gotten home, and now I'm wearing my comfortable frayed shorts and a T-shirt. Thanks to eating healthier and regular work-outs, I've lost several pounds and like what I see when I look at myself. My legs are long and lean and my breasts appear heavier, a little larger than they actually are, in my Victoria's Secret push up bra. The truth is, even though I've lost the weight and grown curves, I still can't get Jason's attention—or any other guy's, for that matter. Hence my stupid plan.

"Yeah, I'm serious," Valerie says, pulling my thoughts back. "You're one lucky woman and I wouldn't mind being in your shoes. I'd take full advantage of it." She makes some kind of sound, a pleasurable moan, if I had to guess.

"You know his reputation, Valerie. His bedroom has a revolving door." I hold my finger up and swirl it, even though she can't see me.

"Which is why I'm jealous. Imagine having that man's undivided attention for one night, or better yet, the whole long weekend. Ummm, just think about it...three sexy days with those capable, controlling hands touching you, bending you to his will...or over the kitchen counter."

Do not think about it. Do not think about it.

Oh, God, I'm thinking about it.

"That is so not happening. I don't even like the guy," I counter.

Then why are you tingling all over at the thought of "getting bent" by Brax?

"Hey, you don't have to like him to sleep with him. Take advantage of his revolving door, Eliza. Get in, get a little—or a lot—of sex, and then move on. How long has it been, anyway?" she asks.

"Low blow, Valerie."

Great now I'm thinking about Brax and blow in the same sentence. I'm going to kill my best friends.

"I'm asking a serious question, Eliza. How long has it been?"

Too long.

I take a deep breath, and shut down my inner voice—the one loving Valerie's plan. "Remember, I'm using him to get another man's attention. It's Jason I want, not Brax."

"Yeah, I know, but come on, you two will be sharing a room and—"

"Oh, shit..."

"What?"

I stop pacing, and my heart crashes against my ribcage harder. "I never thought that far ahead."

"Ah, you didn't stop to think if you were bringing your significant other, that boss man would put you in the same room? You're consenting adults, Eliza, and it would look odd if you brought your boyfriend to the retreat and asked for two rooms."

As a new kind of panic grips my throat, I slap my hand to my forehead. "I need to call this off." I leave my bedroom and hurry to my front window to make sure Braxton's not here yet. It's been over two hours since I ran into him, and he went home to get changed and packed for a beachside getaway. It's almost eight. He's likely to be here any minute. "Yeah, I'll text him and call it off. He'll be happy about that, actually."

"If you ask me you're making a mistake."

"Which is why I'm calling it off," I blurt out.

"No, Eliza," she says, her voice low and even. "Your mistake would be in calling it off."

I shake my head. Valerie is so wrong about this. "I have to go. I need to text him right now before he leaves his house." I'm about to hang up, but stop when she continues to speak in that low even tone that means she has something serious to say.

"Don't do it. Let him take you to the retreat. Force him to play the doting boyfriend. Don't you think he deserves to be put in that uncomfortable situation as payback for all the times he called you lizard, pulled your hair, or teased you? He deserves this," she says. "If I were you, I'd make him pay, torture him in return."

Why the hell is she trying so hard to talk me in to this?

Surely to God she doesn't think I *like* him.

"I don't *want* him, Valerie," I blatantly point out, in case she's mistaking the reason for me asking *him*, specifically.

You have a lot of guy friends, Eliza, so why exactly did it have to be Brax?

"I know, but think of how you could torture him in the bedroom," she says.

"What are you talking about?"

"Have fun with this situation you got yourself into. Make it work for you and kill two birds, so to speak. While you use him to make Jason stand up and notice, you can get back at Brax for everything he's done to you over the years. Say you do have to share the same room, the same bed—wear something sexy and torture him. Like you said, you don't want him, but you can make him want you, then walk away. Or better yet, use him in other ways while you have him there for the weekend." She coughs out the words, "Dry spell."

"I am not doing any of that." I blurt out, even as my mind goes straight to the hot little nightie I'd bought but never had a reason to wear. I've been so focused on school, and my career, I haven't been with a guy in a long time. Which must be why I'm visualizing Braxton on the bed, and me walking around the room in something suggestive. Yeah, that has to be the reason because I don't want him. Not one little bit.

"Why not?" she asks.

"He doesn't think of me that way."

"How do you know?"

"Because...because he doesn't."

"Weak, Eliza, really weak."

"Okay, fine," I shoot back, changing tactics. "What if I do wear something sexy, and he doesn't even notice. I can't handle that kind of rejection."

Not again.

"You're not sixteen anymore, my friend," she says softly, her tone sympathetic.

I pinch my eyes shut and will the unwanted, hurtful images away. I can't—won't be that girl again. "I'm calling this off."

As soon as the words leave my mouth, my doorbell chimes. Damn, I wanted to catch him before he left his house. I feel bad for dragging him across town, just to break it off, but I guess the proper thing to do would be to tell him in person. I owe him that much respect, right?

"He's here. I have to go."

"I'm on my way too. I guess I'll see you *both* soon," she says. "And remember—get your vamp on and bask in the takedown of Braxton Freeman."

"No, you'll see *me* soon." I slide my finger across the phone to end the call, take a deep fueling breath and walk to my door. I grip the handle, swing it open and when I come face to face with the hottest guy on the planet, every reason I have for ending this stupid ruse slips from my mind.

With one arm behind his back, his dark gaze roams over me, lingers on my breasts, my bare legs, scorching me from the inside out. His eyes close for a brief second, then he's once again there, taking me in, a stare so dark and penetrating air leaves my lungs in a whoosh. I take a faltering step backward, needing the distance to break from his spell.

What the hell? He's looking at me like he wants to eat me alive. Since he's never looked at me like that before, it has to be all part of the act, getting himself in the role of my lover?

A small smile tugs at the corners of his mouth, and I brace myself, expecting some smart-ass comment, something insulting about my clothes, or my hair, but instead he gives an appreciative nod, blazing heat still in his eyes as they leisurely travel back to mine.

"I...uh. About this weekend..." I begin, needing to get my head on straight. He's acting, nothing more, and I'd be wise to remember that.

"For you," he says and pulls his arm from behind his back to hand me a beautiful bouquet of flowers.

I stare dumbly at the stunning arrangement of wildflowers clutched in his fist. He could have produced anything from behind there—the evening newspaper, carry-out pizza, a water gun to squirt me between the eyes, but...he brought me flowers? Not once in my life has anyone brought me flowers. I reach out and touch the velvety petal of a daisy with the tips of my fingers.

"Are you going to let them wilt?"

The softness of Brax's voice brings my gaze up and if I'm not mistaken, he looks almost as uncertain as I am surprised. My hands shake a little when I take the bouquet from his. I hope he doesn't notice. It would give him one more thing to tease me about.

"I'll put them in some water," I say, and hurry to my kitchen. I take one quick glance at the man in my doorway, then grab a vase from my cupboard and fill it with water. My brother's best friend had grown up wealthy, and was always very generous with his money, so the flowers might mean nothing to him, but they mean a lot to me. More than they should, probably. Then again, maybe they do mean something to him. I mean, how many times did he want to pay Derek's way in life? My dad was a powerhouse attorney, and he left us when we were young. He provided Mom with enough money for us to get a good education at a private school—where my brother met Brax—but mom taught us the value of money, and both Derek and I held down jobs through high school and college. There were times though, I had a feeling Brax was embarrassed by his wealth, always wanting to do more for us. But he worked hard to get where he is today, and he should be proud of that.

I step back into the front entrance way, and find him exactly where I left him. "You didn't have to do this," I say quietly, my mind taking another trip down memory lane, to the Christmas when I was sixteen and wanted a gift certificate for the spa to get a mani/pedi. All my friends from school were getting one. Mom told me straight up we couldn't afford to spend money on frivolous things, but miraculously, on Christmas morning, the gift certificate was under the tree. It was a surprise to all of us, and to this day—even though he vehemently denies it—I had a feeling Brax had everything to do with it.

Exuding a cool control, he tilts his head, and arches a brow. The uncertainty I thought I'd seen before was gone. Brax was back to his old, cocksure self. "Didn't we already establish that I'd be treating you the same way I treat every other woman I take out?"

"About that..." I begin, when he takes a measured step toward me, his clean soapy smell messing with my ability to form a coherent sentence. My gaze drops, takes in his t-shirt, the way it clings to hewn muscles my hands suddenly want to touch.

End this now, Eliza. Before you do something stupid, like actually try to kiss him again, only to get laughed at.

He shoves one hand into the pocket of his khaki shorts, and I take pleasure in the way they ride lower on his hips. Brax in a suit is one thing, but this relaxed version...it's totally messing with my ovaries. Truthfully, I don't understand it. Braxton is rich, successful, gives to charities, and is, by far, the hottest guy I've ever set eyes on. He grew up in a loving family, with two parents, never having been abandoned by one—like Derek and me. He's never been subjected to the pain behind divorce, or what it does to the kids. So why again is he single, leaving one girl for the next, with no hints of settling down in the foreseeable future? I mean, I get why I'm not interested in marriage. I watched my rich father get bored with his wife and two small kids, only to move on to the next pretty, young thing. It's a pattern he still perpetuates —the pattern of the rich, I guess. Brax might not be married, but his rotating door is a sure sign he's a carbon copy of my father.

"We should get going." Brax says, pulling me back to the moment at hand.

"*...use him in other ways while you have him there for the weekend.*"

As Valerie's words ping around in my brain, a bolt of lust curls through my blood. But what if I did seduce him and he laughed at me again? I could never, ever live through that humiliation again.

You're not a chunky sixteen-year-old anymore, Eliza.

I bend down to pick up my purse, needing something to occupy my hands as I think about how to tell him the weekend is off, without coming across as crazy, after begging him to do this for me. When I stand and turn back to Braxton, I don't miss the blast of heat sizzling in his eyes as they slide down my body. My pulse jumps in my throat. Would he look at me like that if he weren't interested in a little bedroom fun? Then again, I am his best friend's kid sister. Would that stop him?

No. No. No. Don't go there, Eliza. He's acting, and you need to end this now.

"I...my..."

"Your overnight bag?" he asks.

"Uh, it's in my bedroom."

He moves past me, his hard body brushing mine as he walks down the hall and disappears into my bedroom.

"What are you doing?" I ask and hurry after him.

"Getting your bag."

"I'm quite capable of getting my own bag." I plant my hands on my hips and follow him to the door of my room. I don't dare go in. The less time I spend in a bedroom with him the better. I find him staring into the bag I had left open on my bed, and at the little bikini I'd tossed into it earlier.

He clears his throat. "Do you have everything you need?"

End this now!

I open my mouth to do just that, and instead find myself saying, "Yes."

"Good."

He's about to zip up the bag up, but I say, "Wait." I walk to my dresser, and pull out my sexy black negligee. I drop it into the bag, and Brax goes perfectly still, the air in the room charging, taking up space between us.

He thumbs the material. "Black lace," he murmurs, his voice so low I have to strain to hear it.

"In case our ruse works, and Jason finally takes notice," I say, a reminder to him—okay, to myself—that we're not enjoying a lovers' weekend away. This is about him helping me, nothing else, and I am going to kill my best friend for putting such crazy thoughts into my head. Brax doesn't want me and I don't want him. We don't even freaking like each other.

His head lifts, and dark eyes meet mine. "Is that everything?" he asks through clenched teeth, his eyes a shade darker, piercing...almost angry.

"I think so." He shoulders the bag, and I shake my head. "I can carry my own bag."

"Yes, but you're with me now, and things will be done differently."

"Are you always this bossy with your dates?" I ask. He's always had a bossy, controlling side to him. I've just never been subjected to it before. Well, maybe that's not entirely true. There was that time he tossed me over his shoulder and hauled my ass out of the party Valerie and I snuck off to. Everyone was drinking, things started to get rowdy and a fight broke out. He showed up out of nowhere, and removed both Valerie and me from a bad situation. I had no idea how he found out where we were, and we never talked about it again.

"Depends on the date." He walks past me and I follow him out the door. I lock up and he's standing on the passenger side of his Tesla when I reach the driveway. He opens the door for me, and I slide in.

"I had no idea you were such a gentleman," I say.

"You're my girlfriend, Eliza. There are a lot of things you're going to find out about me this weekend."

"Technically I'm not your girlfriend."

"There will be no technicalities this weekend. It's all in, or nothing. As soon as you agree to that, we'll get going."

He stands over me, hovering close, and my heart leaps. "You're saying it's your way or the highway?"

He bends, and his handsome face is close to mine. There isn't an ounce of humor in his eyes when they lock on mine. "Yes."

Nervousness bubbles up inside me, as I mull that over. "You mean when we have an audience, right? We go all in for the audience? But behind closed doors—"

"What will it be, Eliza?"

This is your chance to end it, Eliza. He's giving you an out.

I should climb out of the car right now. I really should. So what the hell is stopping me? Could it be because I really want a chance with Jason? Or could it be something else entirely.

"Just so you know," he begins, his voice softer. "I'd never put you in a situation or ask you to do anything that makes you uncomfortable."

"Oh," I say. Is that why he thought I hesitated? "Actually, I never thought you would."

His jaw unclenches, a new softness about him. "Then you trust me?"

I toy with the handle of my purse. Trust him? Yeah, I trust him. The question is, can I trust myself around him? "Yes," I say. "To both your questions. It's all in, or nothing and I trust you."

"Good."

He closes my door, and I shift restlessly in my seat as he climbs into the car. I try to settle myself as I pull up Google maps and give him directions. We drive mainly in silence, my thoughts going too fast to remain on any one topic. Half an hour later, we reach my boss's beachside mansion.

"Nice place," he says.

"Not as nice as yours," I blurt out without thinking.

"You like my house, Eliza?"

I shrug and examine the cars in the lot, searching for Jason's. "Sure."

He taps his thumb on the steering wheel. "I was actually thinking about selling it."

My head jerks around. "You're kidding me."

His brow furrows as he angles his head my way. "No, why?"

"It's beautiful, with a great infinity pool, overlooking the bay. Why would you ever want to sell it?"

With his concentration back on the road, he slows the vehicle and puts on his signal light. "It's kind of obnoxious, don't you think?"

"Obnoxious?"

The muscles in his jaw bunch as I glance at him, but he turns his face from me. Not before I catch the embarrassment in his eyes. Others might not see it, but there are things this man can't hide from me—never could.

"I think...it's just...a house like that for one person. All those rooms and space. It's kind of much." I frown, hating that he feels guilty for his wealth. He shrugs one shoulder, and goes on to justify his decisions. "I bought it on a whim, you know. Interest rates were down, right time for an investment property." He casts me a quick glance, and I hate how he cares so much about what others think.

"It's a beautiful property and you deserve it," I say.

A smile touches his mouth. "Yeah?"

"Yeah, and believe me, I know all about spontaneous decisions. Sometimes they aren't always the best choice, but you never know. Maybe someday you'll have a big family with lots of kids and fill all those rooms." Without thinking, I slide my hand across the seats, close it over his and give a reassuring squeeze. But the second I do, his gaze lifts to mine—a gaze so hot and so intense it fires every nerve in my body.

Okeydokey...

I reach for the door handle, needing a reprieve from the storm inside my body. I'm about to flee when he leans into me. "Eliza," he whispers, and I practically jump out of my shoes, when he captures my hand, and holds me in place.

"Yeah?" I ask, trying my best to pull off casual.

"Listen, Eliza. If you want to pull this off, you're going to have to stop jumping every time I touch you. I get it, you don't like me, but you're going to have to pretend you do in front of co-workers."

"I know," I say, feeling far too breathless and ridiculous for my stupid body's reactions to this man's *innocent* touch.

He touches my hair, coils it around my finger, and I swear to God, the muscles between my legs clench.

"Take a deep breath," he says softly. I do as he says, then let the air out slowly. When I glance back at him, he's smiling. "Better?"

"Better," I say.

"One more thing." His hand slides to my neck, and his fingers clasp gently as he slowly caresses my flesh with his thumb.

"What's that?"

"I'm going to have to kiss you."

Holy shit!

"I don't think that's necessary, Brax." Jesus, why do I have to sound like I just ran up eight flights of stairs.

The muscles in his jaw clench, and air gusts from his flaring nostrils. "Oh, I think it's very necessary if you want us to look like lovers. We should at least have the kiss nailed, right?"

"Yeah, but..."

"When I sign on to do something, Eliza, whether I want to or not, I give it my full, one-hundred percent. Anything worth doing is worth doing right. I'm not going to make a fool of myself by doing this half-assed, and getting called out. I thought you would have known that about me by now."

I do.

Cripes, I don't think I've ever seen Brax so intense before. I get he's trying to help me and this all part of the act, but holy hell, the man deserves an academy award.

"I...well, I suppose. If you—"

He leans into me and his mouth steals my words. My body ignites. My eyes slide shut but I quickly open them again. Forget all the angst between us in the past; I have to see Brax's face as he kisses me. My chest rises and falls with shallow breaths and his clean soapy scent swirls around me.

His fingers delve into my hair, tugging, controlling, confident in his touch as our mouths move, and tongues tangle.

He slides his tongue in farther, a slow exploration, testing, tasting, discovering with a deeper curiosity. A moan I have no control over catches in my throat, and his kisses deepen, expand, our tongues tangling as curiosity changes to a single-minded hunger that I've only ever read about.

This is what I've been missing?

He inches back, severs the intimate moment and not only am I breathless, I'm speechless—dying from need I never even knew existed, until this second...this man.

Oh this is so not good.

"Well?" he asks. "Do you think we'll be able to pull it off?"

I take more breaths, praying my brain starts working and I can form a coherent sentence. "That was..." How do I put in to words that the man kisses like a freaking God? If I didn't know better, I'd think he was kissing me like he meant it? But of course, I do know better. Right?

"Awful?" he asks.

What? I was awful?

How mortifying!

I swallow down the pain and remind myself it shouldn't matter that he thinks I'm an awful kisser. It's Jason I want. Not him. I repeat that to myself until it sinks back in. "Yeah, awful." I make a face like I'd just eaten a bucket of worms. "Horrible."

"I think tonight, behind closed doors, we're going to have to give that a whole lot more practice if we have any chance in hell of making this work."

OMFG.

I am so in over my head here.

3

BRAXTON

It took everything in me, and I mean every fucking ounce of willpower I possessed, to break that kiss, when all I wanted to do was drag her into the back seat and fulfill all my teenage fantasies—with the one girl who always starred in them.

Seriously though, what the fuck was I thinking? Kissing her was a dick move, and I'm old enough to know better. I might have been lying when I said it was awful, but I wasn't lying when I said anything worth doing was worth doing right. But did I really have to kiss her? Fuck no. I *wanted* to kiss her—wanted to kiss her long before she ever pressed her lips to mine when we were teens. Today, I simply took advantage of the situation. Selfish bastard that I am.

A tortured sound, a half laugh, half moan catches in my throat as she hurries from the car, like she's being chased by monsters. Perhaps she is. It's dark, but the floodlight spilling over the huge stone driveway gives sufficient light for me to stare at her sweet ass, so round and firm in those daisy dukes, just begging to be squeezed by my hands, kissed by my lips. I shake my head to get my shit together. Good thing Derek is in New York, consulting with an architect firm for the big project he'd been hired to oversee. Because one look at me, and he'd know what was going through my dirty mind. I scrub my hand over my chin. My best friend has one hell of a punch and I'd hate to be on the receiving end of it.

But kissing Eliza again would be so worth it.

Then again, I can't risk losing the best friend I've ever had, the one guy one who always cared about the real me and not what I had in my bank account. People treat me differently when they find out who I am, that I'm the son of real estate mogul Phillip Freeman, and made it big in the tech world. But neither Derek, nor his sweet sister, ever let my wealth stand between us, or ever judged me for it, and believe me, I'm always being judged.

Eliza hurries to the back of the car, and I catch her reflection in the rear-view mirror as she waits for me to get our bags from the trunk. I slide my tongue over my bottom lip, and still taste her there. Cotton candy and all things sweet. Great. How the fuck am I going to get that kiss out of my head, especially when we're in the same bedroom tonight, with her using me to catch another guy?

Motherfucker.

My nostrils flare as I think about the douchebag who's too stupid to see what's right in front of him. He'd better be worth all this shit. I climb from the car, press the fob to lock it, and pop the trunk. Eliza glances around, quick, jerky flashes of her lashes as she takes in the empty vehicles lit up under the lights. If I had to guess, I'd say that kiss fucked her up as much as it did me.

"It looks like everyone is here," she says, her chest rising and falling quickly, her expression a mix of nervousness and excitement.

Ah, okay, so now I get it. Jason is here, and that's why she's on edge. It wasn't the kiss after all. Which is a good thing. I am doing her a favor—she doesn't even like me—and I shouldn't be thinking about sex.

What do you want in return?

Don't go there, dude.

I grab her bag and she holds her hand out for it. I snarl at her and toss it over my shoulder. "Lead the way," I say as I grab my duffle and shut the trunk.

She turns and I follow her along the stone pathway leading to the backyard. Noises and splashes reach our ears as we round the corner. I do a quick scan, take in the people swimming, lounging near the edge of the pool or sitting at one of the many tables with a view of the ocean, sipping champagne. I'd say outside of us there are about twenty people gathered.

Eliza opens the gate and I hold it for her to enter. I step through and when it bangs and clicks shut behind us, a few eyes turn our way. I take in her co-workers. Most are male, which isn't unusual in the tech industry

"Eliza," a man in his fifties says as he hurries toward us. Water drips from his board shorts, and he slows when he sees me. The joy in his eyes at seeing Eliza turns to shock when they glance my way.

"Braxton, this is my boss, Richard. Richard, this is—"

Richard holds his hand up to stop her. "No introduction needed, Eliza. I know exactly who this young man is."

"Nice to meet you, Richard," I say and he gives me a power shake.

I return it and he winks. "I had no idea you two were..." He pauses, like he's not sure what to say.

"Dating," I say and step into the role Eliza asked me to play. I put my arm around her and tug her against me. She stiffens at first, but then I gaze at her, a smile on my mouth. "You might have snagged her straight out of Stanford, utilizing this beautiful brain of hers for the better part of the day, which I'm not too happy about, by the way," I say and we both laugh. I let my chuckle die down, and put my hand on the side of her cheek. "But I get her the rest of the time." A pause to let that sink in, and then, "I guess we both know a good thing when we see it."

A warm blush crawls into Eliza's cheek, and I bend down, press a soft, barely there kiss to her open mouth. It takes her by surprise, so I linger there for a moment, wait for her to pull herself together.

"Good?" I whisper. She nods and I straighten.

"I think I'd better show you to your room," Richard says with a chuckle. "Eliza, I put you in the same one as last year. You loved the view so much."

"Thanks, Richard. I really appreciate it." She jerks her thumb toward me. "And I hope you don't mind that I just sprung Braxton on you like this."

"Are you kidding me? Partners and spouses are always welcome, and I am so looking forward to getting to know him, maybe even learning about his business practices. As long as he's not here to scope out any of my team," he says teasingly, but with a hint of seriousness. I can't blame him. Competition is fierce in Palo Alto, but I would never poach from his company. He's been good to Eliza, which makes him A-Okay in my books.

"Wouldn't dream of it," I say and he relaxes a bit. "Eliza tells me you have annual bonding retreats for your top-level management. I think it's a great idea."

His face lights up. "Coming from you, that's a huge compliment."

As he leads us through the crowd, he stops to do a few introductions. Beside me, Eliza shifts from one foot to the other. I follow her gaze, and spot her best friend Valerie talking to some guy who has his face buried in his phone. Jesus, that had better not be Jason. There is nothing I hate more than a guy who pays more attention to his phone than a woman making conversation with him—and that's coming from a guy who built his own tech company from the ground up. It's just plain fucking rude.

Richard stops to introduce us to his wife, a very motherly woman with blond hair and inquisitive eyes. "This is my lovely wife, Michelle."

Richard is about to tell her exactly who I am, when I hold my hand out and say, "It's just Braxton."

Richard nods, like he totally gets where I'm coming from and I suppose he does. "My goodness, Eliza," she says and nudges her. "Where have you been hiding this one?"

Eliza laughs. "Brax and I go way back, actually. It just took the right situation for us to realize how much we liked each other." She smiles up at me and for a brief moment I almost believe she might actually like me, but I'm sure I'm wrong.

"I can tell how much you do." She puts her hands up, like she's warming them near a fire. "I can feel the sparks from here." She gives a sigh of longing. "There is nothing like young love."

Richard laughs. "Come on then, let's get you settled. It's a warm night. I'm sure you'll want to go for a swim and have a drink before lights out."

"Lights out?" I say. "Sounds like you run a pretty tight ship."

"Busy day tomorrow," he explains. "Very competitive group here, and we all need a little shut-eye."

He leads us into his house and I study his mansion. Unlike mine, his has a woman's touch. There are paintings, and flowers, and floral sofas. Mine, well, it's decorated in every shade of gray you could think of. Despite what Eliza thinks, I really should sell it. The house would be better utilized by a big family—one I never plan on having.

I might have grown up with two parents, but they were

never there for me. Dad was always working and Mom was busy with her charities. From the outside it might have looked like the perfect family, but it was a very different story behind closed doors. I'd been in private schools since I was a child and had a no-nonsense nanny at home before I was shipped off to a boarding school in my teens. I was given opportunities others weren't, and I'm truly grateful for that. But there is a part of me that missed out on being a kid, missed out on quality time with my parents. How could I ever get married, or bring a child into this world when I have no idea how to be a husband, or a father? Jake and Eliza might have grown up with only a mother, but she gave them —and me—the love of two parents. I'm so grateful for that. And of course, that's another reason to keep my hands off Eliza. They all deserve that much from me.

We head up the wide stairs, and when we reach the top, Richard points the way, then leaves us to get settled.

"I like him," I say to Eliza and that seems to make her happy.

"I really like the culture at Exact. It's a great place to work."

"Doesn't sound like I'll be stealing you away anytime soon," I say, and give her a little nudge. Okay, now who's the one doing all the touching?

"You weren't serious about that anyway," she says, as she opens the door.

"Hell yeah, I was. I won't poach, but I would have hired you in a minute." I snap my fingers and follow her into the room. She glances at me over her shoulders. "You're brilliant," I add, and mean every word of it.

"Is that a compliment?"

"Just stating a fact," I say and that brings on a grin, but her grin fades as she glances around the room.

"One bed," she murmurs under her breath. I'm about to

tell her I'll take the floor when someone screeches from outside. We both walk to the window to see Valerie break through the water, coughing and sputtering and shoving her wet hair from her face. Her eyes are murderous when she glances at some guy standing on the edge of the pool laughing.

"I think someone just dunked her," Eliza says. Her head jerks my way. "Promise me you won't do that?"

I take in her big brown eyes, the panic backlighting them. I step closer to her, and my knuckles brush hers. "Eliza…" I begin, as her chest rises and falls rapidly. "You know I wouldn't."

She looks back out the window again. "I don't like…"

"I know." I still feel like shit for the time I tossed her into my pool when we were kids. We were going through a heat wave, and Derek brought her to my house one Saturday afternoon, after they'd both gotten off work. She was wearing a cover-up over her bathing suit and for a long time she just watched us in the pool. I was in the house grabbing us all drinks when she finally took it off and decided to have a swim. She was testing the water, when I spotted her in this cute one-piece that showed a curvy body. Fuck, she was hot. My dick grew as I watched her, and I knew if I didn't do something soon, get Derek's attention off me as I handed him his drink, he'd see my erection. So in a dumb, juvenile stunt, I picked her up and tossed her in.

Bad move.

She didn't come up right away, and I jumped in after her. Little did I know she hit her foot on the side of the pool going down. Fuck, I still hate myself for that. She spent the rest of the summer in a boot, all because I was trying to hide a fucking boner. Now she has a fear of the water.

Well done, dude. Well done.

"Come on, let's get changed and get out there before we give everyone the wrong idea," she says, breaking the quiet.

"Or the right idea," I say and put our bags on the bed. She stands there for a moment, hands on her hips, lips puckered.

"I'll get changed in the bathroom." She points to the closed door.

"Okay, but knock before you come out, I might not be decent."

What the hell are you doing, dude?

"I will," she says quickly and unzips her bag. She pulls out her suit and a cover-up and darts into the bathroom.

I tug off my t-shirt, and pull on a pair of board shorts. Eliza might not be planning a swim, but I sure as hell need something to cool me off. I sit on the bed and wait for her. I bounce a little on the comfy mattress to test it. Nice. Not that I'll be experiencing a good night's sleep tonight. No, the only place I'll be sleeping is on the floor. If I have to share a bed with her, it's game over for me. A guy only has so much willpower.

"Brax," Eliza says, followed by a knock, through the closed bathroom door. "You decent?"

My body is but my mind is far from it.

"Yeah, I'm good."

The door creaks open, and Eliza comes into the bedroom dressed in a knee-length bathing suit cover-up. It hugs her curves and hides her gorgeous body. Goddammit, who'd have thought that I'd be jealous of a cover-up. Needing a distraction before I grab her, toss her onto the bed and climb on top, I clear my throat and walk back to the window. I stand there for a moment, let my gaze rake over her co-workers.

"Which one is Jason?" I ask.

She pads quietly across the room, and I listen to the way her breathing has changed at the mention of Jason. Her body brushes mine as she stands at the window, and I swallow down the moan rising in my throat. She scans the pool area, lit by a dozen lights, and then she points.

Son. Of. A. Fucking. Bitch.

"Right there. He's doing something on his phone." She gives a strange little laugh. "Always working. I guess that's why I can't get his attention."

Her eyes dart to mine, and that's when I get it. Little Eliza—Lizard—still feels like that overlooked girl from our youth. Jesus fucking Christ, she doesn't get it. Doesn't get that she's the most beautiful woman at this party and a guy like Jason isn't worthy of her. I said it before and I'll say it again, she needs a guy who's going to worship the ground she walks on.

A guy like me.

Whoa, don't go there.

"We'd better get down there and see what we can do then," I say, and try not to sound as pissed off as I feel.

"Game on," she responds, her eyes wide.

I follow her out of the bedroom and we retrace our steps until we're outside. More introductions are made and when we reach Jason, who still has his nose in his phone, it's all I can do not to knock his teeth out. Eliza is speaking and he's completely fucking ignoring her.

"Jason," she says again, and I slide my arm around her waist, pull her against me, mainly to occupy my hands before I do something I can only regret later.

"What?" he finally asks and looks up at us. He runs his hand through his mess of hair. When was the last time he used a comb? Then again, with a scrubby beard and baggy clothes, he has that shabby look going for him that the girls seem to love. Personally, I prefer to keep my hair short and wear clothes that fit. Still, even I know a good looking guy when I see one. I'm just finding flaws because I don't like him.

"I'd like you to meet Braxton, he's my—"

Before she can finish the sentence, Jason is on his feet. "Everyone knows who Braxton is," he says, cutting her off, and it pisses me off a bit. I know her boss interrupted her, and not in a mean way, but I would have liked for Jason to at least let her finish speaking. She is, after all, here to get him to notice her.

He holds his hand out, and his impressive height allows us to stand eye to eye—his are the same color of blue as mine— and I take that moment to size him up. He obviously works out, and under those loose clothes, he's probably cut. I suppose I can understand Eliza's attraction to him. Truthfully, if he shaved his beard, and dressed properly, we could easily pass as relatives.

"Braxton Freeman. In the flesh," he says, a huge smile on his face as I shake his hand. "I can't believe I'm breathing the same air as you." He shakes his head. "What are you doing here?"

As we shake, I lecture myself on playing nice. I don't want to mess this up for Eliza. Right? "I'm here with, Eliza," I say. "She invited me for a weekend getaway."

For one shocked moment he stares at me, disbelief written all over his face. Then he shakes his head, and turns to Eliza. He gazes at her, giving her the once over, looking at her in a whole new light. Shit.

"Eliza, I had no idea you knew, Braxton. What other connections have you been keeping from me?"

"I'm not keeping anything from you," she says.

"Do you know how long I've been wanting to meet *the* Braxton Freeman?" He turns to me. "You're a legend in this industry. Started your own business from the ground up. Forbes Top 30 Under 30." He wags his brow. "San Francisco's Most Eligible Bachelor."

I hug Eliza tight. A possessive move, I know. If I keep

that up, no one will believe the breakup. "Brax and I go way back," she says and puts her hand on my chest. Her fingers splay, and I place my hand over hers and hold it there.

It takes Jason a second to put it together. "Oh, wait you two are a—"

"Couple," I say, and lean in and give her a kiss right on her open mouth.

Jason clears her throat. "Wow, I had no idea."

"How about a swim?" I ask Eliza.

She smiles up at me, and I keep one eye on her and one on Jason. "Love to."

"Talk to you later, Jason," I say and lead her away.

"Yeah, I'd love to talk to you," he says eagerly. "Let's get a drink later."

I lower my voice and put my mouth near Eliza's ear. "So that's him, huh?"

She nods. "He seems to really like you."

"And his phone," I say. Shit. I'm here to help Eliza win the attention of this douchebag, not point out all his flaws, or come right out and tell her he's not good enough for her. She's a grown woman who can make her own choices and that would be a dick move on my part.

At the edge of the pool, Eliza peels off her cover-up and I nearly bite off my fucking tongue. I glance around, take note of the eyes on her. Jason's gaze slowly lifts from his phone, and they move over Eliza appreciatively. Anger flares through me. What? She wasn't good enough for him until he saw her with me.

Cool it, Brax, that was the whole of idea of the ruse.

Yeah, but that still doesn't mean I have to like it. I dive straight into the deep end as Eliza finds the stairs and wades in. I swim the length of the pool under water and when I come up, I find her talking to Valerie. I have no idea what they're saying, but from their glances I'm guessing it's something about me.

I swim over to them, catch the last of Valerie's words. *"Use him."*

"Hey, Valerie," I say. "Nice to see you again."

"It's been a long time. I'm so glad Eliza invited you."

"Yeah, me too," I say and step behind Eliza. I slide my hands around her body and clasp my fingers around her stomach.

Eliza cranes her neck and whispers, "She knows."

I still don't let go of her. "It's almost like you two really are lovers," she says with a wink.

Eliza breaks from my arms. "We're not."

"I know that." She splashes water at Eliza, then turns to me. "Hey, Brax, I have to go to my cousins' wedding next month. My parents are driving me crazy about getting a guy and settling down. Maybe you could do me a solid and step into the role of loving boyfriend to get them off my back. I mean, you two will be staging a breakup at the end of the weekend and you'll be single again."

My gaze slides to Eliza, who is staring at her best friend. Her eyes are wide, her mouth dropped open. "Valerie, you can't be serious?"

"It'll cost you," I say.

"Oh, and what is this costing Eliza?"

I step back into Eliza. "We haven't negotiated that yet."

"Oooh, Eliza. You should have gotten those terms settled before you started this." She puts her finger on my chest and give a little push, but I don't budge. "Don't you know he's a skilled negotiator?" She grins at Eliza. "Brax always gets what he wants."

My gaze moves over Valerie's face, examining the small smirk turning up the corners of her mouth. She's right, of course. I'm an expert negotiator and always get my way. I'm also able to read my opponents, which gives me the edge up. As I read Valerie's body language and expressions, I can't help but wonder what kind of game she's playing. She doesn't want me at that wedding any more than I want to be there. If I didn't know better, I'd think she was trying to get a rise out of her best friend, a reaction of sorts. But Valerie and Eliza go way back and she of all people should hate me as much as Eliza. Should want me as far away as possible—from both of them.

A splash sounds and Jason surfaces close to us. I move close to Eliza, and she brushes a wet strand of hair from her face as Jason zeroes in on her.

"Brax, come on out and have a drink with me," Richard says, from the outdoor bar area.

My fingers curl under the water when Jason says something stupid to Eliza and she laughs in return. Fuck, I hate that guy. And why the hell is she so nervous around him? I've never seen this side of her before. She's a confident woman with a beautiful brain and body, a girl who can hold her own in an organization filled with men. She must really fucking like him if she's acting all weird and out of sorts. Wait, has she never been intimate with a guy before—is she completely inexperienced when it comes to dating? Has she never been touched? The vision of another man putting his hands on my sweet Eliza sends rage through me.

My Eliza.

Jesus, get it the fuck together, all ready.

"Coming?" I ask Eliza.

"I..." she begins, but Valerie waves me away.

"Why don't you go ahead. Eliza is in good hands here," she says with a grin.

And therein lies the problem, because the only hands I want on Eliza are mine.

4

ELIZA

"Night," I say to Valerie and the others as they all head down the hall to their respective rooms. I follow Brax inside our bedroom, close the door behind me and press my back to it, all the while trying to keep my eyes off his rock-hard body as he confidently saunters to the bed like he owns the place.

Put a shirt on already.

He reaches into his duffle bag and pulls out a dry shirt. I stare at his beautiful hard body, mesmerized as he shrugs into the soft cotton, then, lacking any sort of modesty, reaches for the band on his board shorts.

"What are you doing?" I ask quickly, my voice practically bordering on hysteria.

He pauses, and casts a quick glance my way. "Changing. What does it look like?"

What the hell? I spin around and face the door to give him a measure of privacy. Truthfully, he seems pissed off about something, but I have no idea why or what happened to put him in a shitty mood.

"Couldn't you have at least waited until I wasn't looking?" I shoot back.

"Hey, I'm your boyfriend." He scoffs, an annoyed little sound, and this time I'm certain he's upset about something. "At some point we should see each other naked, don't you think?" he says.

"No, I don't."

The rustle of his clothes reaches my ears as he dresses, and I try not to visualize him naked, those big hands of his on my body as we roll around on the bed.

What the hell, Eliza?

"I'm decent," he says, and I turn back around to find him digging in his bag again. His jaw is clenched tight, the muscles rippling as he tosses half the contents on the bed in search of God knows what.

"Is everything okay? Did I do something to piss you off?"

He takes a huge breath, lets it out slowly, then pinches the bridge of his nose and his taut body relaxes slightly. "No, it's not you."

"Then who. Did my boss say something to upset you?"

Deep line cut into his forehead as he frowns. "No...I'm just...I'm just tired is all."

He digs back in his bag again, and I take that moment to look him over, let my gaze rake over his shirt and jeans. "Is that what you're wearing to bed?"

"Yeah. Why?"

I fold my arms, the air conditioning chilling my body despite the bathing suit cover-up I'm wearing. "Jeans don't seem like they'd be very comfortable to sleep in."

He arches a brow, the corners of his mouth turning up in that familiar cocky grin, and while I always hated him teasing me, I prefer this mood to his last. "I can take them off if you want."

"Very funny."

"I was being totally serious," he says, the teasing edge gone from his voice. He gives a shoulder roll. "I just thought you'd be more comfortable being in this bedroom with me if I were fully dressed."

My insides soften. Sometimes he can be so damn sweet and thoughtful it makes me forget why I don't like him. Wait, this is Brax, the guy who tortured me relentlessly and deserves to be paid back.

"You're right. Good call," I say.

He turns his back to me, showcasing a tight ass in a pair of low riding jeans. Jesus. I link my fingers together as they itch to sculpt his perfect body. Lord, when I came out of the bathroom earlier tonight, and saw him sitting on the bed in nothing but his board shorts, I nearly swallowed my tongue. When we were teens, I'd seen him shirtless of course. But holy hell, over the years his muscles had lengthened and thickened, filled out in all the right places.

He pulls a toothbrush and tube of paste from his bag, finally finding what he was looking for, then stuffs all the clothes back inside. He turns my way and sets his bag on the nearby chair. I let my gaze drop, sliding from a well-defined six pack to take in the very impressive bulge behind his zipper.

Cripes, stop looking at his crotch already.

"Everything okay, Eliza?" he asks, and my gaze jerks back up to his. Dammit, I hope he doesn't think I was checking him out and get the wrong idea...or the right idea.

Good God.

"Ah...just tired, too. But I'm going to jump in the shower, rinse the chlorine off," I say quickly, a desperate ploy to get away from him.

"Okay."

I hurry to the bathroom, turn on the spray and lean against the edge of the sink.

What are you doing, Eliza?

I should not be checking out my brother's best friend when he's here to help me get another guy—no matter how hot he is. I take two deep breaths to pull myself together, then climb into the hot spray. As I grab the soap and lather, I force my thoughts to Jason. I pinch my eyes shut and berate myself for the stupid, insipid way I acted in front of him when he joined us in the pool and focused those blue eyes of his on solely me, like he was finally seeing a different side to the girl he'd always overlooked.

I never thought my plan would have worked so fast. It's great that it did, but who would have thought that when I finally got his attention I'd come across as a babbling idiot, laughing at every little thing he said. I don't have a lot of experience with guys, but I *have* had couple of dates in the past. I should know how to make conversation for God's sake, and not act like a silly schoolgirl with a crush on the quarterback.

Dammit, I need to come across as more put together, more seasoned with the opposite sex. Speaking of sex. Other than that one messy time back in my freshman year, I'm pretty inexperienced in that area, too.

I groan out loud as the water spills over my nipples. That horrible night back in my first year of college was one I'm not in a hurry to repeat. Just then, another thought hits like a punch to the gut. What if I ended up in bed with Jason? Would I come across as suave and experienced, or will I turn into that same inexperienced girl who has no idea what she's really doing. I seriously don't want to make a fool of myself.

Maybe I should take Valerie's advice, and get a little hands on experience with Brax.

As that last thought bounces around in my head, I finish washing, quickly shampoo and rinse my hair, then turn off the spray. I slide the glass door open and listen for signs of

Braxton in the other room. I grab a big fluffy towel from the shelf and wrap it around me. Shoot, in my hurry to get away from Brax, I forgot to bring my pajamas. I walk to the door, and steam escapes to the bedroom as I inch it open to find Brax standing in front of the TV with a remote control in his hand. Since he went all alpha on me and demanded he carry my bag, he'd already seen the contents—including my lacy nightie—so I'd rather him root through it and bring me my pajamas then walk out there in a towel and give him the wrong idea...or the right idea.

Oh, God.

"Brax," I say over the hum of the soccer game on TV.

He lowers the volume. "Yeah?"

"Can you bring me my pajamas?" I point to my overnight bag. "I forgot to bring them in with me."

"Yeah, sure."

I stand there as the hiss of the zipper fills the silence. A second later, he pushes my clothes into my hand. "Thanks," I say and shut the door, locking it behind me. But the second I do, I realize he'd given me my sexy black lace nightie. Son. Of. A Bitch.

Wait!

Why would he do that?

Oh, because this is Brax being Brax. He's messing with me. Playing with me. Being that jerk from my childhood. Heck, maybe I should put it on, seduce him like Valerie suggested and then kick him to the floor once I've gotten his attention. But what if he doesn't take the bait?

What if he does?

I hold the sexy lace in my hand for a moment longer as my brain runs on hyperdrive. He gave this to me on purpose, but I bet in a million years he doesn't expect me to put it on and prance around out there in front of him. All the more reason for me to do it.

Have some fun with him. Pay him back. Kick him to the floor.

Better yet, get a little experience.

I gulp. Could I really do that? Would I be a fool not to try?

I suck in air, and before I can overthink things and stop myself, I life my arms and let the little lace number slide down my body. I hang my towel up, and open the door to the bedroom.

Here goes nothing.

I casually step into the room like I walk around in black lace all the time. "Bathroom's yours," I say and pull my brush from my bag. I step up to the dresser, curve my back a little and start brushing out my hair. I catch Brax's reflection in the mirror behind me. He's standing still, and I'm pretty damn sure he's not breathing. I hide my smile, and arch my back a little more.

"...bending you to his will. Or over the kitchen counter."

Heat climbs up my body, turning my cheeks a deeper shade of pink as a strange, almost tortured growl catches in Brax's throat. My God, I'm getting to him! I'm actually getting to the guy who rejected me, hurt me deeply, when we were teens. I turn, blink innocently at him.

"Is there something wrong?"

"Ah...yes, no...I mean...I...fuck." Her grabs a fistful of hair and tugs.

I point my comb toward the bathroom. "It's free."

"Yeah, right," he says and take three large steps. He closes the door behind himself, a little harder than necessary, and the sound of running water reaches my ears. A giggle catches in my throat, and I put my hand over my mouth to stop it. I really shouldn't be doing this, walking around half naked, but holy hell, I actually got a rise out of Brax. Me. Eliza Banks, the girl he tortured relentlessly when we were kids. A little thrill zings through me to know I can do this to my childhood nemesis.

So what are you going to do about it?

I gulp air, because when it comes right down to it I'm not so sure I have the nerve to seduce him—or the know-how. He comes from the bathroom, and his head is lowered as he throws his stuff back into his bag. I dash into the bathroom, brush my teeth and finish getting ready for bed. When I come out, he's tossing a pillow onto the hard wood floor.

"What are you doing?" I ask.

"I'll take the floor," he says, looking everywhere and anywhere but at me.

"Brax, I can't let you do that." I put my hand on my hip and it lifts my nightie higher on my thighs. Brax's gaze lifts along with it, slides over my half naked body. My pulse leaps as he explores me with heated eyes. "I'm the one who dragged you in to this, and I'm not about to put you out more by forcing you to sleep on a hard floor. You'll never get any sleep down there, and you said you were tired." I grab my pillow and toss it beside his. "I'll take the floor."

"I'm not going to allow you to sleep on the floor, Lizard," he says, his voice a low rough caress, like silk sliding over my nipples. They pucker beneath the lace, and I'm sure one popped free. I don't dare look and draw attention to my arousal.

Or should I?

"Stop calling me that," I say, and grab the blanket draped over the bottom of the bed. I bend forward, lay it out on the floor, and once again a tortured growl fills the air. That's when it suddenly occurs to me that I just presented him with unobstructed view of my bare ass.

"Eliza," Brax says, his voice deeper than it was moments ago.

"Yeah."

"What are you doing?"

I stand and face him, and breath leaves my lungs when I see the heat in his eyes. It licks me from head to toe, and burns through my blood. That's when I realize he wants me as much as I want him. All I have to do is get my nerve up and seduce him.

But what if he laughs again?

What if he doesn't?

I touch my damp hair, curl it around my finger. "I'm getting ready for bed, what does it look like I'm doing?"

He exhales and spears agitated fingers through is hair. "You're not sleeping on the floor."

"You're not either."

"Then what are we going to do about this?"

"We could have a staring contest like we did when we were kids," I suggest.

"You always won those."

"I'm winning this, too," I say.

"Why don't we just share the bed," he suggests. "We're adults, after all."

"Fine, we'll share the bed then."

He scrubs his hands over his chin, and I like the scratching sound it makes as he rubs the fine bristles. "We'll put pillows between us," he suggests.

"Better yet, I can take the top, you can take the bottom." Shit what did I just say? "I mean we can sleep head to foot."

"You want us to sleep in a sixty-nine position?" he asks his voice so low and strained, I can barely hear him.

Sixty-nine. Bodies aligned. Go for it, Eliza.

My knees give a little as I pick our pillow up and toss them onto the bed. I turn the light out with jittery fingers, and slide under the sheets. I swear to God my entire body is vibrating, shaking the bed beneath me. Brax's clothes rustle as he crawls in beside me, his head at the foot of the bed, our *parts* aligned.

I shift restlessly, well aware that I'm in bed, in the sixty-nine position, with the hottest guy I ever set eyes on. My heart is racing, my body urging me to say something...do something.

As I lay there, working on my approach, silence ensues for a long time, then Brax breaks it.

"Eliza?"

"Yeah?"

"What were you and Valerie talking about in the pool?"

Oh, shit.

"Nothing," I say quickly, too quickly.

The sheets move as he sits up and his knee touches my hip. My nipples harden even more and I squeeze my thighs together to ease the hollow ache in between.

"It must have been something. I heard Valerie say something like...use him. Was she talking about me?" Even in a room lit only by the moon I can feel his stare burn into me.

This is your chance, Eliza. Don't blow it. Or rather, blow it. Oh, God.

I give a nervous laugh. "Oh, she was just...well...she thought since you were pretending to be my boyfriend, I could use you to get a little experience."

"Experience?"

"It's...nothing."

"Experience in bed, you mean?" he asks, holding no punches.

I sit up, settle myself against the headboard and pull my blankets to my chest. "Yes," I say honestly.

"You haven't been with many guys, Liza?"

Liza.

Not Eliza, and not Lizard. Just Liza.

He's never called me that before, and I have to say I like

it, especially when it's coming out all sexy and hoarse like that.

"Ah, that's none of your business."

A beat and then, "It's kind of my business, don't you think?" His voice is low, challenging.

"How so?"

"I'm here pretending to be your boyfriend. There are things I should know about you."

"You know enough about me."

"I don't know what you taste like," he says, his breathing changing, becoming faster.

"You kissed me earlier," I shoot back.

"That's not what I'm talking about. That's not where I want my mouth."

OMFG, is he suggesting what I think he's suggesting?

"Brax?" I whisper.

"Yeah," he says. The mattress dips as he shifts position until he's between my legs. His fingers curl around my ankles, and in one quick tug, I'm flat on my back. Air leaves my lungs in a whoosh and my entire body goes up in a burst of flames as I take in six feet of hard man hovering over me.

"What...what are you doing?" I ask.

"Maybe Valerie is on to something."

"We don't even like each other." What the hell am I saying. I want this! But I'm so goddamn nervous.

"That didn't stop you from asking me to pretend to be your boyfriend." He touches my thighs, his big hands widening them, his fingers scorching my skin. Holy cripes, is this really happening?

Oh God, I hope so.

"I've not been with many men," I say quickly.

He grips my thighs harder. "How many?" he asks, a strange kind of possession in his touch.

"One back in my freshman year and it was...awful. I never want to go through that again."

He leans forward, presses his lips to my stomach, kisses me though the lace. His hot breath is like fire on my flesh. "It won't be like that with me, Liza. I promise you that."

A man with confidence. Hallelujah.

"But what if I...disappoint you?"

"Not a fucking chance of that happening," he assures me. "As soon as my cock gets inside you, I'm going to come. Guaran—fucking—teed."

"Brax, I...I don't think...I'm not sure I can..."

"You're not sure you can come."

Jesus, this man can read me like a book. "Yeah. I didn't last time."

"That's because you weren't with me," he says softly, the warmth in his eyes messing me with my insides in strange ways. "I'm going to take real good care of you. You're going to come, babe. You're going to come for me so hard, you'll be feeling the aftereffects come morning."

As his words settle into my brain, I take in his body, the hardness of his cock behind his zipper, the almost desperate need on his face, and my nerves begin to settle. His thumb sweeps over my inner thigh, and my body comes alive beneath his gentle caresses, and the needy juncture between my legs clenches, begging me to spread even wider and invite Brax in.

Do it already!

He lifts his head and I can see the outline of his handsome face. "The way I see it is," he says, his warm, minty breath washing over my face. "I'd be giving you the experience you want, and our intimate familiarity come morning will go a long way in fooling everyone this weekend, don't you think?"

"Two birds," I say under my breath. "That's what Valerie was saying."

"I like the way she thinks." The corner of his mouth twitches. "It's kind of a win/win for you, don't you think?"

"And for you?"

He touches the lace near my breasts, runs it through is fingers. "Full disclose here, Liza. The second I saw you in this sexy little number, I was a goner. My cock was so hard, I nearly jerked off in the bathroom. It's still fucking hard, and I want you in the worst way." He lays over me, and through his jeans, his cock centers on my sex.

"Oh," I say and writhe, shocked at the long length of him, how good he feels pressed up against me.

He growls. "Yeah, oh." He brushes his tongue along the edge of the lace, licking the swell of my breast. "I honestly never thought you'd come out with it on."

"Then why did you give it to me?"

"I wanted to see you in it. You're fucking gorgeous, Liza." He brushed his thumb over my bottom lip. "You know that, right?"

He thinks I'm gorgeous.

His hand leaves my mouth, slides down my body, skimming the outer edge of my breast. I quiver, and a little moan of want catches in my throat.

"I want you, Liza, but I told you before I'd never do anything you didn't want me to do, or anything that hurt you. This is your choice right now. Say the word and I'll stop. But you'd better say it soon, because I'm fucking losing it here."

I wiggle a little more, grind against his hard cock. "What word is it that I should say?"

He goes still, perfect still, like I'd just slapped him across the face. "The word is stop."

I wrap my legs around his body, and tug him to me. "Then

I'll be sure not to say it," I whisper, my bold candor shocking me.

I A little gasp sounds in my throat as he captures my hands, and pins them above my head. I can't breathe, but I don't care. I love the weight of him pressing me into the mattress like this.

"I need to know you're sure, Liza. I know what I want, but I need to know what you want."

My heart wobbles, loving that he's checking in on me like this. "I want you to fuck me, Brax."

His nostrils flare, and he wets his bottom lip. "One thing," he says his voice so deep and serious, it makes me a bit on easy.

"What?"

"When my mouth is on you and my cock is inside your sweet pussy, you think of me, and not him."

"Yes, Brax. I'll think of you."

Like I could possibly think of another when this man is on top of me.

"Good. Eyes open, on me the whole time." He holds my hands with one of his, and runs his thumb over my bottom lip. "This mouth," he says. "I'll do my best not to ruin it with my cock."

Holy Jesus.

"That's what I want, Liza. I want my cock in here." He shifts on my body, puts his hand between my legs. He lightly touches my swollen clit, and our groans mingle. "And I definitely want it in here. I'll try not to be rough with you. I want to do right by you, but I'm going to fuck you so good, baby, you're going to still feel me when this weekend is over."

"Oh, God yes."

"Good, then we're on the same page. Now tell me what you want?" He goes back on his knees, settles between my spread legs and looks over my trembling body, his gaze lingering on my heaving breasts, my nipples poking from the lace to be precise. Intense eyes move back to mine. "All you have to do is tell me, and I'll give it to you."

His words wrap around me, ease my nerves enough for me to confess all my secret desires. "I want to see," I say boldly, my gaze dropping to the bulge in his pants.

He angles his head, lust-imbued eyes moving over my face, gauging me. "You want to see my cock, Liza. Is that what you're asking?"

"Yes," I say, feeling bolder than I ever had before.

He climbs from my body and I whimper, missing his warmth, his weight. But that whimper turns into a moan of want when he removes his shirt, then pulls his jeans and boxers off and kicks them out of the away. Moonlight slants in and lights up his gorgeous body. I go still, and admire the beautiful display of long lean muscles, his magnificent cock. He takes his girth into his hands and strokes.

I swallow, and reach for him. I can't even count how many years I've fantasized about touching this man.

"You want to touch my cock?"

"Yes," I manage to get out.

"You want it in that pretty mouth of yours?"

I whimper my reply as I shift and sit on the edge of the bed. He stands back and continues to stroke himself from base to tip, and I swear to god, I'm about to orgasm just watching him.

"Please..."

"You begging for my cock, Liza?"

I nod, and whimper some more. He finally steps up to the bed, and drops his hands to his sides, giving me full access to his gorgeous cock. I take him into my hands, feel the smoothness of his skin. Pre-cum drips from his crown, and I run my thumb over it, massaging it in. His tortured groans encourage me, and I lean down, run my tongue over his slit.

"Fuck," he growls, and grabs a fistful of my hair. He holds my head as I rock into him, take him deep, until he hits the back of my throat. I choke a bit, a little inexperienced in this area, too. I cup his balls, rub gently as I suck his cock until little hollows form in my cheeks. His groans grow louder, and a thrill races through me. I guess I must be doing something right.

"How could you ever think you'd disappoint me? Jesus, girl, do you have any idea how fucking good you are with that sweet mouth." I work my mouth over him harder, and his veins fill with blood. "That is so fucking good." His grip on my hair tightens, and he tries to ease me off him, but I'm not nearly done tasting him. I never thought I'd love pleasuring a man like this. Then again, this isn't just any man. It's Brax.

Careful, girl. Don't go getting the wrong idea here. This is just about sex.

"Liza, stop," he growls. I glance up at him, and swirl my tongue around his crown, not wanting to miss a drop of his tangy pre-cum. "Jesus fucking Christ, that is hot. But babe, as much as I want your mouth wrapped around me, and as much as I love watching my cock slide between your pretty lips, it's my turn."

"I'm not done," I say, and lick him again.

He cups my chin, and lifts my face until our eyes meet. "Yeah, you are," he says, the intensity back in his gaze and doing the craziest things to my insides. "I'm taking care of you first, and that's not up for debate." My heart wobbles, impressed by his chivalry, and I swallow against the sudden tightness in my throat. "Now get in the middle of the bed, and widen your legs for me. I want to taste you."

As the alpha in him emerges, takes charge between the sheets, I suck in a shallow breath and obey his commands. I go on my hands and knees, giving him a view of my ass as I crawl to the center of the bed. As I turn over, and position myself, I wonder who the hell I am, and what happened to the self-conscious girl who arrived at this seaside mansion a few hours ago. I don't know where she is, or how Brax was able to so easily coax me out of my shell, but a few minutes in his arms, I've turned into a needy girl with little inhibitions. Perhaps it's the ravenous way he looks at me, the dirty way he talks to me. Who knew I'd love a dirty talking, take charge, yet chivalrous man in the bedroom so much.

"Is this what you want?" I say, and lay my hand on my stomach. I splay my fingers, and his gaze tracks my movements carefully as I slide my hand lower, let it fall between my open legs. When my hand stills, his gaze slides back up my body.

"Touch yourself for me," he says, and my body buzzes. "Open that sweet pussy and rub your clit for me." I gulp, never having done that in front of a guy—heck, I barely touch myself in my own bed—but I'm so far gone, I'm pretty sure he could ask me to do anything, and I would.

I touch my wet lips, and inch them open, then slide my finger over my aching clit. "Oh, yesss..." I hiss and my eyes meet Brax's.

"You have the prettiest pussy, Liza." He wets his bottom lip, like he's preparing his mouth, and my whole body quivers. "That one time, back in freshman year..." he begins. "At least tell me the oral sex was good for you."

"We didn't..."

"Oh, fuck." He tugs his hair. "Didn't he know you deserve to be worshipped?" The muscles in his jaw clench. "I'd like to punch that douchebag for not doing right by you. Then again, I'm kind of glad he never had his mouth on you." He reaches out, takes my hand from my pussy and puts it on my stomach.

The bed dips as he climbs on, and positions himself between my spread legs. My body quakes in anticipation, and I close my eyes against the flood of heat.

Oh God, I need his mouth on me. Yesterday.

"Eyes to me," Braxton commands.

My eyes slide open and when I catch the battle behind his, the tightness in his neck, I wonder what we're getting ourselves in to.

"I'm with you," I say, and touch his arm, revel in the way his muscles tense beneath my fingers. He leans over me, tugs my nightie down, and pulls one hard nipple into his mouth, and I grab a fistful of his hair and hold on. His tongue slides, swirls, his teeth nip and tease. My hand goes to my other breast to play with my nipple and touching myself seems to bring out the beast in him. He growls, and sucks harder, drawing my nipple deeper into his mouth, the pull so strong I feel it between my legs. I move under him, lift my hips, buck against him, letting him know in no uncertain terms how desperate I am to feel him inside me.

His mouth leaves my breast and the cool air conditioning in the room rasps over them, the hot cold combination arousing me even more. Brax drops to his stomach, and pushes his hands under my ass. Strong fingers sink into my flesh as he lifts my sex to his mouth, like he's about to feed himself something he'd been denied for years.

"Brax," I murmur, as he buries his face between my legs. That first sweet touch of his tongue pulls a moan from the depths of my throat and I claw at the sheets beneath me. Hot and hungry, his deft tongue sears my sensitive clit as he tastes me. "So good," I whimper, and move shamelessly against his mouth. All thoughts shut down until the only thing driving me is the pleasure between my legs.

He licks from bottom to top, a slow glide that takes me higher and higher. My breathing changes, becomes faster and I go up on my elbows to watch him. He lifts his mouth, his lips wet and swollen from his kisses. Our eyes meet, hold, and something passes between us, something profound, hungry—

something I just might not be able to come back from—then he's once again feasting on me.

His mouth moves, demanding, claiming, eating at me like a man starved. My body quakes, burns from the inside out, the flames reaching new heights as I stand at the cliff, arms spread wide, the world soaring around me. Dizzy, the room spins, but I don't dare take my eyes from him. I cup my breasts, play with my kiss-swollen nipples.

My mouth opens, but no sounds forms when he dips a finger into me, filling me with his thickness. I rock into him, bang my clit against his devouring mouth. From inside, he runs the tip of his finger over the sensitive bundle of nerves, and the dual assault of mouth and finger pushes me over the edge until nothing exists but sweet sensations.

"Brax," I cry out, as my sex clenches around his thick finger.

"Yeah, come for me," he says, the vibrations of his voice rocketing through me and bringing on stronger pulses that make the room close in on me. "Come all over my face." He closes his eyes like he's in total agony, and stays between my legs, lapping at me, forcing the last ripple of pleasure from my body, leaving me sated, exhausted, so goddamn full—body and heart—I'm almost giddy. When the tremors finally subside, I want to move, take hold of his cock and put it inside of me, but my muscles are weak, my brain barely able to hold a thought. With shaky fingers, I reach for him, but he's already on the move, sliding back up my body and closing his mouth over mine.

He kisses me, hard, deep, and when I catch my second breath I cling to him, his mouth like sparks to kindle, my hands move to his back, nails scraping, delirious for so much more from this man. I whimper when he leaves my body, but a second later he's back between my legs, sliding a condom over his beautiful cock.

"Yesss," I say and reach for him. He falls over me, and I touch his taut muscles, feel his restraint. He lightly rubs his tip over my opening, slow, steady sweeps to prepare me. He's taking his time, going slow, trying to make this good for me, even though, from the look on his face, it's killing him. An invisible band tightens around my heart as he grimaces. This man might have teased me relentlessly when we were young, but the truth is, he's one of the best guys I know, and when push comes to shove, he'd do anything for me. Heck, he gave up his whole weekend to *pretend* with me. Only problem is, what we're doing doesn't feel like we're pretending at all. It feels real.

Easy, Eliza.

"Take me, Brax," I plead, a deep, husky command that brings more heat to his eyes. Perspiration dots his forehead as he positions his crown at my opening, and his breathing is so labored, I wonder if anyone else in the house can hear it. I spread wide for him and he slowly slides into my inviting body, giving me one glorious inch at a time. I move, writhe, cry at the urgent need to have him all the way inside me—now—fucking me, losing all control. Surrendering to the raging hunger bubbling below the surface, one he's taking great care to control.

I squirm, take pleasure in his length, his girth, every hot hard ridge sliding into me, pushing against my sex walls in breathtaking ways. Never have I felt so gloriously full, so desired before. His mouth is back on mine, kissing with a frenzy that doesn't match the pace of his probing cock. I whimper, buck, and when he finally seats himself high inside me, it heightens the fever in me, consuming me from the inside out.

He pulls out, a hot slow friction, that blurs my vision. "Harder," I cry out as he holds back, takes his time with me, easing me into intimacy with some chivalrous need to do right by me—the inexperienced girl who always gets over-looked. I totally appreciate it, but I want him unleashed, I want him wild and uncontrolled.

I want Brax to break under my touch, the same way I'm breaking under his.

I put my legs around his back, and he buries his mouth in the hollow of my neck. I lock my ankles, draw him impossibly deeper, until pleasure bleeds to pain and back again. But I don't care. If I only have one night with him, I want it all, everything, every single inch of him inside me, breaking me, ruining me. I want Brax to ravage me, not treat me like a doll who can be broken. We rock together, and he lets out a slow, unsteady breath. It falls over my flesh, and burns through me until I'm a quivering mess. His cock grows thicker inside me, blood rushing through his swollen veins.

"I feel you. I feel all of you."

"Liza," he murmurs. "You've got me right there, baby."

My heart soars, but I don't want to think too much about how happy I am to know that I can take this man to the point of no return.

"Come inside me, Brax," I say, wishing there were no condom separating our flesh. I want his cum in me, I want to feel it drip out of me, a sweet reminder of this night.

"Jesus, I can't hold on, you feel so good," he says, and lifts his head.

"I don't want you to hold on."

His throat sounds as he swallows, a barrage of emotion, everything from uncertainty to pleasure, all over his face. "Eliza..." I lift my hips as he comes down on me. His eyes focus on mine, and his face contorts slightly, every muscle strung tight. He pushes my damp hair from my face. "How could you ever think you'd disappoint me?" He pulls out, glides back in again, then grinds his pubis against my clit.

"Brax," I cry out, as my sex flutters. He pumps again,

applying more pressure, and my breath stalls as a second orgasm blindsides me, a hot, fiery blaze of need that crashes over me steals the air from the room. Drowning, I grip his shoulders to hang on, claw at his skin in my struggle to keep my head above the surface. My body twitches, spasms, sucks his cock in deeper, and all I can do is go with it, ride the waves, let it take me to a place I've never quite been before.

"Holy fuck," he growls, as I grip his cock hard, heat flooding from my body and dripping down his balls, covering my thighs in a glorious mess of release. He stills high inside me, and throws his head back as he releases. Each glorious pulse pushes on my sex walls, and I squeeze around him, milk every last drop until he's panting for his next breath. I hold him to me, and he collapses, driving me deeper into the mattress.

I press my lips to his damp flesh, kiss his muscular shoulder, reveling in the quivering of his muscles. We continue to gasp for air in a room deprived of oxygen. Soon enough, our breathing evens out, and he goes up on his elbows, a small curve of his lips when our eyes meet.

He shakes his head, his eyes holding a measure of disbelief. "That was…"

"Awful," I tease, a reminder of our kiss, which was anything but. My lips still burn from earlier. Laughing, he slowly pulls out of me, and turns. He makes quick work of the condom, dropping it into some tissues to dispose of later, then falls in beside me.

He puts his arm over his forehead, the epitome of male perfection. "If I say it was awful, does that mean we get to do it again, until we perfect it?"

I laugh with him. "I'm not sure it could get any more perfect, Brax. Well, maybe that's not true. I think it could be better without a condom." I shrug, making light of it when it feels very heavy. "You know, for the experience," I say although I'm not sure that's entirely true. I'm not sure why it's so important either, but I need to feel Brax inside me, no barriers, no veils. Just him and me, skin on skin, wide open and holding nothing back.

A moment of heavy silence, and then, "I always use a condom."

My stomach cramps. Dammit, I've asked for too much, more than he's willing to give. Stupid. Stupid. Stupid. *This is just sex, Eliza. Don't forget that.* "Oh, sorry, I didn't mean—"

"No, Eliza. What I mean is I've never had sex without a condom. I'm clean."

"I am, too."

"What about birth control?"

"I'm on the pill." I crinkle my nose. "Terrible menstrual cramps."

He places a soothing hand over my stomach and rubs gently. "I know."

I angle my head. "You do?"

His grin is back in place when he says, "I was at your place, a lot, remember, Lizard?"

I whack his stomach and he lets out a loud oomph. "How could I possibly forget?"

"If sex without a condom is what you want, sex without a condom is what you get. Now come here."

He rolls toward me, and I catch a show of something in his eyes, something warm and soft and...satisfied as he settles me next to him. "No one has ever..." His words fall off.

"What?"

His fingers lightly brush my hair and I wonder if he even knows he's doing that. "I'm sorry, it's crude of me to bring up past relations."

"It's okay, Brax. I've known you for a long time now. I know your reputation."

"I just...no one has ever come like that for me before,

and…I think I'm trying to say I love how responsive you are. I love that I could do this for you."

"I love that you could do that to me too," I say in return, and his laugh fills me with joy. I sigh from the pleasure, a soft escape of air that washes over Brax's flesh. He grabs the blankets, drags them up and cradles me in his arms. Sleep pulls at me as I sink into his warmth, never wanting this moment—this night—to end. Being here with Brax like this, well, truthfully it's something I've fantasized about since I was a schoolgirl. I never knew sex could be so good. Then again, maybe it's only like that when it's with someone you love.

Oh. My. God.

No.

5

BRAXTON

The sound of footsteps in the hall pulls me awake. I open my eyes, but can't orient myself. Where the fuck am I? I blink once, twice, and try to get my bearing. That's when I see Eliza sleeping soundly beside me, looking so goddamn beautiful and sated, it's all I can do not to wake her and take her again.

My mind rewinds to last night, and all the things I did with my childhood crush. Truthfully, it was the best fucking night of my life—years in the making—it's a wonder I lasted as long as I did. The second she put that sweet mouth of hers on my cock, I was done for. So fucking done for I had to pull out every trick in the book to keep from exploding down her throat.

Truthfully, I have no idea where we stand this morning—except that she wants sex again—but last night, for some unexplainable reason, I needed her to look me in the eye, know it was me, Braxton Freeman, who was worshiping her body and bringing her to bliss.

She murmurs in her sleep, and I touch her hair, pull the long dark strands from her face. She breathes deep, an adorable sound of contentment, thanks to a night of mind blowing sex and powerful orgasms.

I want more.

As I think about that, a knot tightens my gut, and a pounding begins at the base of my neck. Jesus Christ, here I am pretending to be her boyfriend, preparing her sexually for another man. How the fuck can we continue with this charade? She wants another guy, and I'm helping her get him. Only problem is, I fucking want her to myself, selfish bastard that I am.

She's not yours, asshole.

What the fuck was I thinking, agreeing to something so asinine?

Oh, probably because this is sweet, Eliza and you'd do anything for her.

"Hey," she whispers, and put her palm on my cheek. "You okay?"

"Yeah, why?"

She sits up a bit, looks me over. "You look like you're in a bad mood again. Is everything okay?"

Shit, I wish she couldn't read me so well.

"I need coffee."

She laughs. "That's right. I forgot how much of a grouch you are before your first cup."

I make a move to go, and her hand drops to my arm. She gives a little squeeze and I turn back to her. "About today," she begins, her lashes flashes rapidly—a nervous little tick of her. "What I asked you to do."

"I got this, Eliza. Don't worry." Really, how hard can it be to pretend to be into her, when no pretending is needed.

"I..."

"When Jason finally takes his eyes off his phone and sees who you really are, he's not going to know what hit him."

I know what I'd like to hit him with.

She gives an uneasy chuckle. "Okay, thanks." She runs her hands along the blankets. "Just checking to see if you were okay and still wanted to go through with this."

"I've come this far, haven't I? I'm not a quitter, Eliza. You know that about me. I see everything through to the end, for better or for worse."

"I know and that's what I love about you," she says, then her eyes go wide and she shakes her head, all that sexy loose hair falling over her bare shoulders. As if realizing she's still naked from the night before, she grabs the sheet and tugs it to her neck.

"Oh, there is something you love about me is there?" I tease, wanting the sweet, relaxed Eliza back, the one who was so open and honest with me last night, one who shed her inhibitions and freely gave me every inch of her body. Body, not heart. Get it together, dude. "All this time I thought you hated every inch of me."

A blush crawls up her throat and deepens the pink in her cheeks. "You do have a lot of inches," she says, then chuckles.

I grin, hardly able to believe what my sweet Eliza just said. I stare at the woman beside me as her lips twitch. Seeing her like this, playful, teasing, all relaxed after the best sex of my night is a total mind fuck. Sexy, smart, funny as hell when she wants to be. The perfect trifecta.

More footsteps sound in the hall, and lacking any sort of modesty, I kick off my blankets and stand, showcasing all my inches in their early morning arousal. Her gaze drops, and her breathing changes.

"You keep looking at my cock like that and we won't be leaving this room any time soon."

She pulls her bottom lip between her teeth. "I'm...sorry."

"Don't be sorry. I loved the way you worked my cock with that sweet mouth of yours. You owned it, Liza. Took me in like you were on a mission and it was fucking amazing. It was all I could do not to fill your throat with my cum."

"Ohmigod, Brax," she says, her eyes wide as she chuckles again.

"What, are you saying you don't like my dirty mouth?"

"...No."

I grin at her, and take my cock into my hand. "That's what I thought."

A knock comes on our door. "Breakfast in twenty minutes," Richard's wife Michelle, says.

"So answer me. Am I crawling between your legs again, or am I tugging one out in the shower."

She points to the bathroom. "Go, or everyone will know what we're doing in here."

"So?"

"So...we need to make the breakup believable, right? If we spend all our time in here, and not out there, it could look suspicious."

I stiffen, her words—a reminder of what this really is—are like a punch to the gut. "Shower it is then."

I step into the bathroom, and shut the door, all the while trying to keep my anger in check. I'm the one who agreed to this, so the only one I can be angry at is myself. I just hope this guy is worth it, and so far he's proving otherwise. Seriously though, what kind of guy only notices a girl when she's worthy enough for another guy. That shit is fucked up.

I shower quickly, rinse the scent of Eliza from my body, and wrap a towel around my waist. "All yours," I say and walk into the other room to find her dressed in yoga pants and a t-shirt her fingers flying across her phone. She sets it down, and I glance at it.

"Everything okay?"

"Yeah, just Valerie wondering what's taking me so long to get downstairs."

"Did you tell her your legs are too tired to carry you because I fucked you last night?"

She laughs. "Yeah, Brax, that's exactly what I told her." She jumps from the chair, and casts me a quick glance. "She said Jason was looking for us." I make a sound, a grunting little noise. "What?" she asks.

"Nothing."

She plants one hand on her hip and studies me. "You don't like him," she says, a statement, not a question.

"I don't know him like you do, Eliza."

"Well, hopefully by the end of the day we'll all get to know each other better." She turns to head to the bathroom, and I wait until the door is shut.

"Can't wait," I say under my breath. I rake my hands through my hair, and tug on my board shorts and a T-shirt. I grab a ball cap from my bag and toss it onto my head. Eliza comes from the bathroom and goes still when she sees me.

"Something wrong?"

She smiles and shakes her head. "With that hat on, you look like you're eighteen again."

"You don't like it?"

"No, it's not that. It's just you pull off a suit so well, and yet...this look."

"What about it?"

"It somehow suits you, too."

"You'd better careful."

"Why?"

I step up to her, toy with the knot on her towel. A quiver moves through her body and her eyes widen. "You keep complimenting me like this and I might get the wrong idea... or the right idea," I say.

She lifts her chin slightly, a show of defiance, but there is something in her eyes, something that looks a lot like lust when she says, "I was just stating a fact, Braxton."

I grin down at her, focus on her mouth, and her lips fall open. Is that an invitation? My gaze flies back to hers. How can a girl with so much desire on her face be chasing another man?

Because she wants you for sex only.

"We, ah, should get going," she says.

I step away from her and adjust my ball cap, bring it lower over my eyes. "You want me to wait until you get dressed, or do you want to meet me down there?"

"You go ahead. I'll follow in a minute."

I nod, and leave her alone. When I step in the hall, I work to pull my shit together, and get my goddamn cock under control. Yeah, she said she wanted to have sex tonight, and by rights I should say no. Why the fuck would I want to prepare her for a douche like Jason?

I make my way downstairs and follow the sound until I find everyone outside, gathered around a large patio table. Three young girls are dressed in crisp white shirts and black dress pants, pouring the coffee. I sit, turn my coffee cup over and give a grateful smile to the server who fills it.

"Thanks," I say, and she nods and walks off. I steal a glance around. To one side of the massive backyard, a beautiful buffet is set up, the food kept hot in covered chafing dishes. I glance around, and all eyes are on me, including Jason, who has yet to remove his phone from his hand.

"She'll be down in a second," I say and take a much needed sip of my coffee. From my peripheral vision I catch the curious way Valerie is watching me, a small grin on her face. I bite back a scoff. Hell, I probably have a night of hot sex written all over me. I hope so, then maybe Jason will realize Eliza's not his.

Goddammit, Brax. That's the whole reason for being here.

"Sorry I'm late," Eliza says as she breezes to the table, looking fresh face, relaxed...well fucked this morning. I pull her chair our and she takes a seat beside me, our legs bump, and as little pulses zap between us, she places her napkin on her lap and sits up a little straighter. "Mmm, coffee. Just what I need." She flips her mug over and one of the servers is right there to pour her a drink. She breathes in the rich aroma, then glances at the cloudless sky. "Great weather for today's activities."

"Perfect weather," Richard says, then does another round of introductions, for my sake, I assume. I gesture a nod to the man named Alex, who is directly across from me. Like me, he's tagging along with his girlfriend for the weekend. I turn my attention back to Richard, who is explaining the plans for the day. "Mason, from Building Bonds, will be joining us shortly to get things under way. We play for a few hours, have a lunch break, then resume afterward. Tonight however, is meant for drinks at the pool and either sunset swims, or moonlit sails." I nod, maybe I'll get some sailing in this weekend after all. Then again, it's not like Eliza will want to join me, and I'm not about to leave her on shore while I'm off entertaining myself. Then again, she might want me to disappear. With me out of the picture, it might give her the perfect opportunity to get closer to Jason.

"If you need me, I'll be at the pool getting a little work done," I say, and try not to look as annoyed as I feel. "Good thing my laptop is in the car."

"Me too," Alex pipes in. His girlfriend smiles at him, and I can't help but think they're a cute couple—without a hidden agenda

"Aren't you going to play any of the games?" Eliza asks.

I put my arm on the back of her chair, a show of possession and stretch out my legs as Jason zeroes in on us. "Not my company, babe. I'm just here because you asked me to be."

"At least agree to be in the tug of war," Richard says. "We could use a good strong anchor like you." Richard grins at

Jason, who folds his arms across his chest, a challenge of sorts. "Give Jason a run for his money this year."

"I'm in," I say quickly, and Eliza's gaze flies to me. So does Valerie's. I ignore them both and drain my coffee.

Richard puts his hands on the edge of the teak table and pushes to a stand. "All right then, let's eat, shall we?"

"Are you really going to work today?" Eliza asks.

"I can't very well join in the bonding games."

"I...suppose." She looks down for a moment, almost apologetic. "Maybe this was a bad idea."

I catch the way Jason is watching us. "I planned to get some work done this weekend, whether I was here or not, Eliza. It's fine. Plus, Richard said something about a sail tonight."

She crinkles her nose. "I took you away from that this weekend, didn't I? I'm sorry."

I put my hand on her cheek. "I can sail here and work. Two birds," I say.

She nods up at me, understanding exactly what I'm saying. "So you brought your laptop?"

"I don't go anywhere without it." Although I do know when it's appropriate and not appropriate to open it.

"This is supposed to be a device-free weekend."

Maybe someone should tell that to Jason.

"I don't think those rules apply to me."

She shakes her head. "I suppose, and I should have realized you'd have work to do," she adds and that's when I realize she's given me the perfect opportunity to set things in motion.

"All work and no play, isn't that what you always say about me?" It's a lie. While I'm a hard worker, I know when it's time to play. It's that balance that makes me a success.

As everyone moves about to fill their plates with breakfast foods, she hesitates for a second. I catch the way Jason is lingering at the table, taking his time to finish his coffee as he eavesdrops.

"Ah, yeah. That's what I always say," she says, clueing in to my tactics as she leaves the table, following everyone to the buffet.

I wait a second until my coffee is refueled again, take a big sip, and follow behind. Jason jogs to catch up with me.

He nudges me, like we're old friends bonding over something. "Women, huh?"

"What about them?"

"A guy like you doesn't get where he is today by taking weekends off."

"Eliza asked me to be here, so I'm here. I'd like to think you'd do the same if she were your girlfriend."

"Oh, yeah, sure. Absolutely." He shoves his hands into the pockets of his board shorts, and fall in place behind me in line. "We never got to have that drink last night. Maybe we can talk later," he says from behind me. I already know what he wants to talk about. My success. My business. If I have any place for him on my team. But I plan to keep my word to Richard, and I'm not about to poach.

Why didn't you keep your word to your best friend?

"Maybe we can take the sailboat out later," he says to me.

"Eliza doesn't really like the water."

"I'm sure she won't mind staying back."

"I'll mind."

From the buffet line ahead, Eliza turns and her gaze lands on me, obviously having heard our conversations. We exchange a long look, then she hurries forward and fills her plate. I load up on eggs, bacon, and toast, and grab my seat back at the table. Soon enough, everyone is talking, and I can barely follow along with the numerous conversations going on around me.

"You sure you'll be okay at the pool by yourself?" Eliza asks me as her knee brushes mine.

Below the table I put my hand on her thigh, and she makes a wheezing little sound that takes me back to when she climaxed around my cock. "Relax." I lean into her, purposely put my mouth to her ear, my words for her only. "This is what you hired me for."

She does a quick check around the table, but there are no eyes on us. Her mouth moves to my ear and when the heat of her breath washes over me, my cock swells, eager to have that sweet mouth wrapped around it again. "Technically, I didn't hire you," she says, her voice a low breathless whisper that matches mine "We do have that whole tit-for-tat thing."

"Yeah, that's right."

"You never did tell me what you wanted," she says quietly.

I inch back, and relax into my chair. "No, I didn't, did I?"

"Are you going to let me know anytime soon, or do I have to guess?"

"Not sure."

"Brax—" she begins, but her boss's voice stops her. All eyes lift in time to see Richard stand and shake hands with a middle-aged man, then introduces him as Mason, today's instructor. After introductions, Mason talks about the games that are going to be played. I quickly excuse myself from the table, set my dishes in the big gray tray, and make my way to my car. I reach into my pocket, fish my keys out and grab my laptop from the trunk.

I grab a lounge chair by the pool, peel off my shirt and settle into it. I open up my email but since I can't really seem to concentrate on too much, I scan through the messages and sort according to importance. I answer a few, yet continually lift my head to see what the team is up to.

"Are you sure you don't want to join them?" Michelle says as she brings me a cold glass of lemonade.

"Positive. I have some work to catch up on, and I'm not part of the team, so it doesn't really seem fair."

"You're kind of a part of it." She gives a knowing little laugh, and I lift my eyes to hers as she perches on the end of my chair. "I mean, you are here with Eliza." She follows my gaze, and watches me take in the group trying to release themselves from the human knot. Every time Eliza laughs, or shouts out an instruction it pulls my focus. She's a strong, take-charge woman at work, and I admire her for that. But fuck, when she handed her body over to me in the bedroom, trusting me enough to know I'd take care of it, well, that shit just messes with my mind, and truthfully it's a responsibility I don't take lightly. I blink my eyes, the rush of last night's erotic memories pulling a groan from me. I cough to cover it, and shake my head to clear the sexy visions. When I open them again, Jason is laughing with her, touching her. He wraps his hands around her waist as they try to break free, and acid fills the back of my throat. The only hands I want on her body are mine, goddammit.

"She's something, isn't she?" Michelle says, pulling my thoughts back. "Richard has so many great things to say about her."

"Yeah," I say. "She's got it all, doesn't she?"

"I heard you two go way back."

"Her brother is my best friend. We met in high school."

"Ah, I see. How does he feel about the two of you?" She laughs, like she's remembering a joke only she's privy to. "I'm asking because Richard was my brother's best friend, and I think he was lucky to walk away with only a broken nose once he found out about the two of us."

I should be so lucky.

"He's fine with it," I fib.

A moment of silence as the sun beats down on us, and then, "You don't have to worry, you know?"

I swipe at a bead of perspiration on my forehead. "Worry about what?"

"Every time Jason goes near Eliza, you look like you want to hit something."

I sit up a little straighter. Maybe this would be a good time to allude to trouble in our relationship. "I just—"

"She's as in to you as you are to her, Braxton, but I have to say, it's kind of sweet to see San Francisco's Most Eligible Bachelor brought to his knees by an adorable, down to earth girl like Eliza."

I laugh. She might be astute, might have picked up on how much I'm in to Eliza, but the girl I'd give my left nut sack just to kiss, well, this is all about sex and experience for her. "What can I say to that, Michelle." I pick up my lemonade, lift it in salute, and take a big drink.

Alex plunks down beside us. Michelle excuses herself, and Alex boots up his computer. As the sun rises higher in the sky, both Alex and I work. Every now and then we make conversation, and I have to say, I like the guy. During our easy conversation, I learn he works in sales for Vericomm, one of America's telecommunication giants. The best part of talking to Alex is, unlike most people, he doesn't want anything from me. When I catch his girlfriend chatting with Eliza during an egg-carrying contest, Alex informs me he and Tamara go way back—high school sweethearts.

Before I can think better of it, I say, "Same here."

I catch the confusion in his eyes. "Really. But I thought..." He shakes his head. "Well, you know what the papers say, so I didn't think you were serious about anyone."

Am I serious about Eliza? Fuck yeah, I am, and when she gets with Jason, that shit is going to mess me up big time.

"Technically I met her in high school, but we didn't get together until recently."

Because she needed to use me to catch another guy…and to teach her all about sex.

He laughs and adjusts his ball cap over his eyes as the sun moves through the sky. "Can't believe the papers anyway."

As I laugh with him, I'm suddenly picturing the four of us on a double date.

Wait, what?

I find Eliza in the crowd, and once again Jason is laughing with her. She's coiling her hair around her finger, a sexy, suggestive move that spikes my anger. The scent of food reaches my nostrils and I turn to see the three servers placing chafing trays on the long table. I push to my feet, toss my hat to my chair, and jump into the pool to cool off—for numerous reasons. I surface at the other end, and find Eliza standing there, grinning down at me with her hands on her hips. I grip her ankles, give her a teasing tug.

"Braxton," she cries out, her eyes wide in warning. "Don't you dare. You know what happened last time."

Guilt eats at me. "I'm sorry, Eliza. You know that, right? I never meant for that to happen."

"I know. It's okay. At least you dove in and saved me."

"Not all lizards can't swim," I tease.

"You're not funny."

"Not even a little?"

"Not even a little." She crouches down, her face close to mine, her cleavage right there for my personal viewing. "Lunch is about to be served." My cock thickens beneath the water when she brushes my wet hair from my forehead. It's all I can do not to pull her in with me, kiss the fuck out of her beneath the water. Or better yet, take her back to the bedroom and show the sweet girl just how dirty I can be. She casts a quick glance over her shoulder then focuses back in on me. "It's going well today, don't you think?"

"Yeah, Jason can't seem to keep his hands off you." I turn

from her. The last thing I want is for her to see how much that bothers me. After this weekend, we have to go back to being friends, or enemies, or whatever the hell we are, and I don't want any awkwardness between us. Her family was like my family, and while I might be all grown up now, a goddamn successful millionaire, there are still some things I can't lose.

"Brax," she says and I turn to her. Her brow wrinkles as her big brown eyes move over my face, hold me hostage. "If you're not comfortable..."

Why the fuck does she keep giving me a way out. Now that she has Jason's attention, she no longer needs me here. I said I'd see the weekend through, but maybe I should just leave now.

I grip the edge of the pool and pull myself out. Water drips from my shorts, and to wipe the worry from her face, I shake my hair and get her t-shirt wet. Only problem is I can now see the sexy outline of her lace bra.

The warm sun dries my body quickly, and I tug on my shirt and follow her to the buffet. I grab a hamburger and hotdog and plunk myself down at the table with the rest of her co-workers. They all laugh and cajole each other, talking about the games they'd played.

"Up next is tug of war. Brax and Alex, we'd love it if you both joined."

"I want Braxton on my team," Tamara, Alex wife says. Everyone laughs.

"Hey," Alex says.

"No offense," Tamara says and drops a kiss onto his cheek.

"No offense? Now why would I take offense to that?" Alex returns, but from the teasing look on his face, he's taking it all in stride.

From beside me, I get a little nudge from Eliza. "Are you going to join us?"

I stare at my hamburger. "Which team are you on, Eliza?"

When she doesn't readily answer, I angle my head, take in the way she's crinkling her nose. Jesus, she is so fucking beautiful. "Jason already asked me to be on his team."

I nod. Of course he did. But seriously, what kind of douche goes after another guy's girl? My hate for this asshole just keeps growing. "Yeah, okay. No problem." I take a bite of my hamburger, chew and wash it down with a swig of lemonade.

"Brax, unless you want—"

"Nope, I don't want," I lie. Oh, I want. I want a fucking hell of a lot from this girl, but that's not going to happen and I can't risk telling her and losing her from my life. "But you do leave me with quite the dilemma, you know."

"What's that?"

"I always play to win, and yet I said I'd never do anything to hurt you. So how am I supposed to win the game and keep you out of the mud if you're on the other team."

"I'm a big girl. I can handle a mud bath. Besides, who says you're going to win?"

I touch her hand, stroke her warm skin with my thumb. "Is that a challenge, Eliza?"

She visibly quakes, and my chest practically puffs out. I do this to her. Me. Not Jason.

"Maybe."

"You're not going to like eating mud," I say.

"Care to make a wager?" she asks with a tip of her chin.

I grin at her tenaciousness. "Okay, sure, if that's what you want. What do you suggest we lay on the line?"

"I'll have to think about it," she says.

I take another huge bite of my hamburger. "You do that, and in the meantime, you might want to change into something old. I'd hate to see you ruin those clothes."

She whacks me, and I nearly choke on my hamburger. "Maybe you should do the same." Her gaze rakes over me, and my pulse jumps when I catch the heat in her eyes. She might be here for another man, but there is no doubt that the physical attraction between us is off the charts.

"What do you want if you win?" she asks.

As my cock thickens, my brain shifts gears. "I'm not sure yet, but I bet it will come to me when I see you all dirty," I say, my voice low for her ears only. "Come to think of it, I do remember you saying something about liking...dirty."

Pink crawls into her cheek. "I...Braxton. I never meant I liked mud," she whispers, and casts a quick glance around the table. Once again, her best friend is watching us, a smirk on her face, like she knows something we don't.

"Yeah, it gets in all those hard to clean places," I say as I envision us in the shower, my hands all over her.

She swallows, and sets her hamburger onto her plate. With a shaky hand, she reaches for her cold drink. Condensation drips off the cup and beads on her flesh I slide my thumb over it, and then brush it over my tongue.

"Ohmigod," she whispers under her breath.

"So you still want to be on the other team?"

"Yes," she croaks out, and I wonder if she's imagining me in the shower with her, cleaning all those sexy crevices.

We finish our lunches, and we're all led to another part of the yard where a great big, man-made mud hole has been dug. The teams get divided, and I walk past the mud. I glance at Eliza.

"Second thoughts?" I ask.

"None."

Alex and his girlfriend take up position in front of me, and Tamara glances at us over her shoulder. "Let's take them down."

"You bet."

"Although I have to say," Valerie says, as she slides in front of Tamara. "Eliza is going to kill you if you drag her through that mud hole."

"Yeah, I know." I wink at her. "But the clean-up will be fun."

"On the count of three," Richard says, and I wrap the rope around my waist and dig my feet in. "One. Two. Three."

We all start pulling, and cheers and laugher ring out. I grin when I see Eliza glaring at me, a challenge in her eyes, and maybe something else. I lean back, tug harder, and we move them a couple of inches.

"Pull," I yell, and Jason does the same as he anchors the opposing team. I might not win the war with him, but I plan to at least conquer him in a tug of war, as juvenile as that sounds.

We gain a few more feet and cheers erupt from our side as groans sound from the other. "We got this," Valerie yells out. "Prepare to eat mud," she says and we all laugh. Another huge tug and we've got them, the person at the front of the rope is teetering near the mud hole and screaming at her team to save her. But there will be no saving. If Eliza had stuck with me, she wouldn't be seconds from eating mud—a hard lesson.

"Okay everyone, one last big pull. Go." We all lean into it, then the rope goes slack and we tumble backward like dominos as the other team lose their balance and get dragged into the mud.

I jump up, untie myself from the rope and follow my team to the mud hole as they reach in and help the others out. Eliza is laughing and wiping mud from her face and a tenderness comes over me as I take her hand in mine.

"You should have stuck with me, Lizard," I say, and she turns those dark eyes on me. I'm about to pull her free, when she tugs on my hand. "Jesus," I yell as my feet go out from underneath me. I land in the water with a splash, and everyone starts laughing.

I sputter, wipe mud from my eyes, and reach for Eliza. I pull her to me as Jason slicks mud from his hair beside her. "You're going to pay for that one, Liza," I say, purposely using my favorite bedroom nickname for her.

Her expression changes, heats as I scoop her up and carry her to the dry grass. Richard, Michelle and Mason are laughing and clapping as we all climb from the mud hole. Richard points to the house. "Okay, everyone to the showers."

I wipe my feet on the mats provided and carry Eliza to our private room. Electricity arcs between us, a new kind of need taking up residency in my gut as I glance at the beautiful woman in my arms.

"Has anyone ever told you how sexy you are when covered in mud?"

"Yeah, right," she shoots back as I enter our bedroom and kick the door shut behind us. Last night Eliza wanted sex without a condom—for experience. That's exactly what I plan to give her right now. It's not smart, it's not wise, considering we'll soon be staging a breakup. But before I do, I need to take this woman again, to see if I can finally get my fill of her and get her out of my system once and for all.

I carry her straight to the bathroom, set her on the counter and turn on the water. I turn back to find her staring at me, like she has no idea what comes next. "Arms up," I say, and when she obliges I peel her shirt off, careful to avoid her face. She remains silent, her eyes locked on mine as I reach around her body and in one smooth move, unclasp her bra.

She lets out a little breath of air. "You're pretty good at that."

I grin, but the truth is, I haven't had as many relationships as most think. No matter who I'm with, if it's a female, pictures are taken and splashed everywhere. I'm not saying I haven't had my fair share of women in the past, but I'm not sleeping with every woman I come into contact with. But now that I've had a taste of Eliza, how the fuck am I ever going to be with another, without comparing her to this woman?

I pick her up from the counter, and set her on the floor. "So dirty," I say as I sink to my knees and drag her shorts down with me. She wiggles out of her underwear and I toss all her wet clothes into the sink.

I frown. "I think they're ruined."

Her little fluttery breath washes over me. "I think it's going to be worth it."

"Think?"

Her entire body quivers as I run a finger up her thigh, imagining the path my tongue will go once I scrub the mud from her body.

"Okay, I know," she says, more conviction in her voice as her fingers rake through my wet hair. "Are you mad that I dragged you in?" she asks, a teasing warmth to her voice. Did she want me mad? Want me to retaliate? Oh, Eliza, you're definitely the good girl I always thought you were, but behind closed doors, you're so much more.

"Definitely, and like I said, you're going to pay for that. I open her nether lips, and nearly bite off my tongue when I see her wet pinkness. She's so fucking hot and ready. For me.

"How do you plan to do that?" she asks.

I grin at her, and swipe my finger over her quivering clit. "You'll see." I stand and take in her nakedness as I make quick work of my clothes. "But something tells me you'll like it."

I back up, and pull her into the shower with me. The hot spray falls over our bodies and I turn her until she's under the overhead rain shower nozzle. She sputters and looks down as the water washes the mud from her hair and body. I reposition her, lather my hands and clean her hair. Once I'm done, I grab the soap pump, squirt a generous amount into my hands, and move her until she's out of the spray. Starting with her gorgeous breasts, I run the soap all over her, taking my time to clean her nipples thoroughly.

Her head falls back on a moan as her nipples swell, and my mouth waters for a taste. "Hands on the wall," I command in a soft voice as I turn her. She puts her back to me, and braces her hands against the tile.

"Time for me to get at all those hard to reach places."

I touch her breasts again, then slide my hand downward, over her quivering stomach until I reach her pubic bone. I linger there for a moment, and place warm, open mouth kisses to her back as my slowness amps up her impatience. She wiggles, trying to force my hand lower, but I'm not done teasing her yet.

"Brax," she cries out, and I fucking love the eagerness in her voice.

"Yeah, baby?" I ask, like I have all the time in the world. I don't. My cock is so fucking hard, I'm ready to shoot a load all over her back.

"I need you to touch me."

"You do?"

"Braxxx...."

I grin. "Where do you need me to touch you, Liza?"

"Between my legs."

I slide my hand between her legs, brush my thumb over her warm inner thighs. "Here?"

"Higher," she murmurs and squirms.

I go higher, and circle her sweet sex, never touching where she really needs it.

"Oh, god, is this payback?" she asks.

I chuckle against her ear. "It's just the start. Now tell me exactly where you want my hand. I want to hear you say it."

"Touch...touch my pussy," she says and it brings a smile to

my face. She moves, wiggles, and I run my finger along the length of her like she asked.

"See all you have to do is ask." I circle her clit, and she trembles.

"My clit," she whimpers. "Please touch my clit."

I do as she demands and her hands slide a little on the wall.

"You do know you have the prettiest cunt I've ever seen, right?" As soon as the word cunt comes from my mouth, the good girl trembles. "What, you don't believe me?" I press down on her clit, and she's a trembling mess beneath my fingers.

"I...believe you."

"Where do you want my fingers now, Liza?"

"Inside me. I want them inside me."

"Inside what? I think you're going to have to be more specific."

"Brax, you're killing me," she pants out.

"I know."

A deep fueling breath and then, "I want your fingers inside my cunt, Brax."

"Yeah, that's it. When you talk like that it makes my cock so fucking hard."

My encouragement seems to do something to her. She rears back as I slide one thick finger into her.

"That's it," she says. "I want you to fuck my cunt with your finger, I want to come all over your hand, then I want to come all over your face, Brax."

Holy mother-fuck. What have I turned this sweet girl into? I have no idea, but I damn well like this wild, open woman who makes no qualms about what she wants. That shit is seriously hot.

"I want you to put your tongue inside my hot pussy, then I want you to kiss me so I can taste it."

My cock twitches, throbs against her ass, and she gives a little moan, a telltale sign that she feels the power and likes it. She's fucking sexy like this.

I push another finger inside her, and the base of my palm against her clit. "Oh, yes, just like that," she whimpers. Her head falls forward, and while I like her in this position, I wish I could see her face. My other hand goes to her ass. I squeeze her lush cheeks gently, the slide my thumb along her crevice. She freezes.

"Brax..."

I press into her ringed opening, just slightly, all the while working my fingers inside her pussy and applying pressure to her clit.

"Oh, Brax," she says. "That feels..." Her words fall off as a powerful orgasm tears through her, sucking my fingers in deeper and scalding them with her sweet release. I stay inside her, moving slowly, prolonging each pulse from her body until she's sagging against the tile, her body a quivery mess.

I step up to her, put my arms around her and hold her to me. I move her back under the spray, warming her body as she comes back down. Her breathing slows, and she turns to me. Her beautiful breasts press against my chest, her nipples scratching slightly as she goes up on her toes and puts her mouth on mine. Her kisses are slow at first, languid, and I match her rhythm. She moans softly into my mouth, a contented little sound that makes me smile. She inches back.

"Something funny, Brax?"

"No, nothing at all. I just really like seeing you like this."

"Like what?"

"Relaxed. Contented. Well fucked." I brush her hair from her face, and say, "I have to say, Liza. I love it when you let go and come undone for me." She frowns slightly. "What?" Shit what did I say?

She steps back, and my raging hard-on juts out. The

elephant in the room. In more ways than one. "Well, let's see if I can do the same for you," she says and drops to her knees. Her sweet mouth wraps around my cock, and I grip a fistful of her hair, push it from her face so I can watch. She works her mouth over me, and my heart squeezes. From her sexy sounds to the way she's worshipping my cock, it's clear she's enjoying this as much as I am. Okay, maybe not as much as I am, but still, no woman has ever given me oral pleasure quite like Eliza. My mind races back to her worries about not being able to please me. Fuck man, they were definitely unfounded. No one can please me like her. Then again, maybe it has more to do with the fact that it's sweet Eliza kneeling before me.

She swirls her tongue, and cups my balls. "Eliza," I groan, doing my best to hang on. Fuck, I don't want to shoot off like a pre-teen who found his first Playboy. I suck in air, gather my control, but the more I do, the harder she tries to get me to break. If I unleash myself with her, let down my guard, I'd be crossing another line, then I'd be totally fucking done for when this is over.

She licks, swirls, takes me to the back of her throat until she's choking. I try to inch out, but she grips my ass, and keeps me locked inside her hot mouth. The water pours over my back, turning a bit cooler, but I don't care. The whole house could be on fire, and nothing or no one could get me to move a muscle. She moans, rocks against me, takes me impossibly deeper. Lightning bolts of pleasure zap my balls, and I punch my eyes shut for just a second, struggling to hang on, but not wanting to take my eyes off Eliza. My blood rushes, my veins fill with blood, yet I continue to fight it. I need to keep some measure of control if I want to walk away from this thing unscathed.

Who am I kidding? I'm already fucked, in more ways than one.

She looks up at me, her tongue pressing against all my

pleasure points, like we've been doing this for years, and she knows me inside out. She eats at me, my cock steel beneath her lips as my chest expands. Goddammit, it's a struggle to breathe.

"I'm going to come," I say and work to pull her off, but she won't have any of that. Jesus, she wants my cum in her mouth, wants to swallow. That knowledge fills me with a new kind tenderness. I jerk forward, once, twice, then let my cum spurt down her throat. She swallows, and swallow and swallows some more and I'm so fucking hot for her, I'm not sure I'm ever going to stop coming. When I eventually do, she eases her mouth from my cock, strokes the length like she's petting a beloved animal. My heart goes into my throat at how much I love her.

Yeah, I fucking love her.

She wipes her mouth with the back of her hand and I shake my head. How can she make that gesture look sexy? I pull her to me, and once again I remind myself what this affair is about—and more importantly what it isn't. Eliza presses her head to my chest, and my heart pounds hard against her cheek. We're day one into a three-day weekend. We're supposed to stage a breakup Monday, but how can I do that? How can I possibly walk away from the woman I want in my arms, my bed...my life? This asinine ruse is actually working, and Eliza's is getting attention from the man she wants, but goddammit, he's not the right guy for her, and it's damn well time I proved it. I'm not sure how I can do that, all I know is that I'm a smart, successful guy and I didn't get ahead by taking a passive stance. No, I'm a guy who fights for what he wants—and what I want is Eliza.

ELIZA

As the last of the dinner dishes are cleared, and the sun begins its nightly descent over the bay, I sit back and stretch out, my body sore after all the physical games we played today, everything from the tug of war to the scavenger hunt. I'd taken a few spills as we raced across the beach and the surrounding trees looking for clues to a puzzle. Then again, perhaps my muscles are aching thanks to Brax and the dirty, delicious way he pleasured me in the shower.

As the sexy image slams into my mind, my entire body quivers. I steal a glance at the man sitting close, but all I see is the back of his head as he chats with Alex, who is seated on the other side of him at the long table. The two seem to have hit it off quite well. I'm happy about that, because Tamara is my good friend at work and a few times we tried to get together outside the office. Unfortunately, we've yet to coordinate schedules. I chuckle quietly. I can't even imagine how hard it would be to coordinate the schedules of four very busy people.

Wait. Shit, what am I thinking?

The four of us will never see each other outside the office. Heck, after this weekend the only time I'll see Brax is during the holiday or special dinners at Mom's. Brax is always invited to those. Of course, I'm sure I'll see San Francisco's Most Eligible Bachelor in the papers, though. A knot forms in my stomach at that thought. Geez, I hate the jealousy that arouses in me. Brax isn't mine, never was. He made that clear the day he laughed when I tried to kiss him.

I shift in my seat and catch the way Jason is leaning toward Brax and Alex from the other side of the table. He obviously wants to be a part of the conversation, not that I know what they're talking about, since Brax has his head turned the other way.

As if sensing my discomfort, his hand slides to my thigh under the table and he gives it a squeeze. His way of letting me know he's not ignoring me, and I appreciate his thoughtfulness. In fact, when it comes right down to it, Brax is always kind and thoughtful where I'm concerned—save for the name-calling and teasing. But really, he's always been there for me, always coming to my rescue one way or another. Warmth spreads through my limbs, followed by a modicum of guilt. If I had my time back, I wouldn't have asked him to pretend this weekend. It wasn't fair of me to put him in such a position, even if I do plan to give him something in return.

Brax turns to me, leans close, his body a wall of warmth. "Richard asked me if I wanted to go out on the boat tonight. Alex is coming, but Tamara doesn't enjoy sailing. She's staying behind, so I think it's just the guys. If you don't want me to—"

"Go, enjoy yourself. You deserve to have a little fun this weekend."

His body brushes mine, and I quiver when his warm breath tickles my flesh. "You don't think I've been having fun?"

Well, there is no denying his arousal—I felt every hard inch of it—and it's clear how much he enjoys being with me sexually. I whack his shoulder. "You know what I mean."

"Hey, are you guys going out on the boat?" Jason asks.

Brax turns to him and his features change, harden. The muscles along his jaw ripple and I've known him long enough to understand that he's not a fan of Jason's? But why? What did Jason ever do to him?

Could it be jealousy?

Wait, is that what I want? For Brax to finally start noticing me as a woman. Is there some small part of me that asked him to play along, because deep down it was him I wanted all along?

Oh, God, I need therapy.

"Yeah, we're heading out when the sun sets," Brax informs him.

"Great, I'll join you," Jason says and finishes the beer in his glass.

Brax turns back to me. "I don't think we'll be too late." He puts his hand on my cheek, his eyes a deeper shade of blue as they move over my face. "Wait up for me?"

"Of course," I say. My heart beats triple time as he gazes at me like I'm the object of his affection. Is it possible that he feels the same way as I do, or am I just making up some ridiculous fantasy? They say sex and intimacy like we've been sharing can affect the chemical balance in the brain. Maybe I'm seeing things that aren't really things. Things I want so desperately, but fear I can never have.

"Okay," he whispers, and drops a soft kiss onto my mouth. I lean into him, and our lips linger, meander, neither of us in a hurry to break apart, despite the audience. When we finally part, I'm breathless, my body on hyperdrive.

"Maybe I won't go," he says and the woman in me feels a measure of satisfaction that I can do this to him.

"No, go," I say. "I know how much you love sailing. We'll just have a girls' night with wine, and talk about you guys." I glance at Val, who is busy chatting with Caleb from accounting. From the way she's leaning in to him, it makes me wonder if she's interested in him. It's a good thing the office doesn't have a no-fraternizing rule. If it did I'd never be able to date Braxton...er...I mean Jason. Although I must say, every time Jason and I talk all he wants to talk about is Braxton. I'm beginning to believe he likes my boyfriend...er...pretend boyfriend more than he likes me.

The plates are cleared, but I do notice how Brax always takes his to the big gray tub himself. I smile. I like that about him. He grew up rich, then made a huge success of himself, but he never takes anyone for granted.

As the guys all disappear, I wave to Val. "Hot tub?" I ask.

She snatches a full bottle of wine from the table and holds it up. "Like you have to ask me twice," she says, teasing. "How about you, Tamara?"

"I'll meet you both there in a few minutes. I have to change."

"I'm wearing my suit," I say and expose the thin strap beneath my summer dress.

"Same," Val says.

I spot Michelle giving her husband a kiss, and wave her over. "Hey Michelle, we're thinking hot tub, wine and gossip."

She makes her way toward us, a smile on her face. "That sounds like my kind of party. I thought we'd never get rid of the guys," she teases but it's clear how much she and Richard are in love. I sigh. They have the kind of love I want.

As Michelle and Tamara dash ahead of us, we make our way to the hot tub. I glance at my friend, who is staring at me with a smirk on her face.

"What?" I ask, my flip flops snapping against my heels as we walk around the massive estate.

Val stops to sniff one of the rose bushes. "Don't 'what' me," she says as she stands back up. "You and Brax have been having crazy monkey sex."

I nearly trip on the stone path, even though there is nothing in my way. "No, we have not," I shoot back in denial.

"Liar," she says and I shake my head. I never could keep anything from her.

Caving, I say, "Well it was all your idea."

"And you are most welcome, my friend," she says as she taps me on the nose.

"How did you know?"

She looks at me like I'm dense. "You both have sex written all over you. You can't keep your hands or eyes off each other. If that wasn't enough to give it away, the noises you both make at night would have."

Mortified, I cover my mouth with my hand. "Ohmigod, no," I say my words coming out muffled.

She waves a dismissive hand. "Relax. Your room is next to mine. No one else probably heard it, and I have to say I'm as jealous as hell."

I let my hand fall. "You should be," I say, shocking myself, as a little giggle bubbles in my throat.

Val laughs. "Who are you and what have you done with my best friend?"

I give a slow shake of my head and think through this crazy turn of events. I can't believe I'm having wild, uninhibited monkey sex with my childhood nemesis. "I've been wondering the same thing." My God, it's crazy how giddy I feel when I talk about Brax. "He just brings something out in me. I feel free to just let go, and..."

"Enjoy?"

I nod. "Exactly."

We reach the hot tub and I hold the bottle of wine as Val lifts the cover. One of the girls who'd been serving us dinner brings us four plastic wine glasses on a tray and sets them on the table near the tub.

"Thank you, that was so thoughtful," I say as I open the wine.

After she disappears, leaving Val and me alone, Val turns to me and says, "I love all the dirty talk, by the way."

My hand stills as I pour the wine into the glasses. "Ohmigod, you really can hear us."

She laughs, and pulls her sundress over her head. "I only listened for a minute, and when I heard you were having fun, I put my ear plugs in." She climbs into the warm water, and waves her hands around. "I'm so happy for you. I knew you two always belonged together."

With two glasses of wine in hand, I take the first step into the water and stop. "What are you talking about?"

Her jaw falls open, then she says, "You can't be serious?"

"About what?" I take the second step, and then hit the bottom of the tub. I hand Val a glass, and grab a seat across from her.

She takes a sip and begins, "Look, I know you've always liked him, and he crushed you when we were kids. But if you ask me, he's *always* been into you, too."

I make a face, like she's lost it. "If he was, then why did he laugh at me when we were kids?"

She shrugs. "You'll have to ask him that. But I'm telling you. I see the way he looks at you. We all do."

A surge of hope rises in my throat. "Do you really think he's into me?"

"I think the two of you need to stop fucking for five minutes and have a talk."

I gulp at her crassness. "You think so?"

"I know so."

Just then Michelle and Tamara come back. They each grab a glass of wine and join us. As they settle themselves, I rest my head on the cushion. Is it possible that Val is right? My pulse beats with hope, and while I've been enjoying all the sex, she's right. We do have to take five minutes to talk— before I go ahead and stage a breakup.

———

Brax asked me to stay up, and I've been trying to. It's well past midnight and there's no sign of him. I heard footsteps in the hall earlier, but Brax has yet to come through our bedroom door. I feel jittery and nervous with the need to talk to him. I toss in the bed, then climb to my feet. I pad quietly to the window and off in the distance, beneath the moon, I see the boat. If they're back, where the hell is Brax?

I swallow against a dry throat and walk to my door. I listen for a minute and when I don't hear sound, I open it. I'm dressed only in my short, cotton nightie that doesn't quite reach my knees, and wouldn't want to run in to any of the guys. I tiptoe to the stairs, and hurry down the long flight. I do another quick check to make sure no one is up, and make my way to the kitchen. I glance around the dark, the kitchen lit only by the glow of under cabinet lighting. I grab a glass from the cupboard, and walk to the fridge. I press the water dispenser, and fill my cup. I'm about to take a drink when I hear a noise behind me.

I jump and turn, spilling cold water over my nightie. But it's the shock of seeing Brax there that has my body quivering all over. I set the glass down. "Ohmigod, you scared me."

"Sorry," he says, although he doesn't look sorry at all. No, he looks hot, needy, his gaze raking over me with heated desire. "We got in late."

I look out the window, but the backyard is empty. "Where is everyone?"

The wicked glimmer in his eyes sends sparks though my body. "They all went to bed. They had a lot more to drink then me, so I told them I'd take care of the boat, make sure it was secured to the wharf before I hit the sack."

I turn to face him, catch the whiff of beer on his breath. "I thought the captain wasn't supposed to drink."

He gives a nonchalant shrug. He's far from drunk, but the drinks seem to have relaxed him a bit, loosened his mood.

"I had a couple of beers on the boat, nothing to impair my duties as captain, or stop me from properly fucking you tonight." He pulls me to him and places a hard kiss on my mouth, a kiss full of hunger and need—a kiss that hints at more. If I had to guess, tonight's sex is about something other than giving me an educational experience. My heart leaps. Is it possible that this man really is into me, that after this weekend we have a chance of something deeper, something more meaningful?

Do I dare hope?

"I was going to ask what you were wearing under this nightie, but I'd rather find out myself." He slides a hand along my thigh until he reaches my bare sex.

"Jesus, fuck, you're not wearing panties." He spreads my wet lips and pushes a finger inside me.

I gasp. "What are you doing?" I ask, and push against him, my actions letting him know I don't want him to stop. It feels so damn good, but anyone can walk in on us.

"Fucking my girl, what does it look like I'm doing?"

"We're in the kitchen, Brax."

Shut up, Eliza, you want this. Anytime, anywhere with this man.

"I don't care."

"We can't have sex here," I whisper, my last working brain cell struggling not to burn out from the lust firing my blood.

"Yes we can," he says as he slides his hand up my nightie, and cups my breasts. Jesus that feel so good, too. "And we will."

"We need to go to our room," I murmur, one last ditch effort to take this somewhere private before we get caught. Then again, maybe that's the whole thrill for him.

"No time," he murmurs through hurried, open mouth kisses to my chin, my neck, my collarbone. Honest to God, I've never seen him like this before. So needy, so carnal...so hungry for me that he can't even wait and take this to our room.

"Need to fuck you, Liza," he pants. "Right here in the kitchen, right on the counter."

The entire room closes in on me as I revel in this new side of him. I inch back and look at him, catch the intense heat in his eyes. Ohmigod, he's going to eat me alive.

He spins me around, and cups the back of my neck like a man on a mission and bends me over the counter. The coolness is welcome against my cheek as my body goes from simmer to inferno. "You want my cock in here?" he asks, putting his hand between my legs again.

"Oh, God, Brax."

"Tell me you want it, Liza," he says, his control hanging by a thin thread that I'm desperate to tear.

"I want your cock," I say, no longer caring if we're overheard. The only thing driving me is this man and what he wants to do to my body.

"Whose cock do you want?"

"Yours Braxton," I say. "It's your cock I want inside me."

He leans over me, nibbles on my ear as he squeezes my ass. "Who are you going to be thinking about when I fuck you and make you come so hard, you won't be able to walk."

"You. I'll be thinking only about you."

Using his foot, he nudges my legs open wider, until I'm

fully offered up to him. "Good, because I'll only be thinking of you too, Liza. It's only ever been you," he says, but I'm so far gone, I'm not sure if I'm hearing him right, or even able to comprehend what he's saying. My sex clenches, eager for him to fill me, take us both to the place we desperately need to go.

He pushes a finger into me again, and I gasp as he fills me. "Jesus, you're so wet for me."

In slow steady moves, he slides his finger in and out, and I move with him, shamelessly taking what I need.

"That's it, Liza. Fuck my fingers. Show me how desperate you are for my cock."

Desperate doesn't even begin to describe it.

I move against him, my breasts rubbing the counter through my nightie, stimulating my hard nipples. Pleasure sinks deep into my core as he slides his finger over the hot bundle of nerves inside me. I gasp, grip the counter, run my nails along it, trying to find something to grasp on to. He pulls his fingers out and I almost cry from the loss, but when his crown nuzzles my throbbing opening, I moan and rock in to him.

Warm hands slide over my back, then take a firm hold of my hips, his fingers biting into my skin hard enough to leave a bruise. But that's okay, I want the bruise, I want to feel him on my body come tomorrow.

"Please…" I cry out.

"Is this what you're begging for Liza?" His voice is hoarse, labored, and his body is tense as he inches into me, no condom, no barrier, nothing but the sleek smoothness of his hard cock entering my body.

Not wanting him to hold anything back with me, I say, "Take me, Brax. Put your cock in my cunt, and take me hard and fast. Take everything you want."

A deep groan fills the air at my dirty little words, and in one quick thrust he's filling me, seating his long length deep inside, the positon allowing him to reach places I've never been touched before.

"Oh, yesss..."

He moves, pistoning in and out of me, his fingers biting harder, like he can't quite get close enough, deep enough.

Like he's claiming me.

I whimper in bliss, and it amps up the urgency in him. His movements become quicker, more desperate, and I get the sense that he's seeking more than release. He slides a hand around my body, presses his finger to my clit. The stimulation combined with his fast pace takes my body to the edge in record time.

"Brax," I cry out in ecstasy as the heat builds inside me—between us—combustive enough to burn for a thousand lifetimes. "Yes," I say as I come all over his cock. My cry mingles with his groan of pleasure as my liquid release scorches him and lubricates his penetrating cock.

His mouth finds my neck as his body presses me into the countertop. I pant, gasp, unable to fill my lungs.

He pumps into me, his cock demanding, frantic as I grind against him. Sensations wash over me, weakening my knees as I revel in the pleasure.

"Fuck, Liza," he growls, and I writhe, squeeze my muscles around his steely cock. "I'm losing it."

"Yes," I murmur as he pounds impossibly harder, his hips jerking, giving me everything he has. "Lose it with me," I say and glance at him over my shoulders. Gone is his guarded look. What I'm seeing instead is Braxton unleashed, wide open, and holding nothing back as he pistons into me, giving me every inch of his body, pounding like he's pouring his entire soul, his entire being into me—no distance between us, physical or otherwise. Excitement flutters in my belly as he finally surrenders to his need.

"Fill me with your cum," I say, as his pleasure becomes mine.

His eyes meet mine, dark, hungry...vulnerable...a man who sees nothing but me as he pummels, slamming home with thrusts that bring on another climax. My pussy squeezes as his cock swells inside me. He tosses his head back and fully lets go, warming my body with his hot cum as he freefalls over the edge, without a safety net.

ELIZA

I glance at the amazing man beside me, a man I love with every ounce of my being. Always have. Last night he gave himself to me fully, and I'm certain we crossed over the line from pretend to real. I need to talk to him, of that I'm certain, but he looks so relaxed and handsome as he sleeps, I don't have the heart to wake him—especially after he'd given so much of himself to me last night.

I quietly slip from the bed, brush out my hair, and pull on a bathing suit. On my way out the door, I shrug into my cover-up and grab my beach bag. Brax might miss breakfast, but I think after last night's exertion, he needs sleep more than anything else right now. I step out into the sunshine as everyone makes their way to the breakfast table.

"Where's Brax," Richard asks, his brow furrowed. "Is everything okay?"

"He was up late securing the boat. I thought he could use a little extra sleep this morning."

I catch Val's eye and she grins at me. Ignoring her all-knowing look, I take a seat and Jason slides in beside me. I angle my head, look him over. He might be tall, well built, features similar to Brax, but when it comes right down to it, no man can hold a candle to the guy I'm in love with. How could I ever have thought I could be with Jason when my heart has always belonged to Brax?

"We have to pair up later for some games," Jason says. "Want to be my partner?"

I hesitate for a second. Yes, I came here with the intention of gaining his attention, but so much has changed, and I don't want him to get the wrong idea.

"That sounds like a great idea," Richard says. "I think you two will work well together."

I nod. "Oh, okay then."

"Mason has some fun things lined up for us this afternoon," Richard goes on to explain. "You can all have the morning to yourself. Go for a sail, a swim, a walk. Whatever you like."

As the morning sun beats down on me, I know where I want to spend my time—lounging at the pool. I flip my cup over when one of the servers brings the coffee, then I head to the buffet and fill my plate, piling it higher than normal, knowing I'll be working the calories off later. I can't seem to keep the smile from my face as I sit back down and dig into my meal. Everyone returns with their food and we all talk quietly over breakfast. As time slips by, I glance up at my bedroom window, missing Braxton's company. Soon the meal is finished and the dishes are cleared. Everyone breaks off to do their own thing and Val and I walk to the pool.

"Have you talked to him?" she asks, getting straight to the point now that we're alone.

"We...ah...haven't really had a chance." I grin at my friend. "I'm hoping to do it this morning."

She shakes her head and laughs. "You must have done a number on him for him to still be in bed."

"Let's just say, I can never look at Richard's kitchen counter the same way again."

"Ohmigod, you're kidding me?"

Heat moves into my cheeks. "Nope."

I peel off my bathing suit cover-up, and take a seat in one of the lounge chairs near the deep end of the pool. Val sits beside me. "What about Jason? He's all over you this weekend. I guess your plan worked."

"I know, and that was the whole point of this weekend. But there is nothing between us."

"I'm not sure he knows that." She gestures with nod, and I follow her gaze to see Jason walking toward us.

"Mind if I join you?"

I shade the sun from my eyes. "Sure," I say and wave to the chair beside me.

He drops into the cushioned lounger and stretches out beside me. "What time do you think, Brax will be up?" he asks.

"I'm not sure."

He frowns, clearly disappointed. He might be noticing me, but I think it's because he wants to get in good with Braxton. I dig into my bag, and pull out my lotion. I pour a generous amount on my legs and rub it in. Then I do my chest, face and arms.

"Mind if I use some of that?" Jason asks.

"Not at all." I hand it to him, then stand to adjust my chair, wanting to get some sun on my back. I lie on my stomach, and exhale a contented sigh and the sun warms my body.

When Jason finishes with the lotion, I say, "Val, can you do my back."

"I got it," Jason says and shifts his lounge chair until it's closer to mine. "So maybe you can talk to Braxton about me," Jason says.

"About what?" I ask.

"My work. You know, build me up."

I should be disappointed that he's trying to use me to get to Braxton, but I can't say as I am. A big cold blop of lotion hits my back, and when he puts his hands on me, I stiffen. Truthfully, the only hands I want on my body are Brax's.

"Eliza."

Speaking of Brax...

Unease trickles down my spine at the coldness in Brax's tone. I flip over, to find him staring at me. His face is hard, his jaw clenched, rage emanating from every pore in his body.

"Brax. I didn't know you were up," I say as I take a second to see the scene before him through his eyes.

"That's obvious." He casts a frigid glare at Jason, then he rakes his hands through his hair. Just then Alex, Tamara, Richard and Michelle head our way, but they go still when they see Brax standing over me like a warrior ready for battle.

"Is everything okay?" I ask tentatively.

"No. It's not. I'm going to take off. Can you find your own ride back?"

My stomach lurches, and despite the heat of the day, goosebumps break out on my skin. I shiver, almost violently as every instinct I possess warns me that Brax is done with this game—with me.

"What's...what's going on?"

"I have some work to do."

I fold my arms across my chest, holding back the emotions that are threating to consume me. "You do?"

"Yes, I do." I flinch at the hardness in his tone, and the backyard goes deathly quiet.

"It can't wait?" I whisper, my throat tight, hot and achy, my pulse thrumming wildly.

He shoves an anxious hand through his hair again. "No, Eliza, it can't wait. And I'm tired of having this conversation with you. Work comes first. It always will. I thought you knew that."

Jason's lounge chair scrapes the stone decking around the pool, cutting through the tension as he inches away from me. Brax casts him a murderous glance, then his artic eyes are back on me again. I wince, the sting of his gaze like a thousand angry hornets.

"I...I didn't realize I was always on your case about work," I say, my heart sinking as I play along. Here I thought Brax was falling for me, thought he wouldn't go through with this pretend breakup, yet here he is playing a part—and breaking my heart all over again.

"Look. I'm going to go." I recoil like I'd just been slapped in the face. "It's best if you get a ride home with someone else." He stares at me for an endless moment, stripping me bare with eyes that had gone glacial overnight. Every muscle in his body is taut, strained, and I clasp my hands, afraid he'll snap if I touch him. I curl in upon myself as he directs that dark, menacing mood my way.

I blink once, twice, and nod my head as his words sink in. This was all a ruse. Brax hadn't had growing feelings for me. Why had I let myself believe otherwise?

Stupid. Stupid. Stupid.

I fight back the tears that are far too close to the surface. "I'll see you around then," I say, hating how real this is for me, taking me back to our youth, when his rejection had ripped through me like a serrated blade.

"I'll grab my stuff and get out of your...way," he says, but what he's really saying is he'll get out of my life. I should do something. Say something. Tell him I love him. But if he loved me back, why would he do this?

He gives Jason one last hard stare. The chill in his eyes freezes my bones as his gaze moves back to me.

"Goodbye," he mutters.

Saliva dries in my throat as he turns, offering me his back as he disappears into the house, and out of my life. I sit there, all eyes on me. The urge to run, hide tug at me, and I'm about to make a move, when Val's hand on my arm stops me.

"Eliza," she says. "What the hell is going on?"

I try to speak, but the knot it my throat won't let the words pass. Without saying anything, Jason climbs from his chair and dives into the pool. I guess I'm no use to him anymore. Cold water splashes up, wets my legs.

I glance at Richard and the others. "Eliza?" Richard asks, concern evident on his face.

I inject a lightness into my voice that I don't feel. "I'll be okay."

Richard nods, and guides Alex and the others toward the beach, giving me the privacy I most desperately need.

A gurgling sound catches in my throat as I throw my legs over the side of my chair and brace my elbows on my legs. Tears sting my eyes and I try to breathe past the tightness in my chest.

"Eliza, honey," Val says and sits beside me. She puts her arm around me and hugs. "You need to go after him. Talk to him."

"This whole weekend was a mistake. I never should have asked Braxton to do this."

"It wasn't a mistake," Val says, but she's wrong. She's so very wrong. I set myself up for heartache again, read more into things between us. I can't blame Brax. Not really. He was only doing what I asked of him, he'd just done it sooner rather than later—ending the stupid fairy tale I'd singlehandedly fabricated.

Acid fills my throat as my chest aches, right around the vicinity of my heart. "I kept checking in with him, giving him a way out of the ruse, hoping there really was more between us than sex, but he never took it, and insisted he see this through to the end. Why didn't I see that? Why did I believe there was more than sex between us."

"I don't care what you say, Eliza, that man is into you."

I shake my head and sniff, then go still when I hear his car door slam, harder than necessary—all for show I suppose. "Then why is he leaving? Why did he cause a big scene in front of everyone, and walk out of here like that?" When I really think about it, it's so not like Brax to cause a scene. Yeah, I was going to stage a breakup, but not one like this, one where Brax came out looking badly. He's a powerful businessman who cares how other see him. How he acts, what he says can reflect positively or negatively on his image, his business. So why did he do this?

"Maybe he did it because he's giving you what he thinks you want."

As my brain races, I ask, "What do you mean?"

"Come on," she begins, rushing on. "You brought him here to help you get the attention of another man, right? Say he's actually in love with you, wouldn't a guy who was in love want to give you everything you wanted despite what it would do to him?"

"Val—"

"Look, Eliza. He came out here and saw Jason's hands all over you. He was enraged. No way was he faking that kind of anger, and I'm guessing he bowed out early because he couldn't handle helping you for one more second. Did you see the way he looked at Jason?" She gives a low whistle. "I though he was going to kill him. That my friend, is jealousy. And where there's jealousy...there's love."

"You think?"

"Yeah, I think. And one way or the other you have to find out where you guys stand, or you'll spend the rest of your life regretting it."

"What if you're wrong? What if he rejects me like he did when we were teens?"

"What if he doesn't?" she says, her voice softer, as she puts her hand on mine.

As I take a moment to digest that, my heart lurches. I suck in two deep breaths and with renewed focus, I look at my friend through watery eyes. "Can I borrow your car?"

BRAXTON

I gesture the bartender for another drink, hoping the whiskey will fill that hollowed-out spot inside me. Jesus Christ, I hated leaving Eliza, but what the fuck was I supposed to do? I promised her I'd see this ruse through to the end, but after giving her every part of me last night, and waking up to see Jason with his hands on her as she sprawled out on her lounge chair beneath him...Christ, I was ready to fucking murder him. But that's when reality hit me. Jason is the guy she wants. The whole reason for me being there in the first place. Fuck man, I never should have agreed to sex with no condom. I needed something, anything to protect me from giving all of myself to her. How does a guy come back from something like that?

The truth is, I might not be the best guy for her, but I'm not sure it's Jason either. In fact I know he's not. But fuck, if that's the guy she wants, how can I possibly stand in her way? I love her, for fuck's sake, always have, and I'm not going to be a selfish prick for one more second. No matter how much turning my back and walking away had gutted me, her happiness comes first and foremost.

"Why aren't you answering my texts?"

Great. Just fucking great. Derek is just about the last person I want to see today. He returned from overseas last night, and I've been ignoring him. For good reason. One look at my face, and he's going call me out on my shit. How can I tell him about Eliza and me? How can I not?

He plunks down beside me at our favorite Irish pub, and gestures the bartender for two more of what I'm having. Then he turns to me, those astute brown eyes assessing me.

"What the fuck is going on with you?" he asks

Jesus, I wish he couldn't read me so well.

"Nothing," I say and finish the whiskey in my glass.

"Don't fucking 'nothing' me," he says. "It's two o'clock in the afternoon, and you're drinking."

I shrug. "So are you."

"When my best friend drinks at two, I drink at two. Now tell me what the fuck is going on so I at least know why we're drinking."

I exhale a slow sigh, and brush the backs of my fingers over my face, a stalling tactic. Another beat of silence, and then, "For starters, I'm a shit friend, Derek."

I twirl my glass, and slowly angle my head until I see the confusion on my friend's face. Derek is the best guy I know, and he doesn't deserve to be hurt by me like this. My fingers curl, as the hate I feel for myself takes up residence in my gut.

He stiffens. "What did you do?"

I can't lose my best friend. I can't. He and his family are everything to me, but I can't keep this from him, either. The guilt will eat me up inside and he deserves to know what an asshole I really am. Here I used to pride myself on keeping my word. Now my word means nothing. I take a breath, let it out slowly and start at the beginning.

"Eliza stopped by my office Friday night and—"

"Is she okay?" he asks cutting me off as he sits up a little straighter, his gaze zinging from me to the door, and back to me like he's ready to bolt. He was always protective of his kid sister. We both were. Still are.

I grunt to let him know what I'm about to tell him is all kinds of insane. "She had her annual retreat at her boss's place, and asked me to pretend to be her boyfriend so she could get the attention of some douchebag she works with."

He shakes his head, incredulous. "What the fuck?"

I scoff. "Yeah, my thoughts exactly."

"Tell me you didn't do it."

The bartender slides us each two fresh shots of whiskey, and Derek shoots one back quickly. Yeah, he really should have a few fast ones before I tell him I ravished his sister.

"Oh, I did it. I did a lot of things." I cast him a quick glance and look away. Fucking coward.

"What things?"

I toss another drink back, and plant my elbows on the bar top. "I crossed a line while pretending to be her boyfriend." One second passes, then two, but they feel like an eternity as I wait for him to say something.

"You slept with Eliza," he announces.

The guilt on my face must have been a dead giveaway. I swallow. Hard. The sound cuts the tense silence between us. "Yeah. I'm sorry. I know you warned me against her and—"

He takes a drink, and slams his glass down on the bar top. "Yeah, when you were nineteen and she was sixteen. Things have changed since then."

"And I didn't mean—" I jerk around to find my friend grinning at me. "Wait, what?" I ask as his words sink in.

"I didn't want you fucking around with my sister when we were teens, asshole. But we're not teens anymore."

"I...what?" I ask again, my rattled brain unable to keep up. I fight to make sense of his words.

"Look, you've been in love with her since the first time

you set eyes on her. You two weren't ready for each other then, which is why I told you to stay the fuck away. I knew eventually you'd find each other, when you were both more mature and the timing was right."

I shake my head, and count the empty glasses in from of me. "I must have had more to drink than I thought."

He puts his hand on my shoulder. "You're not hearing me wrong, pal."

I tense, still not sure he's just fucking with me before he throws a punch. "You're not going to knock my teeth out for sleeping with Eliza."

"No." He raises a questioning brow. "But I am wondering what you're doing here, tossing back whiskey and sulking like a kicked puppy."

"I love her," I say and stare at my drink.

He laughs, and I lift my eyes to his. "Yeah, no fucking kidding, Brax."

I shake my head. "You knew all this time."

"All this time. You're really not that great of an actor." He laughs. Not sure why Eliza thought you could play a role." At the mention of Eliza he glances around the bar. "So where is my sister?"

"At her boss's retreat, with her douchebag."

"Why are you here?"

"I'm not the guy she wants."

He grunts. "I doubt that. She's been in love with you from the second she laid eyes on you too, pal."

My heart misses a beat as a surge of hope and excitement rushing through me. "You think so?"

"I know so."

Unease coils through me, pushing back that burst of happiness as I face my friend. "What if I'm not the right guy for her, Derek? What if I'm not the best guy for her, you know? I grew up in a loveless household. What if I can't do right by her?"

"Brax, you're the best guy I know, and the only guy I'd ever let near my sister." He taps my chest. "I've never met a guy who cared more about people—more about my sister and me—than you."

I put my arm around my best friend's shoulders, and give him a hug. "I fucked up," I say when we break apart. "I totally fucked it all up."

He gives an easy shrug. "Then go make this right."

I stare into my empty whiskey glass like it has all the answers in the universe. "What if it's too late?"

"You're never going to know that sitting here, are you?" He finishes his whiskey, slams the glass back on the bar top. "So go take her away from this douchebag and show her you're the right guy."

I nod, a new kind of desperation burning through my blood. "I need to go find her." I jump from my stool, and turn toward the door, but stop dead in my tracks when it flies open and hits the wall with a deafening thud.

No way!

My gaze goes from Brax to my grinning brother and back to Brax again. What the hell is going on here and why is Derek sitting there smiling like the village idiot?

"Eliza," Brax says and crosses the room until he's standing close. His heat reaches out to me, and when I catch his warm familiar scent, all I want to do is throw myself into his arms, forget that cruel breakup and pick up where we left off last night. But my best friend is right. We need to talk and I need to be honest.

"What...what are you doing here?" he asks, his brow furrowed, his body tense like he's bracing himself. Like I have bad news.

"You weren't at home, or the office, so I thought I'd try here."

"You've been looking for me, Liza?" he asks, his hard features softening as he puts his fingers on my arm and slightly strokes. "You came here for me?"

"Yes, I came here for you, Brax." I jerk my finger behind

me as my eyes search his. "What the hell was all that back there, anyway?"

He shrugs, but his mood is suddenly different from this morning. Lighter. Could that be because the ruse is over and he's free of me. Jesus, don't let me be wrong about us—don't let this be some made up fairy tale in my head.

"Just giving you what you wanted."

"Brax," I shift from one foot to the together.

Tell him how you feel already.

He moves closer, hovering over me, making it impossible to think. "Yeah?"

"We need to talk."

"I know, that's why I was coming back for you."

My pulse jumps in my throat, a bevy of emotions tumbling inside me. "You were?"

Brax was coming back for me?

Breathless, I glance at my brother, who is watching us carefully, too carefully.

"Maybe we shouldn't be having this conversation right here," I say and lower my voice. I'm not sure how Derek will feel about his best friend and sister in bed together.

"Derek knows we slept together. I told him," he says bluntly.

My jaw drops open. "You did? Why?"

"Because he's my best friend, and I needed to tell him I slept with you because I'm in love with you." He gives me a sheepish grin. "But apparently he already knew that."

Brax loves me!

My legs nearly give beneath me, but Brax is there, his arms around me, anchoring my body to his, and coming to my rescue once again. I glance at his handsome face, take in the weariness beneath his eyes. A weariness that says he's been going through his own personal kind of hell, too.

"I...I don't understand. Why didn't you say something?"

Then again, why didn't I? "Why did you break it off in front of everyone? After last night in the kitchen...the way you opened yourself up to me...I thought..."

"I gave you everything, Eliza, but when I saw Jason's hands on you this morning I realized two things. You were finally getting what you wanted, and what you wanted wasn't me."

I glance down, and my hair falls into my eyes. "I...I...don't want him, Brax. I'm not sure I ever did."

Brax touches my chin, lifts my face, and brushes my hair back. There is a new intensity about him as those deep blue eyes stare into mine, like he can see into the depths of my soul. "Who do you want, Eliza?" he asks, everything in his expression telling me our games, our ruse, is behind us. He wants straight-up honesty from me, and that's what I plan to give him.

Throat tight, and my chest expanding with everything I feel for this man, I blurt out, "I want you."

He lets out a heaving breath, like he's been holding it for days. "That's a good fucking thing, because I have a confession to make."

"You...do?" I ask.

"Yeah, I do." He presses his lips to my forehead, then inches back to meet my eyes. "I wanted you my whole life, Liza. Jesus, that time you kissed me at the kitchen table nearly killed me."

"But you laughed at me."

He touches my face. "I know. I've always regretted being cruel to you, but I wanted you so much. I just didn't know how to deal with it. I was young. Stupid." He cups my cheek, brushes his thumb over my bottom lip. "Do you know why I took you in the kitchen like that last night?" I shake my head. "I wanted to get caught. I wanted Jason to see us, to see that you were mine and not his. I know how fucked up that sounds…" He shakes his head, and lets his words fall off.

"No more fucked up than me asking you to pretend to be my boyfriend." My heart is pounding so fast, it's hard to breathe, let along talk. "Why didn't you tell me any of this?"

"I was warned to stay away from you."

I blink up at him, trying to sort through what he's telling me. "I don't understand."

He makes a sound, a half laugh, half groan. "Your brother was so protective of you. He warned me to stay away. I agreed, because he was family. The only real family I ever had. I couldn't risk losing him from my life."

"You had a mom and dad, what are you talking about?"

"I know, but they were never there. We didn't have sit-down dinners like you guys did. We didn't talk about our day, our feelings, our plans. We didn't go to the beach together, or on picnics."

I touch his face, run my fingers along the bristles. "I didn't realize any of this, Brax. I'm so sorry."

"It's okay. I'm okay. I had Derek, your mother…you. I couldn't risk losing any of that. But Liza, I can't keep going on the way I've been going."

"Seattle's Most Eligible Bachelor?"

His brow furrows. He hates being called that as much as I have being called Lizard.

"I was never that. That was hype."

I nod. "I have a confession, too." He arches a brow. "I think on some level I asked you to come to the retreat and pretend to be my boyfriend because all along it was you I wanted. I was hoping the weekend would have ended differently." My mind races back to the breakup. "You caused quite the scene, Brax." My heart squeezes, worried about the repercussions of his actions. "I can't imagine what everyone is saying about you right now."

"I don't care."

My head rears back. "You don't?"

"I only care what you, Derek, and your mom think of me."

I go up on my toes, press my lips to his for a deep, soul-searing kiss. "Does that tell you how I feel?"

He holds me to him and his heart pounds hard against my body and he gives me a teasing grin. "Yes, and I think it's time for me to tell you what I want." He gives me a playful wink. "You know, for agreeing to help you this weekend."

The shift in his mood warms me to the depths of my soul, and I laugh, giddiness welling up inside me. "Oh, really?"

"Yeah, I want you, Eliza. I want you in my arms, and in my bed. I want you in my life...forever."

A gasp catches in my throat. "Are you asking me—"

His eyes sober, hold me captive. "I'm asking you to marry me, and since you love my house overlooking the bay, we can live there together, and fill it with kids. Say yes, Eliza. Say yes and together we'll turn my house into a home."

I swallow against the tears pressing against the back of my eyes. "I thought you didn't believe in marriage or family?"

"I used to say that, used to blame it on my parents' loveless marriage, blame it on the fact that I didn't really have a father figure, and wouldn't know how to be a good husband or dad. But the truth is, I only ever wanted to marry you. No one else ever compared."

"I never believed in marriage either," I say as a tear drips down my face.

He brushes it away and gives me a warm smile. "I know."

"I painted all rich guys with the same brush as my father."

He runs the backs of his fingers over my cheek. "I'm not him. I'd never do anything to hurt you, Liza."

"I know that." I briefly close my eyes, take a second to go over this amazing turn of events. When I open them again, I find Brax staring at me, his gaze so full of love that my heart nearly explodes. "I said I never believed in marriage, but I believe in you, Brax, and that's all I need."

"What exactly are you saying, Eliza?"

"I'm saying yes. Yes to being in your arms, your bed, and your life forever." He presses his lips to mine, and despite the audience, kisses me with everything he has inside him—holding nothing back this time—and I know I'm the luckiest girl in the world.

Someone clears their throat and we break apart to find Derek standing next to us. We were so lost in each other, we didn't even hear his approach.

"Looks like I'm going to be part of the family, bro," Brax says, pulling me against him and holding me tight as he puts a hand on Derek's shoulder.

Brax puts his arms around both of us for a group hug. "You always were, Brax. You always were."

After a long moment, Derek breaks the hug, takes a measured step back, and glares at my fiancé. His look is hard, deadly, as he curls his fingers at his sides. "So, you slept with my sister, without coming to me first," he says. "You broke the bro code, dude."

Brax scrubs his chin and takes two steps back, like he knew this was coming. "Oh, shit."

Bound by a vow with his friends, hotel tycoon Nathan Archer refuses to settle down and tie the knot. His only commitment is to bachelorhood. Granted, that contract was made when he was 15 years old... and in a treehouse. Still, a promise is a promise. And Nate takes his promises seriously.

But when cute little Eleanor Marshall walks back into his life, this blast from the past is no longer the timid little girl he used to know. When Ellie propositions him for a night of sizzling, unattached sex, Nate can't refuse. Besides, it's only one night. And Nate is never going to settle down.

Never say never...
This book was previously published as Never Say Love by Carly Phillips and Lauren Hawkeye

1 *5 Years Earlier*

The gash on his cheek hurt like hell.

Nate Archer traced his fingers over the fresh wound and his fingers came away slightly sticky. Shame coiled in his belly as he padded barefoot into the shallows of Ruby Lake, scooping up handfuls of icy cold water to rinse the blood and sweat from his face.

He could see his buddy Chase's house from here, could view the beams from flashlights already arcing through the treehouse where he and his best friends planned to spend the night.

Chase, Lucas, Gavin—none of them would comment on the cut on his cheek, the split in his lip, or the swelling around his eye. No, they wouldn't say a word, but they would see it. And they would know that not only could bad-ass Nathan Archer not protect his mother, he couldn't even keep himself safe from his asshole stepdad's fists.

Nate straightened and waded out of the water, working his wet feet back into his black canvas Converse sneakers.

Shielding his eyes against the last blaze of the fading sun, he looked back to the treehouse, to the shadows moving inside.

Part of him, a really big part, wanted just to take off. To run away from shitty small-town Ruby Beach and never return. The ache to escape the fucked-up circumstances of his life called to him, a seductive whisper that was almost impossible to ignore.

But he couldn't. No matter how good it sounded, he just couldn't run. Though he was always pissed off that his mom didn't leave his stepdad and get them both the hell out of there, the fact remained that if Nate took off, Hannah Archer would have no one. The knowledge weighed him down as he trudged across the rocky beach to the fence and gate that surrounded Chase Marshall's yard.

Standing with his hand on the gate, he stopped for a second, closed his eyes and listened to the familiar sounds of his three best friends. They'd been friends since eighth grade, were sixteen now, and as close as brothers.

If he left, they'd follow.

He wouldn't ruin their lives by making them chase after him. So it seemed that, for now at least, he was stuck.

Spirits slightly lifted by the laughter of his friends, Nate reached for the gate latch that he'd opened a thousand times over the years. Swinging open the heavy wood, he pushed through, then shouted when he collided with something solid.

"What the—" Nate reached out and grabbed hold of ... a person, his grip landing on soft upper arms. The scent of ripe strawberries hit his nose, and he *knew* it was Ellie Marshall before he made out her features in the fading light.

"Shit!" The sunshiney blonde glared up at him, a finger reaching up to shove her thick plastic-framed glasses back up her nose. "Watch where you're going, Nate!"

"Better not let your parents hear you talking like that,

Blondie." Nate arched an eyebrow at Chase's baby sister, younger by two years, and much of his anger at his stepdad dissolved.

Especially when she saucily planted her hands on her hips and glared at him.

"Where'd you learn to talk like that, anyway?" he asked.

"From you and my dopey brother, duh." Ellie hiked a thumb over her shoulder, gesturing in the direction of the treehouse. "Gavin and Lucas are already here, cackling over some magazine with boobs."

"*Ellie*." Nate wasn't the type to get embarrassed by the female body. In fact, he was the first of his friends to have gotten his hands on a pair of tits, thanks to Janey Bloom, a girl in their class who liked to put out. But hearing Chase's younger sister toss out the word so nonchalantly had the barest hint of a flush creeping into his cheeks. "Don't talk like that."

Ellie rolled blue eyes, the color of Ruby Lake on a bright summer day, then shoved her hands into the pockets of her jeans, looking up at him. Nate squirmed a bit under the assessing glare. Yeah, he was the badass of Ruby Beach High, but he'd always felt like this smart girl could see right into him.

Ellie's smirk died as she took in the cuts on his skin. She hissed in a breath, rising onto her toes with a hand outstretched to touch.

"What happened, Nate?" The tips of her fingers were cool on his heated skin. Though his instinct was to jerk away, instead he found comfort in the simple touch.

But only for a moment. Then the raucous laughter of his friends from up in their treehouse broke through the calm, and Nate jerked back from Ellie's curious touch, the aching humiliation of his stepfather's beating back in full force.

"None of your business." He shrugged his shoulders with

irritation, now doubly embarrassed because he'd found some comfort in the innocent caring of a kid. Worse, she was Chase's little sister. "And don't ask me to explain," he said, anticipating her next response. "You're too young to know."

As he'd expected, Ellie bristled.

Truth was, at fourteen years old, she was the smartest, most mature person he knew, and that included all of the so-called adults in his life. But lately he'd started having these weird dreams about her. Like, *kissing* dreams.

Nate liked kissing just fine, but again, she was Chase's *baby* sister.

He didn't even need a warning from his friend. He was warning himself. *Hands off.* He didn't have to be told—he wasn't good enough for her, and he never would be.

"You guys are such assholes." Ellie narrowed her eyes at him, her slender fingers curling into fists. He felt exactly like what she called him, but instead of showing it, he smirked, nodding at her in dismissal.

And when that strawberry scent lingered in his nose as he walked away, then climbed the sturdy ladder to the treehouse, well, no one had to know but him.

"What's up, bitches?" Wincing as the forced grin tugged on the cut in his lip, Nate swung himself through the trapdoor in the floor.

His body ached as he clambered through, taking his usual spot on top of the pile of sleeping bags in the treehouse, the word sounding super juvenile. The wooden structure perched in the sturdy oak tree was more like their fortress. The four of them had spent countless hours here over the years, and now that they were juniors in high school, it was still where they gathered to hide away from the adults and talk about important things. Mostly about sex.

Nate reached for the small cooler shoved into the corner and fished out a dripping can of Dr. Pepper. It wasn't until he'd cracked open the lid that he realized how silent the others had become.

He looked up, glancing at each of them in turn. Chase, with the same blond hair and blue eyes as his sister, had grown up in a strong nuclear family. And even if his mother had a stick up her ass and a problem with Chase's *lower class friends* ... Chase had a good life. He'd never known Nate's kind of pain. Gavin was Nate's partner in crime when it came to being bad, and Lucas was the one who hid his brains behind black clothing and an emo haircut, but neither of them had ever been beaten.

He knew each of them as well as he knew himself. And as he weighed their stares, he knew that this time they weren't going to stay quiet.

"Dude." Lucas ran a hand through hair dyed raven black. "Why does your mom stay with him?"

He didn't ask why Nate stayed with his mom. They all already knew. They'd probably do the same for their own mothers.

"Dunno." Nate shrugged, uncomfortable, even under the familiar stares of his best friends.

"When we were kids, your mom was awesome." Gavin, the biggest of them all and star of the football team, frowned. "She would have done anything for you. So why is she letting Tom beat the shit out of you now?"

"I—" Nate swallowed thickly. Now that they were asking, it was hard to answer. "She used to be... different. She changed when she met Tom."

Tom. The man who had charmed his mom with the attention she hadn't received in years, not having dated since Nate's real dad had died. But that sweet attention, the flowers and fancy dinners and jewelry, had so gradually and insidiously changed into shouts and fists that it was hard to say when life went to shit.

Yeah, marriage to Tom had changed his mom. Had changed *him*. He was never going to make the same mistake. Nothing good could come from tying himself to one person forever.

"I'm never getting married." The words came out more viciously that he'd intended, but none of the other guys appeared shocked.

In fact, as he watched he saw first Gavin, then Lucas, and finally Chase all nod in turn.

"I'm with you." Gavin's face looked like it was set in stone, but there was the barest hint of something in his eyes that told Nate that the other guy was serious. "Never."

"Me, either." Lucas, too, seemed determined.

And Nate felt... well, he felt a lot of things, most of which had to do with a bonding with these guys he called his friends. They got it. They understood. A big lump rose in his throat, but he swallowed it back. He wouldn't admit a thing. He wasn't a freaking girl. "No marriage, no way. I don't care how big her boobs are."

They all snorted with laughter. Finally Chase, well-adjusted Chase, held his hand out. "Let's make a pact. All of us, we'll remember this night. We'll remind each other. Marriage is bad news."

"Yeah." Gavin nodded, placing his hand on top of Chase's. "Let's swear it. None of us will get married. Ever."

"Are girlfriends okay?" Lucas held out his hand, then snatched it back. "'Cause I'm not vowing to keep my dick in my pants forever, no matter what you old ladies think."

Nate rolled his eyes.

"Girlfriends are fine." Chase scowled at Lucas. "Just no rings. Are you in or not?"

Lucas nodded, contemplating, then placed his hand on top of the pile. "'Kay, I'm in. No weddings here either."

The three boys turned to look at Nate, whose throat felt

strangely thick. This—this was what mattered. Friendship. It would last longer, be stronger than any stupid wedding.

Finally, slowly, he placed his hand on the very top of the pile. He felt strength emanating from the heat of his friends—they were stronger together. They always had been.

"No weddings," he agreed, his mood as solemn as the words he spoke.

"Never."

CHAPTER 1

Present

The curvy redhead pulled a pair of sheer stockings up her shapely legs, and Nate did his best to enjoy the view. He wasn't sure what it said about him that all he could muster was a lukewarm reaction to the woman sitting on his bed.

She caught him looking and grinned, making a deliberately seductive show as she stood, sliding her feet into high-heeled pumps that brought the top of her head level with his eyes. Nate forced his face into a flirtatious smile, but he just wasn't feeling any of the usual sensual pleasure that should be present.

"Get your thoughts out of the gutter." Tapping a scarlet-tipped finger against his chest, Addison, the woman currently warming his bed, reached for her designer purse. A stack of his unopened mail sat on the polished table in his entryway, beside the sleek leather bag, and she plucked a heavy cream-colored envelope from the top of the pile.

"You should open this. Looks important." She handed the large envelope over, then started to dig in her purse, muttering about putting her keys in a special place. Nate was only too happy to turn his attention away from the lack of sexual desire to the heavy paper in his hand.

It was addressed to him, lettered in ornate script that, in his opinion, was barely legible through all the loops and curves. His appreciation for the change of subject disappeared as he realized what was inside. Hell, he'd been avoiding thinking about it since he'd gotten the call from Chase a few months ago. Still, he couldn't ignore the return address that had strange feelings churning in his stomach.

Chase Marshall and Meredith Olsen

7 Scarlett Way

Ruby Beach, WA 98227

With fingers that suddenly felt thick, Nate tore open the envelope and pulled out a slender stack of elegant-looking paper. Several of the smaller pieces fluttered to the floor as he held the largest card, foreboding making his stomach turn.

Together with their families,

Meredith Elizabeth Olsen

and

Chase Nicholas Marshall

Request the honor of your presence at their marriage.

Marriage.

"Son of a bitch." Nate stared at the piece of paper, his insides chilling as though he was standing outside in the dead of winter. Yes, Chase had been dating Meredith for a couple of years, and yes, Chase had asked Nate to be a groomsman, but he'd thought if he put the matter out of his head, the day of reckoning would never come.

A streak of probably unreasonable betrayal stabbed into his gut. What about their vow? Yeah, they'd made it fifteen years ago, but they'd reaffirmed it all the way through college and in the years since. Although not recently. He was forced to admit he'd lost touch with his best friends ... his brothers, but he'd been busy building the Archer Hotel empire. A twist of guilt added to the mix of emotions churning inside him. He had no excuse good enough for avoiding the guys.

And deep down, he knew that the strength of his reaction wasn't really about some vow made when they were kids. No, it was because all he'd been able to think about since finding out about the wedding was *her*.

"Ooh, a wedding?" Addison peered over the edge of the invitation, reading it upside down. Casting a glance at the papers on the floor, she nudged one with the toe of her shoe. "And it looks like you're a groomsman, too. Need a date?" she asked.

Nate swore to himself and as Addison's words sank in, he slowly raised his head to look her in the eye. "A... date?"

She averted her eyes and he mentally grimaced. It was time, he thought. *Past* time. Catching her by her shoulder, he tugged gently until she looked back up at him.

"Addison, what do you think this is?" he asked carefully.

"Relax, I wasn't proposing marriage." She pasted a bright, clearly fake smile on her face and patted him on the cheek, pretending not to be hurt in the least. "See you later."

Nate groaned out loud, watching those long legs walk out the door, probably for the last time.

He'd been in this position too many times to count. Except this time, he thought he'd picked correctly, believing he and Addison were in agreement about sharing some good, no-strings-attached fun. Great sex without any of the obligations that came with commitment. Hell, Addison had been the first to say that she didn't want a relationship, he thought, running a frustrated hand through his hair.

Looked like she'd changed her mind. And though Nate had been perfectly clear from the start, knowing that didn't erase the jagged discomfort caused by hurting her feelings.

But wasn't it better to let her go than to lead her on when his head was full of someone else?

He could still coax a response from his body when it came to Addison, or to any sexy woman, for that matter. But somewhere along the way he'd stopped enjoying the lifestyle he'd so carefully cultivated since taking that vow with his best friends. In fact, he could pinpoint the moment he'd stopped savoring the freedom and lack of commitment. From the time he'd heard Chase was getting married—and realized he'd be seeing Ellie again.

The invitation still clutched in his hands, Nate thought back to the last time he'd seen Chase's sister. He'd been eighteen, and he and Chase had been headed off to college. Of course, he'd been sporting a fresh bruise on his temple, courtesy of his stepdad, but at least this time he'd managed to inflict a few marks of his own.

When he'd stopped by the Marshall house to pick up Chase, his car packed full of boxes, sixteen-year-old Ellie had answered the door. As always, the cornflower blue eyes behind their thick-rimmed glasses missed nothing. She'd immediately noticed his wounds and her pretty eyes radiated pain on his behalf.

She was the only female in the world who seemed to see past the cocky image he'd built for himself of the tattooed bad boy—the only one who cared about how he felt inside. And it was that, even more than the way her little tank top clung to her ripening curves, that had him aching for her in ways that would cause her brother to kick his ass. That would cause him to kick his *own* ass.

And then Chase joined them outside, yelling at his sister to put some clothes on. Nate and Ellie had both slipped back into the roles that they played outside of those rare moments of connection—he the brooding big man off to college, and her, with her smirks and smart mouth, giving hell to her brother. Jesus, even at sixteen she'd been sexy, *and* he'd liked her—a dangerous combination.

She was off-limits for so many reasons. Even if she wasn't Chase's little sister, Chase would kill him for even thinking about touching innocent Ellie with the dominance that he craved during sex. Plus, even though he could only admit it way deep down inside, the opinion of Chase's family, of the town, echoed inside his head. He came from a broken, white-trash background and he was beneath her. She was all that was good and right with the world. And he'd rather die than dim her light.

In the years since, Nate had clung whole-heartedly to that anti-marriage vow, throwing himself into a string of emotion-less relationships—and thanks to the press and the damn gossip mill, he was a well-known playboy. It hadn't been hard to stay true to the promise, the image, not when the only woman he wanted was out of reach. And he knew he'd never give in to love, not while he had breath in his lungs. He couldn't. His fear of the long term was too shaky, his lack of trust in women too ingrained.

But that didn't mean he couldn't wait to see Ellie Marshall again.

———

Closing the door behind her with more force than necessary, Eleanor Marshall tossed her duffel bag to the floor and flopped face first onto the hotel room bed.

"Ow!" She quickly sat up again, rubbing her cheek and adjusting her plastic framed glasses.

The bed, while wide, was hard as a rock, the duvet the color of a bruised peach and made of cheap synthetic material that pulled at the skin.

"Figures," Ellie muttered as she pulled off her eyeglasses and rubbed at her temples.

This day had gone wrong from the start.

Running a hand tentatively over the cheap bedspread, she contemplated 'accidentally' sleeping through her brother Chase's rehearsal dinner... and she was only half joking.

"Come on, Ellie. Order some coffee, brush your hair, and get dressed. You have sisterly duties tonight." After everything it had taken to get to the small town of Ruby Beach, in Washington's Olympic National Park, she was damn well going to paste on a smile and wish Chase and Meredith well.

Even if her own love life had crashed and burned, quite spectacularly, at eight forty-two that morning. A glutton for punishment, Ellie worked her iPhone out of the pocket of her wool pants. She already knew what the words said—had read them over every time she'd had a chance throughout the day —but she still couldn't help doing it one more time.

TEXT:

To: Dr. Eleanor Marshall

From: Dr. Miles Karim

Message: Ellie, I need some space. I think we both know this isn't working. I feel like we've been together for years... and we've only been dating for five months. I need some excitement, both in and out of the bedroom, and despite our many talks on the subject, it's not getting any better. Sorry to break things off this way, but I made the decision last night, and thought it was best to let you know right away.

He needed some excitement, both in and out of the bedroom. Right. Dark clouds of frustration and the requisite tears welled up as Ellie read the text yet again. She'd tried to make things good between them... *especially* in the bedroom.

Miles had been good-looking enough, with tasty golden skin, dark mocha eyes, thick black hair, and a health club fit body. Despite all that, he'd never been able to make her feel more than lukewarm between the sheets, and though she'd wanted more—so much more—her body hadn't responded in kind.

"Argh!" Standing, Ellie grabbed one of the hideous fringed pillows from the head of the bed and hurled it across the room.

There. That felt a little better.

She was *not* frigid, damn it.

Nor was this breakup all her fault. She was smart, wasn't she? She was a well-respected optometrist who had run her own successful Seattle practice for the last three years. She was responsible. Though she didn't typically work on Friday afternoons, an elderly patient had called her emergency line right after she'd closed for the day, complaining about seeing a bright flash of light followed by a curtain across her vision. The symptoms indicated a potential retinal detachment, something that needed to be treated right away, and though Ellie had needed to get on the road for the wedding, she'd taken a look before referring the patient for an emergency appointment with an ophthalmologist.

She wasn't some weak, whiny woman, either. She was capable. When her car had broken down on the freeway five miles from the lodge, she hadn't gone into hysterics. She had simply sighed, called Triple A, then, with a glance at the ever forward-moving minute hand of her watch, had slung her duffel bag over her shoulder and hiked the rest of the way. In the snow. Her sensible shoes had finally served a purpose.

Smart. Responsible. Capable. Yep, there was a recipe for an exciting woman in the bedroom.

CHAPTER 2

"**N**o. I'm better than this." Swiping a sweaty lock of hair back from her damp forehead, Ellie allowed herself one last, long sigh. Then she hauled her duffel bag onto the bed and, unzipping the roll-up compartment at the bottom, pulled out the swath of nude-colored silk so she could get ready for the rehearsal dinner.

Her dress for the evening wasn't her usual style at all—but her soon to be sister-in-law had purchased it for Ellie especially for this occasion. It would be rude to refuse the bride's present simply because it made her feel naked. So she could add polite to her list of attributes.

Unfastening her work pants, Ellie let them fall to the floor, then kicked them aside. She fisted the hunter green of her wool sweater and tugged it up over her head. The whoosh of air felt fantastic on her sweat-dampened skin—she was in shape, but it had been a long, hot walk in her work clothes from her car to the lodge.

"Hmm." Looking down at the creamy white camisole and bikini briefs that she had on, she surveyed herself critically.

She was curvy, always had been, but what woman didn't

wish that her ass was a bit smaller, or her stomach a bit flatter? And Miles had been attracted to her. She had the right equipment, even if she was more comfortable with it hidden beneath sweater sets and loose trousers. She might not be feeling great about herself at the moment, but she was attractive and the dress on the bed would show a lot of her ample cleavage. Enough of it to find *someone* to have one night of hot, sweaty sex with?

She blinked, surprised at the path her thoughts had taken ... but why not?

What better way to soothe her bruised ego? Her brother had lots of single friends, lots of decent looking co-workers who would be at the wedding tonight.

"Yes." Biting her lip, Ellie made her decision before she could over think it. A one-night stand.

She was going to do it.

Suddenly a face flashed through her memory, one with dark hair, charcoal eyes, and a sexy smirk. Her brother's best friend Nate, who she'd harbored a crush on since her teenage years. But just as quickly as the notion popped into her head, she shoved it right back out. Nathan Archer was a millionaire, a tycoon now. And if the tabloids and her brother were to be believed, he was still one hell of a player. He dated supermodels and actresses. She might not have low self esteem, but she wasn't stupid, and tonight she was feeling fragile. It wasn't the time to set herself up for failure.

Her iPhone vibrated on the dresser across the room, the alarm she'd set for five-thirty chiming. She flicked it off. She had half an hour to make herself presentable and to get from the "charming" overflow lodge she'd gotten stuck in, to the beautiful hotel where the festivities were actually being held. As the sister of the groom, she could have easily had a room at the luxurious Ruby Beach Lodge down the road... *if* she had bothered to pay attention to the booking dates.

Ruby Beach was a small town, and it was full up with wedding guests. In the end, she'd been able to find nothing else but this place. Not even her parents or her brother had been able to help get her a room at the wedding hotel. She was lucky to at least have a place to sleep.

She removed her dress from its protective plastic, and laid it out on the bedspread. Bending at the waist, Ellie opened the back zipper of her dress. Strapless, it had a boned corset-like bodice that splayed into a sensual flare of lace and chiffon ending at her knees. Studying it, Ellie felt a tremor run through her at the thought of feeling so ... exposed. Squaring her shoulders, she prepared herself mentally to don the sexy garment. After all, the nearly sheer dress would help her on her mission. One night of steamy, no holds barred sex.

"Frigid *this*, Miles," she said, reaching out a hand for the dress.

A sound at the door had her whirling around, clutching the dress to her scantily clad body. Before she had more than a second to gather her thoughts, the door swung open and she let out a startled shriek.

One that was cut off as a male intruder entered the room, a garment bag slung over his arm, snow melting in his hair.

At a glance, she pegged him as tall, dark-haired, and gorgeous.

He froze in his tracks when he spotted her. "What the hell?" His voice was rough, like the burn of whiskey, and tickled at her memory.

Though it had been years, she placed him immediately. Speak of the devil.

Last time she'd seen him, he'd had shaggy hair and a bad boy vibe that made the high school girls drop their panties with one look. At least, that's what the rumors and the girls had claimed. And though he still had the bad boy look to him, now he dressed in a black business suit that fit his mouth-watering body like it had been tailor-made for him, which, from what she knew about his large empire, it probably had.

Standing in the doorway, as if her thoughts had conjured him, was Nathan Archer, her childhood crush. A tattooed badass who'd made something of himself with a lucrative chain of trendy boutique hotels. The sexy-as-sin playboy, known for his revolving door of women, stood in her room, exuding sex appeal and looking as perplexed as she felt at the moment.

Okay, maybe not quite as perplexed, because he definitely looked her up and down, taking note of the fact that she was almost naked.

What was he doing here?

She opened her mouth to ask him exactly that—but he beat her to it.

"Ellie Marshall? What are you doing here?" Those storm gray eyes swept over her again, and since the dress she was holding up in front of her was so skimpy, there was still plenty of it to see.

His eyes heated as they slid over the creamy expanse of her exposed skin. Even with her glasses off and being hopelessly near-sighted, she couldn't miss the flush that rose to his cheeks.

She blinked, processing the fact that Nate Archer had noticed her as a full-blooded woman, looking like he wanted to eat her alive.

And she wanted to let him. She always had.

———

Nate had had a hell of a long drive from Seattle, for a trip he didn't want to make, for a wedding he had no desire to attend. To top it all off, he'd arrived in town only to discover that his new secretary—make that his *former* secretary—had accidentally booked him a dingy hellhole instead of the luxurious Ruby Beach Lodge, where the wedding was taking place, and there were no other rooms available in the entire area.

With the beginnings of a migraine coming on, he'd walked into his room and discovered the woman who had been haunting his thoughts since the wedding invitation had arrived—Ellie Marshall. A barely dressed Ellie Marshall. His imagination had paled in comparison to reality. She was all grown up, and she was fucking gorgeous.

Stepping further into the room, Nate shook off the snow, dropped his hand-tooled leather suitcase and tried to keep his eyes on her face. It wasn't easy—though she still had flyaway hair and wasn't wearing a lick of makeup, it was all too easy to see that Ellie's teenage plumpness had settled into curves in all the right places. Places that were pretty visible because she was wearing nothing but innocent white panties, a camisole, and some scrap of flimsy fabric clutched to her very nice breasts.

He'd always been able to keep his feelings for Ellie on the back burner, simmering but never bursting into full flame. But they'd never been adults, alone in a hotel room, and as he met her gaze, the connection that had always existed between them snapped into place, making it feel like the universe had thrown them together on purpose.

But, he reminded himself, nothing had changed. She was off limits and always had been. He'd come a long way from his own beginnings, but a sweet, innocent woman like Ellie was meant for better men than him. Which meant he had to fix this mix-up ... yesterday. But first he had to figure out why she was here.

"Well? What are you doing in my room?" he asked again, this time harsher than he'd intended. But what could he do other than deflect, when he was sporting a hard-on he didn't want to her to notice?

She was his best friend's little sister. He'd snapped the strap of her first bra, for heaven's sake. Now he was straining to make his cock behave as he thought about filling his hands with the rosy breasts he'd caught only a glimpse of but wanted to see more.

"For your information, *you* are in *my* room. You can't just walk into other people's rooms while they're half naked!"

He held up his hands in self-defense. "This is my room, or the key the front desk gave me wouldn't have opened the door."

Ellie reached for an ugly wool sweater that lay on the bed beside her and held it up against her chest as added coverage, too. But not before the movement made her generous breasts jiggle, causing Nate to think feverishly of ice. Lots and lots of ice.

"Okay, obviously there's been a mistake. And it's nice to see you and all, but I have had a really shitty day, and I have to put on this excuse of a dress for the rehearsal dinner. I don't have much time." Her eyes sparkled with tears that she was trying ferociously to hold back and he groaned.

All he wanted was a hot shower and a glass of Jack on ice. Was that too much to ask? Obviously yes, because he found himself faced with a woman on the edge of a breakdown, instead. One whose day had clearly been as stressful as his. The media might love to play up his heartbreaker status, but no way was he going to force a female with teary puppy dog eyes out into the hallway.

"Room forty-two. Reservation was in my name. No problems checking in. You?"

Ellie blinked and shook her head. "No problems for me either. Obviously. And I was here first." She met his gaze.

As he looked down into her wide cornflower eyes, he

caught a flash of heat in the blue depths. The ribbon of space between them seemed to shrink and he knew that he wasn't the only one feeling this spiraling sexual attraction. Transfixed, he watched as her cheeks flushed and her tongue darted out, moistening her lips. The messy blond hair and wide-eyed expression turned her sex kitten body into a lethal combination of cute and hot. Not his usual type, but then, wasn't that why Ellie had always been special to him?

Down, Archer, he warned himself.

Swallowing thickly, Nate cleared his throat. They hadn't stood this close together since that morning he'd left for college. But this... this was entirely different. She was all grown up now. And, since Chase couldn't see inside his head, Nate could admit that not only was she beautiful, but he wanted her. Badly.

Bending awkwardly at the waist, Ellie picked up her iPhone, unlocking it while keeping her eyes on Nate. "There's obviously been a mix-up. I'll call—oh, shit! It's so late!"

CHAPTER 3

Dropping the phone—and the clothing she'd been using as a shield, Ellie bent to paw frantically through her bag, finally pulling out a pair of strappy heeled sandals and a small beaded purse. "Could this day get any worse?"

Blowing air out slowly, Nate squeezed his eyes shut against the breasts offered up to his eyes by the skimpy camisole and Ellie's bent position. At that moment, he didn't care what the hell had happened to the room, he just needed her to put some clothes on before he lost his mind.

"Here's the plan." His cock was threatening to stand at full attention, so Nate grabbed his suitcase, heaved it on top of the dresser, and made a show of sorting through it. "You do whatever it is *you females* do to get ready for things like this. I'll get dressed out here. We'll stop by the front desk on our way to the dinner and get this sorted."

Behind him, he heard an inelegant snort and looked over his shoulder to see Ellie's panty-clad ass scurrying to the bathroom.

Despite his amusement and accompanying grin, his cock

hardened further at the wiggle of her hips, and he cursed under his breath. "You have something to say, Blondie?" The nickname he'd called her in their teens fell from his lips easily, as if the long years since then had disappeared.

Closing the door all but a crack, Ellie poked her head back out, her lips schooled into a smirk.

"I'm sure you're quite acquainted with 'us females' in general." As she disappeared behind the closed door, Nate frowned at the comment.

He'd had his share of women, true enough—but he was nowhere near the playboy that the tabloids liked to portray him as.

Okay, maybe he was.

What the hell did it matter what Ellie thought if he couldn't have her?

Fuck. Shedding his suit and tie, he set them aside and drew his jeans up over his hips, adjusting his cock inside his black briefs so that his arousal would be less noticeable. The denim was a dark wash and had been expensive too, but at least they were comfortable. He spent enough of his time in suits—and he'd be in a tux for the entire wedding—so tonight he was going for casual.

Chase's mother, who had never approved of him, would shake her head, but he'd never given a damn what she thought of him.

He still didn't.

But he wondered what Ellie would think of his less than formal attire. She hadn't mentioned a date—and he sure couldn't be hers—but he was forced to admit that what she thought of him, what she saw with those big eyes, mattered. More than it should have.

The bathroom door opened and Ellie emerged, dropping her sandals to the floor so she could step into them.

One glance and Nate was struck dumb. "Blondie. Wow."

He couldn't stop himself from looking—the woman was absolutely spectacular. Her hair was up in a messy bun, leaving her creamy shoulders bare. Her face was only slightly touched with makeup—something shiny on her lips, her lashes long and sooty, and her skin looked just as it always did, clear and fresh and innocent. He found it infinitely more attractive than the layers of makeup that most women in his social circle always buried themselves under.

Then there was the dress he'd caught a glimpse of earlier. It stopped at mid-thigh, showing off shapely legs and cut low enough to make his mouth water. And the color... The golden silk made him think of her naked. Gloriously naked and beneath him.

"Don't say it. I already know I am so not the kind of woman to wear this dress." Setting aside her glasses, Ellie screwed open a contact lens case and, with the ease of an expert, plopped the watery looking discs into her eyes without a mirror. "Meredith gave it to me specifically to wear tonight. I couldn't say no."

Nate was a bit disappointed that she had put in contacts instead of her glasses. He liked the way the tortoiseshell frames set off the cornflower blue of her eyes. But with the glasses off, she had nothing to hide behind. He found himself enjoying that little side benefit as she lifted a hand to adjust the frames that weren't there, then dropped it to the side and squirmed.

She was really cute when she squirmed.

"Hate to break it to you, Ellie."

Clenching her fists, Ellie turned and resolutely looked Nate in the eye.

He wondered why on earth she looked like she was preparing to take a punch to the jaw. "You are absolutely the type of woman to wear this dress."

Ellie huffed out a breath, clearly in disbelief.

"Ellie," he said more gently. "This dress was made for you."

Confusion softened the self-doubt on her face, and then both were gone as she pulled her shell back around herself, as surely as if she'd put on her glasses. "Really? Because today I was dumped via text message specifically because of my lack of sex appeal, so please don't give me flowery words because you think I want to hear them."

Avoiding his eyes, Ellie stuffed a bottle of eye drops, her driver's license, a wad of cash, and a slender tube of lip gloss into her tiny purse. "I'm not one of your female admirers. I don't need to hear fake compliments."

Nate schooled his mouth into stern lines to hide his irritation, both at her summary of the type of guy he was – never mind that she was right – and that some asshole would hurt her that way. He wanted to wring the guy's neck for causing her to question her femininity.

"Do you really want to be with someone who would dump you via text anyway?"

"No, but that's not the point."

"Then what is?" he asked, confused.

Sucking in air as if she was downing liquid courage, she placed her hands on her hips and turned to face him. There was a look of determination in her eyes that he didn't quite understand. "I want to find a one-night stand tonight. Do you... do you think I can?"

Fuck. Me.

Nate felt his mouth go dry. One-night stand? His cock jumped to attention again—he wanted to be the one to touch her, to finally lose himself in her and he clenched his fists at the thought of another man's hands on that flawless skin.

Hands off, Archer. Bad idea, remember?

He closed the distance between them, using her question as an excuse to look his fill. Lifting his hand, he ran his knuckles over her cheek—an innocent enough gesture, but he felt the heat flash through him.

From Ellie's sharp inhalation, she felt it too. The tension between them was hot, heavy, and urged him to bend his head and dive right in with a kiss hot enough to melt that flimsy dress right off her body.

But he couldn't. If she knew what he liked to do to women, she'd run screaming into the night.

"You look great. Seriously."

"Thank you."

He knew he was going to regret the next words, but he forced them out anyway. "This is definitely a one-night stand kind of dress. And hey, I'll even be your wingman."

Ellie blinked at his words, glancing away. She smiled, but he couldn't quite tell if she was truly pleased by his offer.

"I'll take you up on that." Smoothing her hands over her thighs, she pulled a woollen coat over her shoulders, then walked toward the door, wobbling a bit on her heels.

So. Freaking. Cute.

And it was the combination of sex appeal which she clearly didn't know she possessed, vulnerability, and her genuine adorable allure that got to him most.

"Let's stop at the desk quickly on the way out to ask about getting you another room," she said.

"Yeah. The room." Nate cursed under his breath as they exited into the parking lot, not thrilled at the idea of being separated from this unique creature who had all but dropped into his lap.

CHAPTER 4

"I already told you; there's no mix-up. Eleanor Marshall and Nathan Archer are both booked into room forty-two. The bill split between the parties." The girl manning the front desk was maybe sixteen; hair dyed inky black, eyes ringed with matching pencil.

She cast Ellie a smirk, the ring in her lip glinting in the fluorescent light. "What's the matter, you two have a fight?"

Her name badge read "Stephanie", and Ellie didn't miss the way her eyes took a leisurely trail down Nate's body. Wow. When she'd been that age, she never would have dreamt of being so forward, especially with someone older. Hell, she still wouldn't act like that.

She cast a sidelong glance at Nate at the thought. He had that effect on women. He had that effect on *her*. But she was relieved to note the narrowing of his eyes, which told her that he didn't much care for the teen's scrutiny either.

Still, he stepped closer to the counter and leaned onto it like he and Little Miss Stephanie were best friends already. "I know this wasn't your fault. No one is saying that."

He winked, and Ellie barely refrained from rolling her

eyes as a bright red flush stained the teen's otherwise ghostly pale cheeks. "But maybe you could just see if there's another room available. See, this lady and I are both invited to the same wedding, but we don't know each other. So being stuck in the same room together would kinda suck, you know?"

Smart man. Flirting with the goth girl to ease her attitude and hopefully get them separate rooms. Which she'd need if she was going to pick up her own man for the night.

The thought of going on the prowl for someone who *wasn't* Nate... well, it left her with a hollow ache in her chest. Which was ridiculous. She hadn't seen him in years. So what if she still had the hots for him? It was never going to happen.

"I'm really sorry." The girl batted—actually batted—her eyelashes up at Nate before tucking a lock of hair coyly behind her hair. She tapped on the keyboard with long nails painted dull gray. "We had computer issues last week, so my guess is that it somehow dumped you two together. But we don't have any extra rooms. The entire town is full up for some fancy wedding over at the Lodge."

"Right." Nate smiled, but Ellie saw the hint of strain behind the easy gesture, making Ellie wonder if he had a headache.

She wouldn't be surprised if he was in pain, his day had obviously been as frustrating as hers. Her fingers itched to massage his temples and ease his stress, and she curled them into fists, suppressing the gesture.

"Well, can you please let me know if a room opens up?" he asked, sliding a business card with his number across the counter to the girl.

"Of course." The sweet smile she sent him was in shocking contrast to her makeup and attire. "Can I get you anything else while you're out? Extra towels or pillows? Mints?"

Ellie thought she heard Nate snort beneath his breath.

"I'd like a bottle of chardonnay in a bucket of ice waiting in the room when I return." Nate flicked a glance at Ellie, and she felt her heart skip a beat. "Charge it to my card, and add a tip for yourself while you're at it."

"Of course! Any particular kind?" Stephanie bounced up and down like a puppy. "There's a yummy Naked Grape one that my boyfriend gets for me... I mean... that my mom likes to drink."

Nate actually winced and Ellie held back a laugh. He turned over his business card, reached for a pen, then scrawled down a few lines.

"See if one of these vintages is available. If not, please look for something in the two to three hundred price range. And if you don't have any wine glasses available here, please also purchase them." He slid the card back across the counter.

Stephanie squeaked at the price, and Ellie very nearly did, too. Two to three hundred dollars for a bottle of wine? She made a great salary as an optometrist, but she considered it a good day if her wine had a screw cap instead of coming from a box. Not that she'd be tasting this expensive Chardonnay, and... wait a second.

"What exactly am I supposed to do while you use this fancy wine to seduce whatever woman you've brought back from the rehearsal dinner?" she asked.

They stepped out of the tiny office into the blazing light of an Olympic sunset in December, and Ellie squinted, shielding her eyes. Her sunglasses hadn't fit in her tiny purse. "For that matter, what if I find someone the way I planned? What do we do?" she asked.

"We could always have a foursome." Nate grinned, stuffing his hands into his pockets.

"You're joking," she asked after a long pause, not quite

sure whether he was kidding or not. He had always been wild …

Her pulse thundered in her chest as he pinned her with that sexy stare.

Finally he shook his head and groaned. "Any man that doesn't want to have you all to himself is very stupid, Blondie."

His gaze worked its way up and down her body, and Ellie tried to hold back a tiny gasp. Just having his eyes on her—it was more exciting than actual sex with Miles had been. In fact, it made her wonder … Miles *who*?

She leaned closer, like a magnet being pulled ever closer to its twin.

"We'll figure out the room issues later," he muttered, straightening his body away from hers.

She blew out a breath, unsure if she was relieved or disappointed he'd chosen distance.

"Well, that's me," he said, pointing across the parking lot to a shiny black Porsche Carrera. "We might as well ride together."

A Porsche. Of *course* that was his. Seeing the sleek ride next to the Ford Focus that had been towed in from the highway just emphasized how different they, and their respective lifestyles, were. No matter that her childhood crush had deepened in the last forty-five minutes.

"Sounds good." Shooting him a bright smile, Ellie started to make her way across the parking lot, struggling not to wobble in her high heels. "Now let's find me a one-night stand."

Nate muttered something beside her, and she cocked her head. "Sorry, didn't catch that?"

He shook his head, then smiled back, his expression bland.

"I said I'd buy the first round."

———

As Ellie followed Nate into the large dining room at the Ruby Beach Lodge, she tugged at the hem of her dress, unsure if she was more uncomfortable with the dress or the prickly tension between herself and Nate. The ride from the motel had been short, but Ellie couldn't figure out what was bothering Nate to cause the sudden awkward silence. She'd escaped the car, relieved.

But even relief at escaping the tight confines of the car wasn't enough to make her race into a room filled with her too-predictable family. And leave it to Nate to attempt to urge her on ahead of him—a perfect gentleman.

She took her time dropping her coat at the coat check before forcing herself into the party.

Ellie took a look around the lavishly decorated room and smiled. Meredith was an event planner, and from the sumptuous decor, it was easy to see that her future sister-in-law was very good at what she did. She'd combined the holiday season with the wedding event perfectly.

Centerpieces of crystal and pale blue roses, swaths of light that ran from the palest of pinks to deep rose, even the smartly dressed waiters who circulated with trays of wine— Meredith hadn't missed a single detail. She'd even managed to make the hanks of mistletoe hanging overhead looked as if they'd grown there.

"Would you like a drink?" Nate asked, his warm fingers pressed to the bare skin at the small of her back.

"That would be perfect." She managed the words as he rubbed his thumb over the small expanse of naked skin, where his hand still lingered. A simple touch shouldn't make her pulse race, but it had, even though he surely hadn't meant anything by it.

With a nod, he headed off toward the bar, and her breath

actually caught in her throat as she watched his lean figure move through the crowd, owning the space as he walked. But no sooner had he arrived than two women surrounded him there.

"Oh, for the love of ..." Ellie turned away, sliding her tongue across her glossed lips, trying to understand this push and pull between herself and Nate. She shouldn't care who he talked to. And she hadn't seen him in years. Yet all of the old feelings had bubbled to the surface the second he'd stepped into their room, making her teenage crush seem small in comparison.

Before she could think further, a screechy voice called out her name.

"Eleanor Anne Marshall, it's been years!" A claw-like hand grabbed Ellie by the shoulder, spinning her around. Teetering on her high heels, she found herself face to face with her worst nightmare—her cousin Holly.

Holly Adams had made Ellie's life *hell* in high school, mocking her for preferring books to guys, and making fun of her J-Lo-esque rear end. And while it might be cliché, harboring resentment for the prom queen, she suspected that most women didn't get to call said prom queen family. Sadly, Holly hadn't grown up and consequently the biting comments hadn't stopped when school did.

"Holly." Ellie swallowed a grimace as the saccharine scents of hairspray and perfume hit her nose. "What a... surprise."

"Well, it shouldn't be!" Holly rolled her eyes, and Ellie ground her teeth together in irritation. "Where else would I be this weekend?"

Where else, indeed? Holly still lived here in Ruby Beach. She'd been a cheerleader, prom queen, and was still reigning over the high school as an administrative assistant in the front office.

"So that's an interesting look for you." Holly made a show

of looking up and down Ellie's dress. Her expression said that this was not a compliment. "Decided to step out of the box a bit, hmm?"

"It was a gift from Meredith." Ellie smiled tightly, counting to ten in her head. The scrap of blue lace that her cousin wore was way skimpier than her own dress—actually, it wasn't really even appropriate for an elegant wedding event. Still, Holly always bared her legs and boobs and whatever else she could get away with. And because she owned it, she made it work.

"Of course it was." Holly smiled, the expression not quite reaching her still-assessing gaze. "I should have known you'd never choose something like that."

Ellie clung to the confidence she'd felt with Nate's strong hand on her back and opened her mouth to hopefully come up with some witty reply, but once again, Holly beat her to it.

"So you still sell glasses for a living? That's... fun." Holly dug through her sequined purse as she spoke, as if she was just making conversation and couldn't care less about the answer.

"I am an *optometrist*." How was the woman managing to insult her when *she* had never even left the high school she'd once terrorized?

"I'm sure that's fascinating. Miss Eleanor Marshall, purveyor of spectacles." Holly did that eye roll again.

God, what a bitch, Ellie thought, her temper beginning to snap along her spine. "That's *Dr.* Marshall," she said to her cousin, enunciating the words, wanting nothing more than to slap that simpering smile off of her cousin's face. But she couldn't, of course.

Nice girls didn't get into fistfights at weddings.

CHAPTER 5

The woman clutching Nate's elbow would not stop talking.

He wasn't listening—he hadn't wanted to be in this conversation in the first place. But the woman—Sara? Dara? They'd hooked up a few times back in high school, but by the squeal she'd let loose when she'd set eyes on him, he'd have thought they were long-lost, star-crossed lovers.

He nodded and grunted at appropriate intervals, but his attention was fixed across the room on Ellie, who looked as trapped as he felt, caught in a conversation with her mother and her cousin Holly—And Nate remembered Holly. The woman had pursued him relentlessly all through senior year. Well, not just him—she would have been happy with Gavin or Lucas, too. They'd all agreed that they'd rather get their dicks caught in a mousetrap than inside that woman.

As Nate watched, Ellie's expression turned strained under the attention of her mother and cousin. The brightness that he'd always loved about her drained away, and he couldn't handle just standing by and watching it.

"Excuse me." Abruptly he pushed away from Sara-Dara, but before he took a full step, she grasped his elbow.

"Wait!" She smiled in what he imagined was supposed to be a seductive manner as he half-turned back, impatience in every muscle. "Do you want to maybe meet up after this? Relive some old times?" She leaned in closer, brushing her breast against his arm.

Man, he should be used to these come-ons by now. For years, he'd even enjoyed them. But he'd grown tired of the game, something he'd been forced to recognize since discovering that Chase was getting married and that he'd be coming face to face with Ellie again.

"I have other plans." He shrugged off the woman's touch, feeling a slight pang of guilt as he heard her noise of dismay.

His fingers tightened on the drinks that he still held in his hands—a fruity martini for Ellie and a plain old domestic beer for himself. He would have preferred wine, but the selections had made him shudder. His feelings for Chase's little sister may not have changed, but his taste buds surely had.

As he approached the small cluster of women, he heard Holly's voice, unmistakable even after all these years. And a glance told him she was smirking as Mrs. Marshall spoke to her daughter.

"You'll let Holly help you with your makeup for the wedding, Eleanor." The older woman pursed her lips as she studied Ellie, who flushed under her mother's harsh inspection. "I don't know how many times I've told you. It takes more than decent clothing to look polished. Don't you wear makeup when you see your clients?"

"Patients, Mom. They're patients." Ellie sighed, sounding annoyed even from a distance. "Because I'm a doctor, remember?"

"An *eye* doctor, not a medical doctor." Mrs. Marshall

sniffed. "I still don't understand why you didn't go further and become a real doctor, rather than taking the easy way out."

"I like my profession, mom."

Good girl, Nate thought, taking a long sip of his beer, fortifying himself. Ellie was a smart, successful professional woman. Who the hell did they think they were, putting her down?

"I'm going to introduce you to someone tonight, Ellie. Since we're still waiting for *your* wedding," Holly interjected, her smile just a touch too bright. "Harry is an ex of mine. He's a *real* doctor."

"I don't think—"

"You can't stay single forever. It's not healthy," her mother said in agreement.

Nate, on the other hand, vehemently disagreed. If she wasn't with him, then he was quite happy with Ellie staying single. As long as he was nearby, no other man was going to get near her.

Leave it alone, Nate. Who she dates isn't your business, he reminded himself. He'd agreed to be her wingman, after all. He frowned at the reminder, pushing those thoughts aside. For now, his mission was to get Ellie away from the women who were doing their best to steal her smile.

"There you are." Moving quickly, Nate slid through the last throng of people and placed his hand on Ellie's back. The warmth of the skin there was addictive, and he couldn't resist rubbing his fingers over her flesh in a small circle.

"Nate!" He'd never seen a woman look more relieved. Damn it, but he liked how real she was. With Ellie there was never any of the phoniness always a part of the women he usually spent time with.

He pressed the martini into her hand, smothering a laugh when she downed half of it in one swallow.

"Mom, Holly, you remember Nate Archer."

"Indeed." Mrs. Marshall looked him up and down, lips curled in distaste, and he stared right back, impassively. "How... lovely... that you could make it," she said, her words clearly at odds with her real feelings.

"Yes, I'm sure you're thrilled that all of Chase's oldest friends could be here." He cast her a benign grin, one that would never let her know her attitude stung.

She'd never forgiven him for coming from the wrong side of the tracks and befriending her son. He could only imagine how she'd feel if he made a move on her daughter. Still, it felt damned good to face the woman after all these years, knowing he'd made a success of himself, a fact even she couldn't dispute.

He slid the hand touching Ellie's back up to rest on her shoulder, hugging her to his side. Despite his touch being casual, she stiffened, and her unexpected rejection took him off guard. Ellie had never been embarrassed to be seen with him in the past, and it never dawned on him that she'd have changed.

Had she? Or was he misreading her signals?

"We're wanted at the bridal party table," he said, determined to find out.

"Bye, Mom. Holly." Without a backward glance, Ellie hurried away from the conversation. She tilted her martini glass to her lips as she moved, draining the rest of the liquid, then blinked down at the empty glass in surprise. "Oh. I didn't mean to drink that so fast."

"I'd say you deserved it." Snagging it from her hand, he handed it off to a passing waiter. "Good thing I showed up to rescue you from your family."

Craning her neck up—man, she was a little thing—she narrowed her eyes up at him. "I can take care of myself."

"You can. But a little help never hurts." He smirked down at her.

"True." She flushed and started to move in the direction of the wedding party table, but he wasn't ready to let her go.

Her reaction to his public touch niggled at him, wounding him deeply. Placing his hand on her shoulder, he steered her toward an emergency exit that was almost invisible behind one of the lush fabrics covering the wall.

"What are you doing?" Ellie asked. "I thought we were needed at the table."

"I just said that to get you away from your mom and cousin." He pushed through the heavy door and they exited the room. The air was thin and icy, a welcome relief after the heat inside.

Nate suddenly craved a wild Washington snowstorm, one that would wash away all the strange, painful, uncertain feelings that accompanied him being back in his hometown. A storm that would set he and Ellie on a clearer path.

He watched as she turned her face up to the sky, inhaling deeply. She'd clearly needed the break as much as he had and he gave her a moment to settle herself.

"Ellie."

She met his gaze, curiosity in her big blue eyes.

"If you don't like me touching you, I'd prefer you just say so." He kept his voice mild, but inside he was feeling anything but. He didn't *want* to stop touching her... he wanted his hands on her again and again and again.

"*What?*" Ellie's eyes had been closed, but they snapped open at his words. "What on earth gave you the idea that I don't like you touching me? I mean, why would you think ..." That adorable flush stained her cheeks and his words obviously flustered her.

Interesting, he thought. Pushing his insecurities aside - and wasn't that a kick, Nate Archer having insecurities when it came to women - he moved closer to Ellie. "When I put my arm around you in front of your mother, you stiffened. Why?"

He fixed his stare on her face, searching for clues, intrigued by the flush spreading over her skin.

Ellie stared up at him wordlessly for a moment, and he found himself shifting restlessly under her bright stare, frustrated with his inability to read her thoughts.

"Oh, Nate." She finally spoke and their connection clicked in again, the pull between them honest and real. "Of course I don't mind you touching me in public. I never cared what my mother thought. I never will."

He released the breath he hadn't been aware of holding. She wasn't ashamed of him, she never had been.

God, he'd been an idiot.

Ellie looked up at him with sky blue eyes. "You know, Nate, you have enough of a reputation with the ladies that I kind of figured you'd be a little less dense than this." Huffing out an exasperated laugh, she patted him on the shoulder.

Freaking *patted* him, like he was a puppy – and had she really just called him dense? But she'd done him a favor, breaking not just the tension but his embarrassment at baring his soul and a weakness he'd preferred not to show.

"So we're all clear now right? Touch me all you want." Her eyes opened wide at that statement. "I mean ... we're fine."

They were, he thought, aware that her sudden discomfort and rambling were signs. Damned good signs. Maybe he *had* been dense when it came to her, but now he wasn't. Not anymore.

"Anyway, thanks for taking me out here and giving me a second to breathe. Now let's head back in," she continued, quickly turning and brushing past him in a sudden rush to get to the door.

He shifted deliberately so that she had to press up against his chest to get by. Her gaze flicked up to meet his, and she sucked in a startled breath. At the same time, her nipples beaded into hard points against his chest, and her lips parted, ready for a kiss, confirming his suspicions.

It wasn't that Ellie *didn't* like him touching her—it was that she *did*.

The realization, combined with that heady and familiar strawberry scent that seemed to emanate from her very skin, had him hardening uncomfortably against the harsh denim of his jeans.

They stood there for a long moment, lightly pressed together, breath mingling, the air around them thick with unspoken words and longing.

With any other woman, Nate would make his usual slick moves, kiss her and take her to bed. But this was Ellie. The woman he wanted most in the world—the woman who, he was now sure, wanted him back. But she was also the woman he'd thought he could never have because she was special. And she deserved more than perfected moves that meant nothing, so he let her go.

He'd need to approach her differently, he thought, processing the fact that not only was she different to him, but she caused him to act differently as well. It was worth letting the moment pass ... for now.

She was worth the wait.

Nate took a moment to breathe a last mouthful of crisp air before he followed her back in, eyes trained on the sway of her body as she hurried across the room to their table, well aware that a distinct and irrevocable shift had just taken place. Before, he'd never considered that he could have Ellie. He'd never been good enough, and he hadn't wanted to put Chase in the position of having to point that out.

But now that he knew Ellie wanted him too?

Holding onto his determination to keep his distance just became infinitely more difficult.

CHAPTER 6

Nate arrived at the large circular table designated for the wedding party and caught up with Ellie. He touched her elbow and opened his mouth, planning to tell her that they weren't done talking. But the words were swallowed in a chorus of hellos from friends he hadn't seen in years, along with introductions to the others at the table.

"Nate. Son of a bitch." Gavin pounded him on the back and Nate choked on a mouthful of beer. He glanced up to find the other man grinning, obviously pleased to see him.

Warmth suffused him and he turned away from Ellie to greet his old friend. "Shit, it's been way too long."

"Well, we've got time to catch up." Gavin pounded on him again, his heavy thump on his back strong. Ex-soldier strong. "Sit down. Let's drink," Gavin said.

He gestured to a seat across the table from Ellie.

Too far. It wasn't going to work for Nate. "I'd rather sit here." He winked at his friend, then very deliberately slid into the seat next to Ellie instead.

She reached for her glasses, which of course weren't there,

a sure sign his nearness flustered her. Her reaction was really fucking cute, something that had never appealed to him in anyone but Ellie. And something he would have warned himself against thinking, but that little exchange outside—the realization that she wanted him too—had the alpha beast inside his ribcage pounding on its chest and declaring her as his.

Nate took another long swallow of his beer, listening to Gavin and Lucas with one ear as he eyed Ellie. As he watched, her gaze flickered over his guy friends, assessing them in a purely female way.

Nate narrowed his gaze, well aware of what she was doing —sizing them up for that one-night stand she was so hell-bent on having. And that same alpha beast inside him let out a low growl. She'd leave with Gavin or Lucas for a wild romp over his dead body. He refused to let anyone touch her but him. And oh, how he wanted to touch her. All over. To lay his palms on the sweet curves of her ass, and watch them flush with his mark.

He sobered at the thought. The other reason he ought to keep his distance. What would Ellie think if she knew what he liked when it came to sex? How would this strong, sassy woman feel about submitting in the bedroom? Would she hate him for his needs? The thought had a ball of ice forming in his gut.

He watched, on edge, as she talked to Gavin and Lucas, and when she laughingly dismissed them, turning away, relief filled him from head to toe. And when Ellie looked at him, then flushed and dropped her gaze, an electric current whipped over his skin.

Maybe... just maybe she wouldn't be as opposed to his sexual preferences as he'd believed.

———

The other members of the wedding party were all seated at the same table, and once Ellie had had another drink and chatted a bit with most of them, she relaxed. While some of her family might make this weekend hellish, with these people, she could enjoy and be herself.

"So if I told you that you had a nice body, would you hold it against me?" Gavin Hunter, one of her brother's groomsmen, settled back in the chair on one side of Ellie, and grinned at her, tilting his beer up to his lips.

"Been sitting on that one long?" Ellie rolled her eyes, but his compliment made her feel good, and she couldn't help smiling. She gestured to his drink. "And how many of those have you had? That sentence had like twenty words. Don't you usually settle for two?"

"Got to get through this charade one way or another." Gavin shrugged and took another sip.

Ellie cast him a sidelong glance, assessing him as a potential candidate for her night. He'd always been a good-looking guy, even back when he thought that having a cigarette hanging out the corner of his mouth equalled irresistible sex appeal. With his rock-solid body, close-cropped hair, and pale green eyes—in a perfect world, he'd be a prime candidate for her currently empty one-night stand list.

Ellie stifled a sigh as she reached for her own drink, shooting down that thought immediately. Lame pickup line aside, she couldn't muster up more than a whisper of attraction for him, and she knew exactly why – the man sitting on her other side.

Nate leaned in so close that Ellie could feel his warm breath the back of her neck. "Does Chase know you're saying things like that to his baby sister?" he asked Gavin.

He spoke mildly, but when he placed his hand on Ellie's shoulder and squeezed, the sensation of his fingers pressing into her skin felt... Well, it felt like he was marking her. And she couldn't lie, it made her breath come a little faster and her pulse quicken.

"And why do you care, old buddy, old pal?" Gavin grinned before thumping his empty beer bottle down on the table. "Nate and Ellie, sitting in a tree..."

She rolled her eyes at his childish behavior. "Gavin, grow up," she muttered, though her cheeks flamed in heated embarrassment.

She ought to be used to this old rhyme directed at her. Back in high school, when she'd actually had a crush on Nate, her brother had teased her mercilessly, as had Gavin and Lucas, and she hoped no one remembered or brought that up tonight.

She waited for Nate to react but he remained silent. Remembering their interaction outside, her heart pounded against her ribcage.

Gavin, who was obviously already a few steps past tipsy and on his way to drunk, pushed away from the table, presumably to get another. The chatter from the rest of the group—Lucas, another groomsman, and two bridesmaids who'd introduced themselves as Kate and Harper, along with Harper's much older date—was loud. Almost enough to cover the sudden, heavy silence from the man seated on her left side.

"So he's being ridiculous, huh?" she asked Nate, needing something to break the tension after Gavin's teasing.

Bracing herself, she twisted in her seat to look at Nate. The mixture of emotions she found in his expression—definite heat, a touch of tenderness and a bit of possession—were startling and more than a little confusing. Because earlier when she thought for sure he'd lean in and kiss her, he'd backed off. She didn't know what to make of his hot and cold behavior. And she wasn't going to figure it out in the middle of a crowd.

"I'm going to get another drink," she said, needing a break. She started to rise from her chair, and suddenly his fingers were at the small of her back again—and oh, she liked the way he touched her there.

Slowly, she sank back down into her seat.

"I don't like Gavin hitting on you," Nate said, a bit of dark surprise in his husky words.

"I didn't like it either," she admitted. Gavin wasn't the one she wanted flirting with her.

In fact, there was only one man here tonight who made her blood sing—and he was staring at her, the corners of his lips curling up and a storm swirling in his eyes.

She'd never dreamt that Nate might actually be *interested* in her. And though she'd never been particularly adept at flirting, she'd have to be blind to miss the heat he was throwing out.

Without warning, a hand clamped down on her shoulder, interrupting her thoughts and causing her to jump.

"Evening, folks." Her brother grinned down at them, interrupting and breaking the moment. "I'm so happy you're here! You all came!"

She pushed aside the little hum of her interaction with Nate and turned to her brother. "Of course we came." Ellie looked past Chase to where Meredith stood beside him, and they shared a mutual eye roll. "I'm your sister, remember? And these are your best friends? Where else would we be?"

"I know. But..." Chase exhaled deeply, then cast a look down at Nate, whose own expression seemed a little... tight. "I knew *you'd* come, Ellie. But Nate... I'm really glad you're here."

Why would Chase doubt that Nate would come? Before she could ask, Meredith pulled Chase along with her to greet the other bridesmaids. Ellie shrugged off the odd encounter as she watched Chase and Meredith settle into their seats.

Despite the fact that he was a little bit tipsy, Chase doted on his bride. The expressions on the couple's faces made Ellie sigh a bit inside as she watched. She was happy enough being single—she'd never been the type to feel like she needed a man to complete her. But even with Miles, she'd missed the companionship that came with having someone real and true by her side.

And she'd be a big fat liar if she didn't cop to missing sex. Oh she'd had sex with Miles. Nice sex. But she'd wanted hot, panty-melting sex. The kind she'd never experienced before. The kind a guy she desired badly could give her.

She cast a sidelong glance at Nate to find him watching her in return. The heat in his stare stoked the low flames already burning in her belly. She wanted him. And she was kind of getting the idea that he wanted her too—though she had no illusions that it would be for anything more than one night. His reputation assured her of that. But one night was all she needed to scratch the itch, right?

"I'm going to make a toast!" Chase banged his butter knife against his water glass, hard enough that Meredith winced and took it away from her fiancé, laughing.

"Easy, hon." She placed a hand on Chase's shoulder, and the look he cast her was so... just so *full*, that Ellie felt her heart swell.

She wanted that, too. Someday.

Chase got to his feet, not seeming to notice that Meredith had placed his water glass in his hand instead of the wine, which made Ellie giggle. "Everybody listen up!"

"Aren't *we* supposed to be toasting *you*?" Lucas leaned back in his chair and grinned.

Ellie glanced around the table, catching Meredith's sister Harper as she cast him an annoyed glance. But then Chase found his butter knife and knocked on his glass again, forcing Ellie's attention back to her brother.

"Meredith and I are so happy that everyone could make it tonight." Chase beamed around the table, reaching down at the same time to run a hand tenderly down Meredith's cheek. "All the people we care about are here. But I especially want to give a shout-out to my three best friends."

Beside her, Ellie felt Nate shift in his seat. Turning to look at him, she found his face set in unreadable lines.

"Luke, Gavin, Nate. You guys know why I thought you might not come." Chase took a sip of his drink, drunk and happy enough to still not notice that it was water instead of wine. "But I'm so happy that you came to support me anyway. No matter what we told ourselves when we were kids— Meredith is the real deal. So here's to the friends who are like my brothers."

"What is he talking about?" Mystified, Ellie pinned Nate with a puzzled glance as Chase sat back down.

Nate paused, mouth pinched tight, and she waited for an explanation. Finally he shook his head, and when he stilled, his features had smoothed out again. "He... was worried that we ... wouldn't approve of Meredith."

"Why not?" Ellie shot back, instantly defensive of her soon to be sister-in-law. "She's fantastic. And perfect for Chase."

"It's a long story." Nate groaned, and when he again looked at Ellie, the look was assessing. The naked heat in his stare would have made her knees buckle if she hadn't already been seated.

She leaned forward, just a bit, leaning in for... well, for what, she wasn't entirely certain but by the look in his gaze ... he was going to kiss her. Her heart pounded wildly in her chest.

"Ellie." His warm breath fluttered over her mouth.

Was he going to kiss her?

No. He couldn't. She couldn't. Chase would kill them both.

She didn't care.

She had to care. They were sitting right across the table from her brother.

Embarrassed heat suffused her skin, her own breath came out heavy as she straightened, certain her feelings must be obvious to everyone around them.

"Wait." It almost killed her to do it, but she pulled back from Nate.

He blinked at that single word, then slowly, as if waking from a trance, he shook his head, that guardedness returning to his gaze. "I'm sorry. That was... inappropriate."

He reached for his beer, which Ellie noted was empty and rose to his feet. "I'm going to get another drink," he said in a cool voice. "Would you like one?"

She immediately thought of their conversation outside, and realized what he'd read in her withdrawal. She waited for him to look back at her; when he didn't, she grabbed his hand. "Nate."

He met her gaze with his colder one.

"Remember what I said outside? I don't care who sees you touching me."

CHAPTER 7

She waited for what felt like forever for her meaning to sink in. "Just... maybe not at my brother's rehearsal dinner? While he's sitting right there?"

Nate cocked his head to one side, and in that moment, as his stare raked over her, she felt as though he could see through her, read every nuance of her intense feelings.

Finally he nodded, the corners of his lips turning up in the barest hint of a smile. "I'll be right back."

Her pulse thundered as she watched him walk away from the table.

Wow. Just... wow. She'd come here tonight hoping for a one-night stand. Hot guys were everywhere tonight. And, she thought as she looked down and discreetly adjusted her dress, her boobs looked damn good. It would probably be smarter not to put her heart on the line, to find someone else.

But this thing between her and Nate, whatever it was, ensured nobody else would do. It was Nate. Or no one.

Fidgety in Nate's absence, she decided to head to the washroom for a quick makeup check, only to be stopped when someone sank into the seat that Nate had just vacated.

"Hi," her new companion said, sending her a flirtatious smile.

"Um, hello."

She regarded him in return, slightly puzzled.

He looked vaguely familiar, but she couldn't quite place him. He bore more than a passing resemblance to John Mayer. Boy next door, with an edge. He was dressed in a gray suit that hinted at a nice body, and when he shifted in his seat, the whiff of cologne that reached her nose was pleasing.

"You must be Ellie. I'm Harry." The man offered a hand, casting her a shy but sexy smile and she found that she couldn't help but smile in return.

"I'm sorry, but do I know you?"

"Your cousin Holly said she mentioned me?"

"Oh! Yes." In that earlier conversation, where Ellie's attention had been focused on Nate.

And when a look over her shoulder told her that Nate was deep in conversation with Sara Stone, who Ellie distinctly remembered was one of his high school exes, she experienced a heavy pang of annoyance.

She knew Nate would come back. But damn it, she wanted him now.

Shifting in her seat so that she didn't have to look at Sara flirting with Nate, she focused her attention on Harry. He really was quite attractive. He seemed well-groomed, and the smile on his face said he was eager to please. Compared to the heat Nate's smile generated or the tingles his touch on her back set off, though, she felt less than nothing. But, surrounded by her family, she had no choice but to be polite.

"Um, you're the doctor, right?" she asked him.

"I hear that I could say the same to you." Harry smiled, clearly more at ease now that the conversation had been initiated. "Optometry, is it?"

And not a single mention of the fact that her family didn't see her as a *real doctor*. Well, that was nice.

She didn't want nice. She wanted tall, dark and dangerous.

"Ellie." A fresh martini appeared in front of her, accompanied by that rough voice that made her tingle. "Here's your drink."

"Nate." She looked up, and as soon as her eyes met his, she felt it—that slap of heat. "Care to introduce us?" he asked, glaring at Harry.

Ellie blinked. "Yes. Nate, this is Harry. Harry, Nate."

Harry stood and smiled, offering his hand, but the smile slipped off his face at the ferocity of Nate's expression.

"Nathan Archer," Nate said in a low growl.

"I've followed your career, it's been very impressive," Harry said, attempting to make polite conversation.

"Thank you."

"My cousin introduced us." She stood, unable to stop herself from moving closer to Nate. "Harry is a doctor."

Looking Nate right in the eye, she cocked her head, arched an eyebrow. Dared him without words to make the next move, to declare himself as more than her wingman for the night.

He grinned and heat shot straight through her. He wrapped an arm around Ellie's waist, the feel of his fingers digging protectively into her skin causing electricity to flow through her body. Every inch of her responded to his possessive hold and the look of ownership on his face.

Alpha men had never really been her thing—at least, the men she dated certainly didn't fall into that category. But having Nate go all macho caveman over her? She needed a tall glass of ice water. Maybe a fan. She'd never admit it out loud, but if he wanted to grab her hair and drag her back to his cave, she wouldn't put up much of a fuss.

Harry looked from Ellie to Nate, then back to Ellie again,

before taking a step back. "Well. It was nice to meet you, Ellie. I think I'll be getting back to my table."

"Nice to meet you," she murmured.

"Right." Harry cast her an uncomfortable smile before walking away. The second he was out of earshot, Ellie leaned into Nate.

"And what was that, hmm, wingman? I think you might have just cock-blocked me." She'd never been much good at flirting, but this thing with Nate was like a force of its own, carrying her along in its wake.

"Damn straight I did." Nate closed the space between them. Cast a surreptitious glance around their table, eased back just a bit. "If anyone is going to have his hands on you, Ellie, it's going to be me."

Ellie fought shivers that took hold of her body and yes, her emotions, leading her to acknowledge that yes, she was going to pay for this moment at the end of the weekend. When Nate walked away.

Right now? She didn't care.

He slid his hand from her waist to her lower back, pulling her in closer and she shivered, her body trembling in delight.

"This isn't a good idea, me holding you like this," Nate muttered.

"No, it's not," she said softly. The buzz of voices surrounded them, but she couldn't see anyone or hear anything else, her world entirely focused on Nate.

"If you knew what I wanted from you, you'd be disgusted."

Her pulse stuttered at the raw admission. He wanted her. All she had to do was meet him halfway.

But that comment ... "Are you talking about the kinky stuff?"

Surprise painted his face before dark interest dawned. "Explain."

She squirmed under his gaze. "Well, the tabloids. There

have been articles about you ... about things that you like. In the... bedroom." And she'd be lying through her teeth if she said that those articles hadn't fuelled her curiosity, hadn't powered more than one hot, sweaty, sexy dream.

He cleared his throat. "And if you knew what those things entailed, you'd run. You'd be smart to." He dipped his head, his breath warm against her ear, his voice harsh. "I like my sex hard and hot, Ellie."

Ellie wasn't sure what a hot flash felt like, but she was pretty sure that his words had just given her one. She grew dizzy listening to his words, knowing that at the end of this conversation she'd have Nate.

"Perfect for my one-night stand," she said, biting her bottom lip, her breath catching in her throat.

"Blondie," he said on a low growl, with a smile so wolfish and seductive she could almost believe he wanted to take a giant bite out of her, and her heart slammed hard against her ribcage.

But behind that grin was a seriousness that told her he wouldn't touch her unless he was absolutely sure about what she wanted. "Think about what you're saying."

"I've thought about it for years. I've thought about you." She swallowed after forcing the words out. "This is what I want."

His expression darkened, and he laced his fingers through hers, tugging her up. "Come dance with me. Take time to be sure."

She didn't have to think about this, she already knew. She wanted... oh, she knew what she wanted. The dampness between her thighs, and the way her heart pounded hard in her chest, made her need perfectly clear.

But this was Nate. Dangerous, delicious Nate who would take what she gave ... and be gone in the morning. That's why she had to take his advice, and think.

It was easy to say she was okay with a one-night stand. Another to go through with it when the man in question was the answer to all her dreams. But if she wanted Nate, she had to accept his terms.

And if knowing he'd be gone in the morning made her feel hollow inside... well, she was a big girl. She'd deal with her emotions when the time came.

———

Finally, finally Nate had the woman of his dreams at his side. And rather than throwing herself at him, she was still focused on a one-night stand. He just barely held back a crazy laugh.

As he guided her onto the dance floor, he thought that fate really was a cruel bitch.

"Nate?" Ellie watched him with those careful blue eyes as he drew her into his arms. The tip of her tongue darted out to trace over her lips, and he barely stifled a groan.

She couldn't possibly understand the depth of what he wanted from her. If she did, she'd be running far, far away. But at this point, the primal instinct to mark her as his own won out. Though they were the only ones on the dance floor, he gave into the need, tugging her against him with one hard movement.

She gasped but didn't push him away. It pleased him immensely that her gaze didn't so much as flicker from his own.

Her sweet curves molded to his body and he thickened, hardening against the stiff denim of his pants. His hips moved reflexively, seeking her heat, and her soft moan had his blood pumping harder in his veins.

He wanted to sink into her, immerse himself in everything that was Ellie, and he wasn't just talking about sex. But she'd made it clear that that wasn't going to happen.

He knew exactly how she saw him. The player, the kinky guy who'd oblige her curiosity for a night.

Knowing that hurt more than he'd imagined it could. And he knew that for the first time in his life, this would be more than sex. Would leave him in a world of hurt. If he was smart, he'd stop this right now.

But if she wanted to take a walk on the wild side, he'd be damned it she did it with anyone but him.

She shifted restlessly against him, and his body responded. He hoped like hell they looked like old friends sharing a dance and catching up, because he'd drawn her closer than was appropriate and didn't much feel like letting go. And when he shifted on his feet, her soft thighs cradled his erection, driving him mad.

"Jesus, Nate." Ellie's nails dug into his shoulders, and he hissed at the delicious bite of pain. Threading his hand into her hair, he gave it one quick little warning tug before releasing and returning his hand to her back.

The small gasp, the low moan—ah, fuck. Those intelligent eyes of hers were blurred with need from that little taste of dominance, something he'd never expected from her.

Any thoughts of walking away flew right out the window. This woman, her insecurities, her hidden sexuality was his, and he meant to claim her. "Yeah, you feel it, too."

"I'd have to be dead not to feel it." Ellie buried her face in his neck, just for a second, but the moist heat of her breath on his skin made him growl.

This connection between them was intense. Never before had he been so desperate to get a woman alone, to get inside of her, and he knew that need stemmed from the feelings he had for her that had nothing to do with sex and everything to do with the warmth around his heart. Pressing his fingers to her back, he gave another subtle little roll of his hips, and almost swore out loud at the sweet, sweet sensation.

CHAPTER 8

Drawing on every little shred of self-control that he possessed, Nate pulled back, placing just the thinnest ribbon of space between them. It was physically painful.

"What's wrong?" Ellie's voice was low, breathy, and he could just imagine her panting out his name as she came.

"I need you to be clear about what you're getting into." Nate watched her expression carefully. One hint that she wasn't on board, and he'd walk away. It would kill him, but he'd do it.

Ellie huffed out a laugh, her lips curving into a wry smile. "Not sure how to break this to you, Nate, but I've done this before."

Oh, had she now? He knew she meant that she'd had sex before, but just the reminder that another man had put his hands on her brought forth a blinding fury. Forgetting his well-worded warning, he pulled her flush against him again and growled.

"I don't think that you have, Blondie." He smiled down at her as well, but this time the tone held a mocking, hungry edge. "Unless you're telling me that you've been with a man who took everything that you gave him and demanded more? A man who wanted to claim you, to mark you, to make you forget you've ever met any other man?"

"I—what?" Ellie's fingers scrabbled for purchase against the muscles of his back, and he just held her tighter.

"You heard me." Christ, but when she looked at him like that, her eyes already blurry with pleasure when he'd barely even touched her...

Ellie was silent for a moment, but he felt her shiver, as though a fever had overtaken her.

"Are you talking like... Fifty Shades of Grey kind of demanding? That's what you'd want from me if we... sleep together?"

Was the woman serious? She didn't even look put off by the notion, just intrigued.

Nate was done for.

"Well, I left my whip at home." He savored her soft gasp and decided not to enlighten her that he was joking—mostly. "But the basic idea, yes. I want to own you. And make no mistake, we will not be sleeping together. I will be fucking you. Hard."

"Well, when you put it that way." Ellie sucked in a deep breath. Nate studied her face, looking for any sign that she was at all unsure.

There was none. Instead, her every look, her every shiver seemed to mirror the clawing need that he felt, too. Their eyes locked, the connection between them pulling tighter. Ellie's fingers slid from his back, playing over his shoulders and working their way into the non-existent space between their bodies. She grabbed the front of his shirt, lifted her chin.

He wanted to kiss her. Needed to taste her lips, to explore that hot, wet cavern of her mouth. To own it.

Just in time, he remembered where they were.

"Ellie." It almost killed him, but he pushed them the slightest bit apart. "Too many eyes here."

He wanted to press his erection against her sweet heat again so badly that he *almost* didn't care. Only the thought of her embarrassment, Chase's anger, and the set-down that Ellie would get from her family for hooking up with that good-for-nothing Archer boy, held him in check.

Ellie blinked and swallowed heavily. For a moment it looked like she didn't care either. Then she nodded ever so slightly, inching back, putting space between them.

Nate hated the distance. If he had his way, he'd have her naked and on the floor beneath him, never mind who the fuck was watching.

"We need to leave." Ellie swallowed, and he watched, fascinated, as she tried to pull her mask of cool composure back into place. "I have to move some of that alcohol to the reception venue for my mother first. Why don't you... go on ahead and say goodbye to Chase and the others? I'll meet you out at your car in fifteen minutes?"

Blondie thought she was going to dictate how this went down, did she? Nate grinned to himself as he ushered her to the side of the dance floor.

Catching a finger in one of the flimsy straps of her dress before she could scurry away, he leaned in to whisper in her ear.

"Fuck moving the alcohol." Her earlobe was right there, a pretty pink shell that he wanted to bite, but there were too many people around. "We have better things to do."

Ellie arched an eyebrow at him. "My mother asked me to."

"No." Nate fought back the urge to crush her against him and run his hands down the length of those luscious curves. "This is what you're going to do. You're going to forget about the alcohol. You're going to go to the ladies room, and you're going to take off your panties."

"*What?*" Ellie's mouth fell open. "Are you insane? I'm not doing any such thing."

"I told you that I would demand everything from you." Nate leveled her with an intent stare. "If you don't want to do as I ask, then it's best we don't start at all."

"I—" Ellie flushed a pretty shade of deep pink as she visibly struggled with the order. "I don't—"

For one long, agonizing moment, Nate thought that she was going to bow out. And it would crush him, but he'd respect her decision. But then she straightened her spine, tossed him the single sexiest glare he'd ever seen in his life, and marched out of the large room—as much as she could march in high heels.

So. Cute.

Blood humming, he loitered for a few minutes, making small talk with the people milling around him. When he saw Sara-Dara heading toward him like a steam engine, he figured he'd hung around long enough and beat a hasty retreat.

He walked into the hallway. Ellie was standing just outside the women's bathroom, her cheeks stained red and the fingers clutching her small purse in a death grip. She narrowed her eyes at him as he approached, but her pupils were dilated and her nipples were puckering against the thin silk of her dress.

"I did it." The words were partially defiant, partially aroused. "Can we go now?"

"In a second. Put them in my pocket first."

"I'm not taking them out of my purse here!"

"Yes, you are." He smiled lazily, nodding politely at a woman who exited the bathroom. "You'll pull them out of your purse and place them in the pocket of my jeans, right here, right now. Know why?"

"Why?" she asked.

"Because once those little panties are in my pocket, my cock is going to get harder than it's ever been." He smiled at her sharp intake of breath. "And that's the way you want me. Hard and ready for you."

"For heaven's sake, Nate." Ellie wiped a hand over her brow. "I can't *think* when you talk to me like that."

"I'd say you're still thinking too much if you can form that sentence." With a quick glance around, he noted the nearly abandoned coat check.

For what he had in mind, it was just perfect.

"Come with me." Without waiting for her reaction, Nate strode toward the door of the coat room.

The door was meant for employees to enter and exit through while people checking their coats would pass them over the bar-style opening. With so few items inside, however, no one was manning the station, and the dimly lit interior was empty. Still, Ellie dug her high heels into the carpet as he tugged her through the entry.

"Oh, no. Not here."

Ellie was strong, but she was so very little, especially compared to his six-plus feet. Pulling her into the coat check after him required about as much effort as it would take to lift a kitten.

"Nate!"

"If you seriously mean no, then say red. Understand?" Body humming from being so close to her, Nate slammed the coat check door shut behind them. He pulled her tightly against him, just the way they had been on the dance floor, and waited for her to nod.

She did. And he continued.

"Tonight I'm going to do a lot of dirty, dirty things to you." Dipping his head, Nate nipped at that delicate earlobe that had been taunting him all night. "Things you've never done. Things that might make your mouth say no, out of habit, when you really mean yes. So red is the word that means you want me to stop. Got it?"

"I..." Ellie flicked a quick glance to the side, to where the wide bar-style opening yawned. Where they were, in a corner against the door, they were hidden - unless someone leaned right over that bar. Still, the chance that someone could do just that, could see whatever he was about to do to her...

He watched as the potent combination of nerves and excitement and, finally, surrender painted her face.

"Red. I understand." Then, astounding him, she fisted her fingers in the front of his shirt and tugged his mouth down to hers.

"Ellie." His need to take control reared its head, but then their lips were glued together, greedy little murmurs coming from her slender throat as she opened beneath the flick of his tongue.

This. This was the kiss he'd been waiting for, dreaming about, ever since they were teenagers. The room spun as though he was drunk, and he worked his fingers into the golden ribbons of her hair, freeing it from its bun and anchoring himself in her warmth and scent.

She whimpered against him, her fingers digging into the muscles of his chest until he felt a bite of pain. With every slide of her soft lips over his own, his control slipped away, disappearing with the need to be inside her, to be part of her, to be *consumed* by her.

No. No consuming. He didn't get lost in women. He dominated them, he owned them, he sent them out of their minds with pleasure... but he never, ever lost himself.

He needed to bring some of that control back.

"Press your cheek against the door." Using the hands in her hair as a guide, Nate turned Ellie until she faced the closed door they'd just entered the room through, pressing her against it. "Hands flat against the door. Do not move them, no matter what I do."

He watched as she sucked in a great mouthful of air, her chest heaving in a way that made him curse under his breath. Slowly, she did as he asked, lowering her face to the metal of the door, then sliding her hands across the surface until they came to rest above her head. She shivered, goose bumps prickling her soft skin even though her body was fever-hot beneath his.

"What are you feeling?" Pressing his front to her back, Nate grabbed her hips, then slid his hands up her torso, palming every curve, absorbing the sensations. "Tell me."

CHAPTER 9

"It's like... fire and ice," Ellie said as he worked his hands between her breasts and the door, teasing her with circling strokes. "The door is cold. But I'm... I'm so hot. Everywhere. Like I'm on fire."

"You're going to get hotter." He rolled his hips as she bucked back against him, the delicious friction making his eyes roll back in his head.

With his teeth, he slid one of the delicate straps of her dress down the sensual slope of her shoulder, then moved to the other. She was naked beneath, and he felt his cock grow impossibly harder as the slip of silk fell to her waist and he caught her nipples between his fingers.

She cried out sharply as he tugged on the hard peaks, and he laughed into that warmly scented tumble of hair.

"No noise, Blondie. Even though I'm going to do my best to make you scream, no sound until we're alone..." He rolled her nipples, savoring the way they continued to tighten beneath his touch.

"Nate, God!" Using her hands as leverage, Ellie pushed back against him, grinding her sweet ass into his erection. For a moment, he gave into the rising tide, tugging her back against him and pushing against her, chasing the dark need.

"I can feel how wet you're getting, Blondie. Hot and wet and ready for me." With one hand, he continued to toy with her nipple, enjoying the way she pushed back against him with each tug. With the other hand, he moved down her body to cup her between her legs, finding her aching core. With her panties in his pocket, there was no barrier between his questing fingers and her slick heat.

"Nate. I need you." Ellie shifted, trying to line up her damp folds with the tips of his fingers. He chuckled darkly and slid them forward until her mound rested in the palm of his hand.

"I know what you want." Rotating his wrist, he ground the heel of his hand against her clit. Her thighs trembled, squeezing him. "You've always been a good girl. The kind of girl who would never let me fuck her in a coat closet. But that's exactly what you want, isn't it? You want me to slide right between these sweet thighs and fuck you hard."

"Yes! Yes! That's what I want."

Releasing her breast, he slid his wrist in front of her mouth. "If you need to scream, bite."

"*Nate.*" Ellie pressed down against his hand, her slickness coating his fingers. "God, please. *Please.*"

"Please what?" Slowly circling his hand, he worked his palm against her clit, the tightness of her thighs telling him that her pleasure was mounting. "Say the words."

"Please make me come!" Her whisper was a scream as she writhed against his touch. Losing it because of him was... he didn't have words to describe it. Never mind that this was just going to be for tonight—he wanted to ruin her for the touch of any other man, ever.

She needed to come? He'd give her the orgasm of her life.

"Hold on, baby." She was so wet, so ready, there was no

need to take it slow now—bending her at the waist, he speared two fingers inside her.

She gave a strangled cry against him, her body pushing down, silently begging for more.

"That's it." He worked his fingers in and out of her impossibly tight heat. "The second time you come for me, it will be when you're stretched around my cock. But I don't think you can wait that long, can you, Blondie? You need this. Need what only I can give you."

"Yes. Dammit, yes, Nate. Please!" Her forehead knocked into the door as her writhing became more frenzied, but his wanton little minx didn't even pause. "Now, now, now!"

"Since you asked so nicely." Dipping his head to lick a trail up her neck, Nate scissored his fingers inside of her, loving the way she clenched around him. He did it again, felt her response ratchet up a notch in intensity, and then did it one last time, twisting his wrist so that he hit the soft flesh inside her, just the right spot for her to let go.

She gave a low cry, stiffening in his arms. Delicious licks of pain bolted through him as she sank her teeth into his wrist, a definite scream just barely muffled by the fabric of his shirt.

She squeezed the hand trapped between her legs hard, greedily wringing every last drop of her orgasm from his fingers. The ferocity of her response had him sinking into that fog again, the one where all he could think, taste and see was her.

Now. He had to have her now. Before his brain caught up with his body, he was reaching for the condom tucked into his pocket, determined to sheath the erection that had grown painful and in turn, guide himself inside all of that wet heat.

"What do you mean, she was with someone?" A female voice cut through the air from just outside the coat check, and both Nate and Ellie froze. "Ellie didn't bring a date. I know she didn't."

"It was Nathan Archer." The voice was male—it was that doctor who'd been hitting on Ellie earlier. Even though he couldn't blame the guy for trying, he still stiffened with possessiveness. "They really seemed like they were together."

"Nathan Archer?" The pair were in front of the counter now—Nate could just see their shadows.

Ellie shoved frantically against him, and he couldn't quite hold back his chuckle. Sliding his fingers from where they were still nestled inside of her, he gave her clit one final rub, enjoying her intake of breath before letting her free. Still, he shifted to cover her while she straightened her dress, just in case someone got too curious and poked their head into the room.

"No, that's not possible. I don't think they've even seen each other since high school."

The voices faded as Holly and Harry passed by the coat check, and Nate couldn't help but chuckle again when he heard Ellie's massive sigh of relief from behind him.

"Come on then, Blondie." Turning, he met Ellie's stare. Her eyes were still bright, her skin flushed bright from her recent orgasm and knowing that he was the one who had brought those beautiful changes out in her had him forgetting about everything but the driving need to be inside of her.

Nate had only had the smallest taste of this woman and he craved so much more. He didn't understand why. He just knew he felt more when he was with her. Protective, in ways he'd never been with another woman. And, as he guided her from the Lodge with a hand at the small of her back, he wondered if just this one night was going to be enough to get his fill.

———

Ellie's nerves hummed the entire ride back to the motel. She was entirely focused on the man in the driver's seat next to her. Every shift of the muscles in his thighs, every quick glance he cast her way made her stomach clench with delicious anticipation.

It did something funny to the area around her heart, too, but she wouldn't let herself focus on that. This was just sex. Hopefully really, really amazing sex with the man she'd dreamt of for so long.

The scene from only minutes before played on a looped reel in her head, telling her that her imagination had barely even touched on how good this was going to be. She'd just gotten mostly-naked with Nathan Archer. And the depths of her response to him had blown her mind.

She was keyed up; her skin stretched tight. She wanted to put her hands on him again. Wanted his hands all over her.

Nate remained silent as he pulled into the small lot of the Ruby Sunset Motel, sliding the car into a spot close to the door of their room. Ellie's pulse began to beat double-time as she realized that this was it—she was going to walk into that room with Nate, and then they were going to have sex.

Flushing all over at the idea, she busied herself undoing her seatbelt. Before she could unlatch the metal buckle, Nate's strong fingers did it for her. Grabbing her around the waist, he hauled her over the centre console so that she was sprawled against him.

"Last chance, Blondie." He caught her earlobe between his teeth—God, *God,* she'd never even known before tonight just how hot that made her. "We go through that door, and you're mine."

"Then why are we still in the car?" Ellie barely managed to get the words out before Nate's mouth was on hers, his tongue demanding entrance in a slow, skilled kiss that was dirtier than any actual sex that she'd ever had before.

His mouth slanted over hers, and his hands tangled in her hair, guiding her movements. She couldn't catch her breath, because every time she thought he was going to pull away, to break off the kiss, he pulled her even further under.

The interior of the car heated, their panting breath steaming the windows, just from this kiss.

Restlessly, she wiggled on his lap, jolts of satisfaction shooting through her when she felt the very hard evidence that said he was as ready for this as she was. Freeing one of her hands, she reached down and stroked his arousal, working her fingers up and down the rigid length, through the fabric of his jeans.

Nate caught her around the wrist, stilling her movements. "I don't think so."

She stretched out her fingers and danced them over what she could reach, causing him to hiss. "Why not?" She grinned when he reflexively thrust his hips up against her. "I want to return the favor."

"You are far dirtier than I ever imagined you'd be, Blondie." With a groan, Nate dragged her hand away from his length, placing it safely back on his chest. "No touching until I say so."

"That's so not fair." She tugged against his grip, felt another surge of excitement when she noted the predatory spark in his eyes.

He set her back in her own seat, quickly exited the car, then rounded it to open her door.

"Fair has nothing to do with what's about to happen." Nate extended a hand for Ellie. She slowly tangled her fingers in his. "We're going to do things tonight because I want them... but also because you've given me your permission and told me that that's what you want, too. You want to be taken over by me as much as I want to lose myself in you."

CHAPTER 10

A full body shiver took her over, emotions far beyond the physical wracking her every sense. She knew, she *knew* that this would never become anything serious. It couldn't. But she'd never had a man say anything like that about her before, and she couldn't quite stop her heart from doing a little dance.

"Hope that wine's ready." He grinned down at her, the expression wolfish, and Ellie's heart thundered.

Except... the wine. Right. The wine that he'd ordered because he'd known he would be bringing a woman back to this room. It was just convenient that it happened to be her.

Though she tried to hide it, her smile faltered.

"You know, I had big plans for that wine before you decided you wanted to jump my bones." Nate's voice was mild as he led her to the door of their room and slid the old-school metal key into the lock.

"I'm aware," Ellie couldn't stop herself from snapping. "This isn't really a great time to bring that up."

"You're cute when you're jealous." He brushed a kiss over her lips, just a whisper, and it still stole Ellie's breath. "Yeah, I had big plans. See, when I ordered it, I already knew that the only woman I wanted was you. But I tried to convince myself that it was a bad idea. I planned on getting drunk on good wine until I passed out, so I wouldn't have to think about you getting naked with whatever asshole you'd decided to scratch your itch with."

"What?" This was so far from what Ellie had expected him to say that she stopped still.

"I didn't have plans with any other woman tonight." Nate arched an eyebrow, gesturing back toward the parking lot. "You were my first choice. My only choice."

"I ... just ... wow. Okay."

He grinned. "Glad we got that cleared up." Nate splayed a hand across her back and walked her into the room, shutting the door behind them. "Because I believe you said something about returning a favor."

Just like that, the entire world narrowed until it was just her and Nate, and the heat pulsing between them.

Before she could lose her courage, she reached for his waistband, gasping when he pushed her hand away, pressing her up against the cool metal of the door.

"I said no touching." Slowly, deliberately, he undid his belt, pulled it from the loops. Let it fall to the floor. "Not until I say you can."

As he regarded her intently, Ellie watched, breathless, trembling just the tiniest bit as he untucked his shirt from his jeans and loosened the top button. Undid the front zipper of his jeans.

Ellie couldn't stop herself from looking, and also couldn't hold back the small murmur of pleasure when the head of Nate's cock, straining to be free of the black underwear, made itself known, glistening and ready.

"Lose the dress."

Ellie's attention snapped back to his face. Surely he didn't expect her to just strip for him?

She'd pictured this more as a frenzy of them ripping each other's clothing off, a frantic coupling that left no room for thought.

Nate remained still, watching her. *Apparently not.*

She hesitated, not sure she could do this. Good girls didn't do erotic stripteases for demanding lovers, right?

Well, good girls didn't have orgasms in coat closets, either, and she'd already done that. What was one more step into craziness?

Raising her chin, she reached around back for the short zipper that fastened her dress. She could reach it easily enough, but the position felt awkward, thrusting her breasts forward, putting them on display.

Nate didn't offer to help. Instead he just continued to watch her with that serious expression, missing nothing as she slid the straps from her shoulders, then, with a great big breath, let the dress fall to the floor.

She was naked except for her shoes. Oh God, oh God. Her hands fluttered, anxious to cover her breasts, the embarrassingly damp space between her thighs, but a low growl from Nate stopped any movement.

"Don't you dare." He caught her hands, tugged, arranging her so her hands were clasped behind her back. Something about being so exposed while Nate watched her hungrily was as awkward as it was exciting.

"You agreed that tonight you're mine. And if you try to hide what's mine, there will be consequences." The harsh words were contrasted with a sweet, wet kiss.

Nate clasped her chin in his fingers and guided her movements as he took her mouth. She had the fleeting notion that she should be a more active participant, but after always giving in to what everyone wanted and needed, it just felt so damn good to let go and let him be in control.

By the time he ended the kiss, she was warm and relaxed like she'd just drunk a big glass of wine while soaking in a hot bath. One of those wolf-like glances from Nate, though, and the searing need came rushing back, right into her veins, making her high.

"Are we agreed?" he asked.

"Agreed," she whispered.

"That makes me very happy, Blondie." He grinned as his hands returned to the waistband of his jeans. Ellie felt her mouth go dry as he slid them and his briefs down over his hips, freeing his rock-solid erection.

"Now, back to returning that favor. Leave the shoes on, and get on your knees."

———

Nate was feeling the pressure.

He'd imagined this exact scenario a million times, in a million different ways, but he'd never fully realized the weight that he would feel when it happened.

He wanted to make this good for her.

More to soothe his own nerves than hers, he walked deliberately across the room to where the clerk had left the bottle of wine chilling in a plastic ice bucket. Classy, but it served its purpose, he supposed.

He knew that Ellie's gaze was on him as he picked up the bottle, approved the label, then uncorked it. He made a show of pouring an inch of the straw-colored liquid into the cheap glass, then lifting it to his lips and sampling.

When he turned back toward her, her eyes were bright, intent. Focused on his face, even though his jeans were still hanging open.

He moved to the edge of the bed, sat, then patted his thigh.

"Come here."

She made a choked sound, her hands twitching, and he knew that her instinct was to cover herself again. In response he simply arched an eyebrow and waited.

After a long moment in which she flushed the prettiest shade of pink, Ellie crossed the room, closing the space between them. It was obvious that she felt exposed, but that was the way he wanted her—exposed, open, on edge.

Now that he had her here, he was damned if it would just be about sex, never mind what she believed about him.

"Sit." He again patted his leg, and couldn't hold back the smirk when she squirmed.

"Nate. I can't sit on your lap while I'm naked." She reached again for her glasses, hissing with frustration when she found nothing there.

He waited without comment. Finally she heaved a great sigh, then settled herself gingerly on his leg.

Before she could catch her breath, Nate tugged her flush against his chest. She gasped when he ran his fingers through her hair, stroking her like one might an overly excited animal. With a small sigh, she settled into the touch, and Nate felt his pulse stumble.

He knew that she believed he was just a playboy, not capable of anything more. Hell, until he'd heard the news of this wedding, *he'd* believed that too. But he knew that after he'd been inside of Ellie Marshall, after he'd shared this experience with her, there would be no going back, at least for him.

The thought was terrifying and liberating at the same time. And from the way she shivered against him, he wasn't the only one who felt that way.

"Drink." Holding the glass up to her lips, he tilted until

the golden liquid tipped into her mouth. She hummed a sigh of approval, then opened her lips for more.

He let her have one more sip, then took one himself, laughing at the noises she made as she swallowed.

The sexy, sexy noises.

"Sorry." Ellie caught him looking and twisted her lips into a wry smile. He tracked the movement of her tongue as it darted out over the curves of pink. "I don't think I've ever had such expensive wine before. I don't know if it's worth what you paid for it, but it's damn good."

"I have high standards. And I only indulge in the best." Nate held the glass up to her lips again, tugging it back when she reached for it with her own hands. "No. Hands on your thighs. Let me give this to you."

He'd been referring to more than the wine with his comment, but when she didn't seem to notice, he didn't push. Something told him that this particular woman needed to be shown how special she was, rather than told.

She tilted her chin up for more wine, and he let her have one final sip before tugging it away. Her gaze flicked from the glass to him, and he watched as her chest heaved with a deep breath.

"Aren't you going to finish it?" Her voice was pitched low, painted with a husky tone that he'd never heard there before.

It was like a siren's call, and suddenly his capacity for patience, his desire to take it slow and draw out her pleasure were stretched tight and thin.

"Oh, I am." Keeping a careful grip on the wine glass, he used his other arm to slide her from his lap to the bed. Her thighs parted, cradling him as he settled her onto her back, then knelt on the floor between her legs.

"What are you doing?" Ellie pushed herself up onto her elbows, staring at him down the length of her body. There was nothing sexier than seeing the beam from those sapphire eyes, looking down at him from that expanse of silken skin.

She was clearly aroused, flushed and short of breath, but he wanted more. He wanted her screaming his name, wanted her writhing beneath him.

He wanted to take her further than she'd even gone before. Wanted her to remember this night for the rest of her life.

Lifting the glass, he tilted it until a trickle of the gilded wine poured over the edge. It landed on her breasts, and he savored her gasp as he drizzled it down the soft plane of her stomach, then the swathes of her upper thighs.

"Nate! What are you doing?" She jerked up, gasping. Tossing the glass aside, he pressed on her belly with the flat of one hand until she laid back down.

And then he laid his tongue on the glistening dampness that lay on her thigh, sliding the wet heat into the crease where leg met stomach. She moaned, and he felt a surge of triumph, knowing it was him and only him that was making her feel this way.

"I'm finishing the wine."

CHAPTER 11

athan Archer is licking wine off of my skin.

Ellie arched her back, pushing herself into the touch. The sensation as his tongue dragged over her body was so much better than anything she'd ever imagined—and she'd imagined plenty.

"So have I." Nate's voice took her by surprise.

Ellie didn't realize she'd spoken out loud until he'd replied to the thoughts churning through her head.

"I've thought about you like this since long before I should have," he said.

Nate licked a trail up her stomach, following the lines made by the spilled wine and she gasped.

"I—I had no idea. And it's ... hard to believe."

A sharp smack on her left hip shocked the words out of her mouth, and she stared up at Nate open-mouthed.

"If we're going to do this, then you need to trust me." He arranged himself over her, but held himself just far enough back to make her long for his touch. "That means that if I tell you something, I expect you to believe it. Understand?"

"Yes." She wiggled beneath him, trying to get in contact

with his touch again. He delivered another light slap to her upper thigh, and the world around her begin to whirl. "What was that for?"

"You can't just say that you believe me." Dipping his head, Nate brushed his lips over hers in a touch so light that it ignited more than it satisfied. "You have to actually believe it. Or there will be a punishment. Do you understand?"

Holy. Hell. The intensity in Nate's stare, the way he'd set her skin on fire, the flutter in her chest—she'd never felt so alive.

Aware that Nate was waiting for an answer, Ellie nodded, frantic to have his hands back on her. As he crushed his lips to hers again in a feverish kiss and she melted into the embrace, she fought to remember that this was nothing more than sex to him. Sex and friendship.

And that was how she wanted it. How it had to be.

Right?

"Care to share with the class?" Breaking away, Nate smirked down at her, and Ellie flushed as she realized that he'd noticed her little internal argument. And what was *wrong*with her, getting lost in her own head when this was happening around her?

"I'm sorry." She placed a tentative hand on his chest. She was a strong, professional woman—no way was she about to admit her insecurities to him. The kind of women he usually had his bed probably had egos the size of the Statue of Liberty. "Where were we?"

He shifted his weight onto his knees, braced above her. He regarded her for a long time, and she felt as though those charcoal eyes could read into her very soul.

She hoped not, because then he'd be able to see that, more than aroused, she was having an awful lot of very fluttery feelings in the depths of her belly.

"Interesting." Still rising above her, he began to unbutton his shirt, one fastening at a time.

"What's interesting?" she asked, then she no longer cared at all.

Her mouth went dry, struck dumb by the sight of a well-cut shirt being shrugged off of wide, extremely well-sculpted shoulders. Not even if those shoulders were covered with dark, intricate ink, and not even if the rock solid chest boasted...

Oh, sweet Lord. Nate had a nipple ring, a simple silver hoop looped through the left side. Before she could stop herself, her hand was reaching up to touch.

He let her dance her fingers over the small piercing, hissing when she stroked, fascinated by the contrast of the cool metal and the hot skin.

"*This* is what's interesting." Eyes dark, he caught her hand, pressed her fingers against him. With his hand over hers, he helped her to tug on the ring, and they groaned in tandem at the touch. "You're a dirty girl, Ellie Marshall. And all these years I had no idea."

"I... I don't know what to say to that." Propping herself up on her elbows, she let her hand rest on his chest, absorbed the steady thumping of his heart beneath her fingers. "I've never thought that way about myself before."

"Haven't you?" Before Ellie could blink, Nate had both of her wrists caught in one of his hands, pressed into the quilt above her head. He grinned down at her as she tugged, then squeaked, realizing that he had her pinned.

"When I take it slow, your mind wanders. When I'm nice, your response is lukewarm." Dipping his head, he pressed his lips to hers, his tongue demanding an entrance that she immediately yielded to. "It's when I show you my piercing and pin you down that you get all excited. So yes, Ellie, you're a dirty girl. And if I want to ruin you for all other men—and believe me when I say that I will—I'm going to have to take you farther than you've ever imagined going before."

What?

"Nate—what—"

His hands pressed her wrists into the mattress hard, and then he backed off of her, standing on the floor between her knees.

"Don't move an inch." The muscles of his arms, his chest rippled in the low light that filtered through the window coverings as he hooked his fingers into the sides of his opened slacks. Ellie almost whimpered when he inched them down his lean hips, letting them fall to the floor.

He was absolute perfection. Over six feet of lean muscle, golden skin decorated with intricate designs that made her fingers inch to touch. That tantalizing and unexpected piercing, and an erection big enough to make her catch her breath.

He was swollen, the head already leaking. *Was that really for her?*

She didn't realize that she'd sat up, that she'd moved toward him until he growled low in his throat.

"I told you not to move."

She barely had a moment to appreciate all that was his hard, naked body before she was flipped onto her stomach, a pillow pushed beneath her belly.

"Oh, shit." The words escaped her lips as he clasped her hips, canting them up. She froze against the pillow, her fingers clenching the fabric. She'd never been in this position before, so open and exposed.

Knowing that he could see—probably *was* seeing—that most intimate part of her cleared her mind of thoughts of everything apart from what was happening in the moment.

"You're wet already. Do you know what that tells me, Ellie?" His hands came to rest on the curves of her ass, and she shuddered. "That tells me that you like this. You like being open to me, and you like me telling you what to do."

I just like you! The words reverberated through her mind, but then his palm landed on the curve of her behind, and all words were lost.

The sound of the blow was a sharp crack in the small room. The strike wasn't hard, but it was a scarlet shock to her system. She cried out, rearing up, only to have a gentle but firm hand placed between her shoulder blades, pressing her back down.

"Is this—are you—punishing me?" Another blow landed, making it hard to get the words out. "For not believing you earlier?"

A wicked chuckle sounded from above and behind.

"I should. Yes, I should punish you for that." One more blow, right over the division of her ass, and then a finger slid between her slick folds, slipping inside. "But no. Everything we do tonight is for two reasons."

He curled one finger inside of her, rubbing over her inner wall, and Ellie felt her knees tremble. "One, because you've shown me that you *want* to be taken further. Further than even I imagined you would want to go."

The single finger pulled out, and was replaced with two, which forced a whimper from between her lips.

Her hips rocked of their own accord. So close, she was so close. Never mind that he'd brought her to climax less than an hour ago, it had only awakened the hunger.

"And two." The two fingers inside of her curved, finding some spot that made her gasp. At the same time, he pressed his thumb over her clit, and light began to dance behind her eyes.

"Two is because I want to. No more, no less." Just as she opened her mouth to cry out, already anticipating the fall, Nate removed his hand.

"No!" Frantic, Ellie shoved back against him. Instead of placing his fingers back inside of her, he delivered an open-handed slap to the shockingly sensitive flesh of her pussy.

Her mouth opened on a wordless scream.

"We've already taken the edge off for you, remember?" God, but that commanding tone, the one that was like steel and silk, only served to ratchet her arousal up higher. "Now it's my turn."

With one smooth movement he rolled her onto her back again, her head cushioned on the pillow. Eagerly, she reached for him, but he pulled back with a warning glare.

"Tilt your head back." She did as he asked, and he adjusted her body before climbing off the bed and rounding it. His hips were level with her lips, her head hanging upside down off the bed, and anticipation wracked her body as she understood what he was about to do.

Her lips had already parted before he'd taken himself in hand and pressed the swollen head of his erection to the warm cavern of her mouth.

She closed her lips around him immediately.

"Eager little thing, aren't you?" His words were rough, but his touch was gentle as he eased forward. His weight was heavy on her tongue, salt awakening her senses as he eased forward, pulled back, then pushed in just a little more on the next thrust.

"I love how much you want it." Her heart jumped at the mention of the L-word, even in this context, and then the thought was swept away when he traced a possessive finger over the line of her cheekbone.

The warmth turned into full-blown heat when he caught her chin firmly and held, forcing her to look up at him as best she could from the awkward position.

"That eagerness is only for me. Do you understand?" Her

blood was an inferno, firing along her veins as she moaned her assent around him. "Just me. No other man. Ever."

His words almost sent her over the edge again. He was talking to her like a... like a *thing*. His plaything. Like he'd take everything she gave him, then demand more. A tiny flicker of thought tried to surface, insisting that she shouldn't enjoy this. Shouldn't be dripping wet from being restrained and told what to do.

But she did. Oh, she did. And he was absolutely right—it was all for him.

"You feel so good around me, Blondie." Nate pushed forward again. This time his length tapped against the back of her throat. She swallowed, certain that she was about to gag, but then he slid home.

Triumph surged through her when a raw groan ripped from his throat.

"So tight. So hot." He pulled back just a fraction, then pushed forward again. Overwhelmed with sensation as she was, she noted that he treated her with care, when he could easily have made this very uncomfortable for her.

She swallowed, pleasure suffusing her at, well, at bringing *him* pleasure.

"Ellie!" The hands stroking over her face tightened, as though he was about to lose control, and then he pulled right out of her mouth with a wet sound.

"What's wrong?" She swallowed, running her tongue over her dry lips to dampen them. Her voice was raw. Struggling to see his face, she slid back on the bed, rolled to her side. "What did I do?"

"I should spank you again for assuming that you did something wrong."

She caught just the quickest glimpse of his face, just enough to discern a ferocious hunger. Then he grabbed her around the waist, adjusting her so that her head was on the pillows at the head of the bed, her body laid out before him.

Nate crawled onto the mattress after her, his rigid cock trailing along her inner thigh before settling against the tender flesh between her legs.

"I should spank you, but I can't right now. I need you, Ellie. I've needed you for so long. And I wanted to be inside of you when you make me come for the first time." Nate reached for a foil packet that he'd set on the bedside table sometime after they'd entered the room.

Crimson warning lights flashed across the front of Ellie's brain. She blinked, need fogging her senses as she tried not to let the tidal wave of emotions caused by his words fill up the tunnel that he'd just dug in her heart.

CHAPTER 12

"Nate. I..." She planned to say something flippant, something that would help to transform the intensity of the moment back into just plain old lust and heat.

But then she heard the crinkle of foil, and his sheathed erection was pushing inside of her, and she couldn't think at all.

"Oh God." Ellie gasped at the intrusion. Her flesh was so swollen with arousal that the sweet invasion was overwhelming. She dug her heels into the bed, arching her hips for more and at the same time crying out because she wasn't sure he was going to fit.

"Easy, Blondie." As he had with her mouth, Nate pulled back, giving her a moment to recover before he continued forward. "You can take me. And it's going to feel so good."

She widened her parted legs, wanting nothing less than all of him. Frustration caused her to grit her teeth and wiggle her hips, and then he pressed in the last delicious inch. Finally home, Nate buried his face into her neck and stilled.

"That feels amazing." Ellie's whisper broke the silence.

He lifted his head. She looked into Nate's eyes, and what she saw there made her heart pulse stutter. Pools of stormy gray, with flecks of amber that she'd never noticed before... and they were focused on her like she was the only person in existence.

His breath misted over her cheek as he braced himself on one arm, then tangled his other hand in her hair. "Ellie."

His stare searched her face, and her belly did a slow roll.

Before she could catch her breath, he rolled his hips, and the emotion combined with the sweet friction of him inside of her had her closing her eyes against the onslaught.

"No. Open your eyes." The hand in her hair tugged, awakening the nerve endings along her scalp and sending a rush of heat between her legs. She arched against him in response, and the pressure on her clit made her cry out.

"That's right. Keep your eyes on me while I fuck you." His voice burnt her senses like a shot of whiskey. "I want you to remember who it is that's making you feel this way."

He slid out, then in, the planes of his taut belly rubbing against her clit with every thrust, and she felt herself rocketing toward that peak again, the one she'd been denied just minutes before. One thought rose out of the spiraling bliss, and she gasped it out, her fingers digging into his biceps as he began to move faster, taking her hard.

"And what about you?" The silver of his piercing winked in the low light, and her left hand slid over his chest to rub over the fascinating detail again. When she made contact, he stiffened, then began to move inside of her harder and faster, which made it seem all the more important that she got her answer right away. "Will you remember that it was me who made you feel this way?"

She cringed as soon as the words left her lips, but still, she wouldn't have taken them back. Nate didn't pause, just dipped his head to nip at the cord in her neck, then trailed his tongue up to dip into her ear.

"I'm definitely going to spank you later for all of this self-doubt." He scraped his teeth over the tender lobe, and when she arched and shivered, he used the hand in her hair to force her to look back into his eyes.

"But for now, listen up." He braced his weight on one hand as he began to move harder and faster, then harder and faster still. She found her legs curving around him to hold him to her even more tightly, her stare riveted to his own.

"I already told you, I've wanted this for longer than I'll ever admit." Harder. Faster. Their hips smacked together, their skin slapping with a sound that shouldn't have been sexy and yet was the most erotic thing that Ellie had ever heard. "It's not possible to forget who is making me feel this way, because I've never felt this way before."

Oh, shit. Ellie's heart trembled, the feelings that accompanied her crush multiplying and then pulling her under. She fought to put up reinforcements, to rebuild the walls that would keep her safe from inevitable heartache, but the tidal wave of sensation rising from her core and spreading to the very tips of her fingers was all-consuming, lighting everything in its path to flame.

"Nate!" His name fell from her lips as the largest, most intense release of her life pulled her under, stealing her breath, coloring her vision. Her cries echoed around the room as he continued to fill her, their heat sealing them together until it was hard to tell where he ended and she began.

As if from a distance, she felt Nate's hard muscles draw tight, heard his pained groan. He pulsed inside of her, his fingers digging into her scalp, his face buried against her neck as he emptied himself inside of her.

It could have been seconds, or it could have been a half

hour before Ellie felt her senses returning to her. She was lying on her side, half draped over Nate's chest, his pulse thundering beneath her fingertips.

She wanted to curl into him and never let go. And the realization had her heart pounding all over again. She was in deep trouble. She'd tried so hard to remember that, even though they were friends, this was just sex to Nate. But she knew that she'd passed the point of no return—her feelings were well and truly engaged.

God, how could she possibly keep sex and the emotion separate when they'd just done... *that*?

And *that* was another matter entirely. She'd always fancied herself a vanilla kind of girl, but being held down, spanked, and taken hard had been the hottest experience of her life. She'd always prided herself on being in control—how could she possibly enjoy giving it up?

Yes, she was in deep.

She needed to get out of this bed. Maybe even out of this room. Needed to get some air, some space, before she lost herself altogether.

————

Complete satisfaction and terror were tightly entwined in Nate's gut, and they didn't seem interested in letting go anytime soon.

Nate wasn't ashamed to admit that he'd probably earned his playboy reputation. Still, he'd never had sex that was even remotely comparable to what he'd just shared with Ellie. It had been far more than the fulfilment of a long-held desire—in the space of an evening, she'd somehow managed to work her way right inside him.

He looked down at the top of her golden head as she shifted restlessly in his arms, rolling his eyes at himself. The fireworks might have only been discharged tonight, but they'd been set to explode for years.

Ellie stirred in his arms again, and he caught a glimpse of her face. The panic that he saw made his gut clench.

"Hey. What's going on?" Adjusting his position on the bed, he pulled himself to a sitting position and tried to wrap his arms around her, but she danced just out of his reach and shimmied to the edge of the bed.

"Nothing. I just... I'm going to go grab a shower." She looked around, nerves apparent in every movement, before she tugged on the loosened sheet, wrapping it around her body.

The symbolism couldn't have been more readily apparent —she was shielding herself, constructing a barrier. But why?

Guilt flamed as a possibility occurred to him. Ellie wasn't like most of the women he took to bed, and right now he couldn't be happier about that. But had he been so wrapped up in finally having her in his arms that he'd missed some signal? Had he pushed her too hard, too fast, and not realized that it was too much?

"Talk to me, Ellie." Catching the edge of her sheet in his fist, he held tight when she tried to stand. She huffed out a breath of exasperation, glaring at him over her shoulder.

He knew her well enough to note the other emotions swirling in her eyes at the same time.

"I'm fine, Nate." She tugged the sheet up, covering her cleavage. "I just need a few minutes to myself, okay?"

"No." Not caring about his own nakedness, he slid across the bed to seat himself beside her. Catching her chin in his hand, he gently tilted her head so that she looked him right in the eyes. "I need to know what just happened. I thought you were right there with me. Was I wrong?"

A battle raged over her face, and his body tightened when he thought she would insist on staying mute. Finally she heaved a great sigh, tension evident in the stiff lines of her shoulders.

"Look. I just... I've always known who I am. I'm the good girl, the one with everything together. The one in control." Her lips were pinched into a thin line when she looked right at him. "I can't reconcile that with what we just did. How can I like you holding me down and telling me what to do? That's... isn't that against everything I believe in?"

He studied the worry in her face, which should have lessened after admitting her fears. She obviously wasn't telling him everything, but then, after having sex just once, he didn't really have the right to demand access to all of her innermost thoughts. They'd tackle what was laid out in front of them first, then.

"Do you think less of me because I like to be in control?" He made sure that his voice was mild, accompanied by a brush of his knuckles over her cheek, a gesture meant to calm.

Ellie blinked, clearly startled. "What? No, of course not. Why would I think that?"

"Then why would you think less of yourself for being on the other side?" He stroked his fingers through her hair, and she visibly relaxed under his touch, though the shadows in her eyes remained.

"I don't understand."

"What we do in the bedroom, what we crave, it's not the entirety of who we are." It wasn't the first time that he'd had this conversation, but this time it was more important than ever that he get his point across. "Enjoying being held down and spanked doesn't have any bearing on any other aspect of your life, not unless you want it to."

She studied him with those wide eyes, and he found himself again missing her glasses, which seemed an integral part of her. She opened her mouth to speak, then closed it again.

"Ask whatever you want."

She shifted and the sheet fell to her waist, but he forced himself to keep his eyes on her face, for the time being at least.

"I don't know if this is something I'll want to do forever." She swallowed thickly, and he found himself wanting to trail kisses down the slender column of her throat. "I think it's something I want because... because it's you."

And that sound was his ego swelling. He had to fight the urge to puff out his chest.

Until her next words, anyway.

"So maybe it would be easier for me to think of it that way for now. I don't usually have flings with men, either. So when I... when I go back to my real life, then I can decide if this is what I want all the time."

She was clearly sorting through her feelings, and that was what he'd wanted her to do. But her words were a scalding hot knife to his soul.

Back to her real life. The life that she had without him. Because she thought he was nothing more than the playboy friend of her brother, the guy who was fun to play with but not to keep.

The notion didn't sit well, but now was not the time to push, not when her emotions were so close to the surface.

"Let's order some food." Changing the subject abruptly, he stood and crossed the room to where the ancient corded phone sat beside the television. He didn't miss the way her eyes tracked his movements.

There was hope. At least, he hoped there was hope.

"We had dinner already." Her voice was cranky, and at this he wanted to smile.

While he sure didn't want to hurt her, he didn't mind getting under her skin.

"I'm not hungry," she said.

"You're forgetting how long I've known you." Absently he flipped through the dog-eared 'locals guide', which contained a few equally worn takeout menus. He pulled out one for a steakhouse that had been around for as long as he could remember. "I've seen you eat an entire pepperoni pizza."

"Wow, that makes me feel sexy." She glared at him, her cheeks flushing crimson. "Why would you say that?"

"Are you kidding me?" He tossed the menu onto the bed, then dipped his head and kissed her, brushing his tongue over the seam of her lips until she emitted a small moan. "Do you know what a turnoff it is to take a woman to dinner and be forced to watch her pick at a salad with little pieces of chopped up chicken on it?"

"I like salad with chicken." She scowled, but when he settled his hands onto her shoulders and started to rub she seemed to relax a fraction.

"Do you know what the real meaning of the word sensual is?" Nate let his hands trace down Ellie's upper arms, stroking feather-light touches over the tops of her breasts, savoring the way her breath hitched. "It means *of the senses*. All senses. And watching a woman take sensual pleasure in a decent damn meal awakens all kinds of other needs for me."

"I—oh." Ellie arched into his touch. He circled her rosy nipples once, then drew his hands back up to her shoulders. She moaned with disappointment when he removed his touch completely, tossing the menu into her lap.

"Now pick something, or I'll pick it for you." He grinned, then tugged the sheet away entirely, making her squeak. Her hands fluttered to cover herself, but as if she'd remembered his earlier order, she instead set them on the bed and clenched them in the sheets.

"Might I remind you, I have to fit into a bridesmaid's dress in two days." Under his stare she shifted restlessly, her breath coming faster, her pulse beating like a hummingbird's wings at the base of her throat.

Watching the way that she reacted just to his stare had his own arousal kicking in, and he felt his cock start to rise.

"Well, if it eases your worries at all..." Lazily, he took himself in his hand and pumped slowly, the simmering heat in Ellie's eyes engorging the flesh. "You'll only be wearing that dress until I can get you out of it."

"What?" she asked.

Her stare fastened on the slide of his hand on his own cock. That, more than the touch itself, had his own need coalescing, his pulse speeding, the blood pumping through his veins.

"I mean... I thought..."

Yeah, he knew what she thought... she thought that they were already done, that by tomorrow he'd have moved on to a new conquest.

He had news for her. As long as she was willing to be in his bed, in his bed she'd be. Starting now. So he closed the space between them, sweeping the menu onto the floor. Seating himself on the edge of the bed, he pulled her into his lap so that she straddled him.

The sweetness between her legs made contact with his cock and he hissed aloud. Fuck, but she was already wet, ready for him.

Sweeping her hair to one side, he dipped his head and licked the soft skin of her neck. She cried out, her legs clenching around his hips, and he let the sensation take him over.

"I thought you were about to force-feed me." Ellie gasped as Nate shifted them back on the bed so that he laid full length, her glorious curves on full display on top of him.

Clasping her hips in his hands, he rocked her against him and swore out loud as her slick heat slid over him.

"I am." Reaching between their bodies, he caught her clit between two fingers, sliding back and forth until she started to pant, then sheathed himself with a condom and slid into her heat. "I definitely am."

CHAPTER 13

N ate slept wrapped around Ellie, sharing the same bed.

The thought circled Ellie's mind as she ordered a second mimosa. The sparkling combination of orange juice and champagne paired nicely with the massive plate of eggs and bacon that she'd grabbed from the buffet before joining the long table of women at Meredith's bridal brunch.

She'd turned toward her habitual Greek yogurt and berries out of habit, and then had remembered Nate's comments about chicken salads. And the truth was, despite the massive order of spaghetti that she'd devoured at two in the morning, she was still starving.

This weekend might make her fat and give her a drinking problem. Being with Nate sure worked up an appetite.

The chatter of the women surrounded her as she took a seat at the end of the table, but to her tired ears it was just noise. Her mind was focused on Nate, churning out a never-ending reel of the previous night's activities in vibrant detail.

He'd spanked her, and she'd liked it. More than liked it—

it had been the single most mind-blowing experience of her life. Intense—that was the word she was looking for.

It had taken everything she had to leave him in the room this morning, and she was already aching for him. Aching for the sex, yes, but also for that camaraderie that had come with the non-sex stuff too.

Damn it, she liked him. Like, *like liked* him.

She was so screwed.

Scowling, she shoved a piece of bacon into her mouth, looking down the table. Her cousin was there, chattering brightly, dressed in a very short, very tight little floral sundress that was completely inappropriate for the weather, despite the cardigan she'd topped it with. Looking at Holly made Ellie think of Harry, and she winced a bit as she remembered that she'd get questions about him today.

Yes, he was nice-looking, and he'd seemed pleasant enough. But after a night with Nate? There was no way she'd be able to settle for 'nice'.

And she hadn't been lying to Nate last night. Giving up control to him had blown her mind.

The thought of giving it up to another man? In fact, the thought of having sex with another man at all?

Not even on her radar.

"Good morning!" Meredith plopped herself into the seat next to Ellie, sunshine evident in her voice. Clad in a sleek navy sheath, she looked absolutely radiant. Her brother had chosen well.

"Someone's perky this morning." Ellie grinned at her soon to be sister-in-law and ate another piece of bacon, trying to push Nate out of her head and enter the moment. "I thought you were supposed to abstain from sex the week before the wedding."

"Ha, ha." Meredith grinned and reached for the silver

creamer, adding a generous dollop to her coffee. After a brief hesitation, she reached for the sugar bowl too. "Screw it, at this point the extra calories won't have time to mess with the way my dress fits. And after that, Chase will be stuck with me anyway."

"Chase wouldn't even notice if you gained fifty pounds and all your teeth fell out." Ellie rolled her eyes, a hint of envy sparking in her chest. What would it be like, she wondered, to have someone who loved you that much—the real you, the one deep inside?

"True. Though he has quite a love for my ass the way it is." Meredith winked, picking up her coffee.

"Please. I don't need to know anything about my brother and your ass." Ellie made a face, sipping at her drink. She glanced surreptitiously at the clock on her phone... and maybe took a quick scroll to the text icon.

Nothing. Not that she'd expected it. But still.

"Expecting a message?" Meredith spooned up some yogurt, grinning at Ellie. "I heard that Holly introduced you to Harry. Surprisingly enough for one of her exes, he's a pretty nice guy. And I heard he was quite taken with you."

"Who?" Ellie tore her eyes away from the screen—damn it, would it have been too much to ask for a *good morning, thanks for rocking my world* message? "Oh, right. Harry. Yes, he was very nice."

"So?" Meredith nudged Ellie's mimosa with her coffee cup. "Did you give him your number? Is that why you're looking? Because the guys are golfing this morning, remember? So don't worry, he'll probably text you later."

"Right. Thanks." Ellie struggled to fight back guilt as she shoved her phone away. She couldn't tell Meredith who she'd actually gone home with last night, because Meredith would tell Chase.

And if her big brother knew what she'd done with his best

friend—and more, that she'd *loved* it—there would be hell to pay.

Never mind that there were already going to be consequences—namely, the state of her heart by the time the weekend was over.

Ellie looked up into Meredith's smiling face and struggled to find something to say to change the subject. She didn't want to dwell on the inevitable outcome of this weekend—she just wanted to savor it while it was here. Was that too much to ask?

Surprisingly, it was her cousin Holly who saved the day by shuffling down the table, landing in the seat next to Meredith. Like Ellie, she had a mimosa in one hand, but the brightness of her smile told Ellie that she'd had a few already.

"All right, ladies. Time to talk about the bachelorette party!" Holly giggled, Meredith groaned, and Ellie snuck another peek at her phone.

Still no message, but Nate's promise to peel her dress off of her tomorrow made her think that they'd be together tonight, too, and the very thought made her shiver with excitement.

It was going to be a very long day.

———

There weren't many options when it came to strippers in Ruby Beach, so Gavin hadn't had much to work with. And as Nate sat uncomfortably on the questionably upholstered chair at Ruby Love's, the first and last strip joint he'd ever stepped foot in, he could see why.

The titular Ruby was the only actual entertainment in her establishment. And since she'd been in her early thirties back when Nate was a teenager, she was now of an age that just wasn't working for any of the guys gathered for Chase's bachelor party.

Well, except for Gavin. Nate was surprised to see that, for the second time in as many days, his serious former soldier friend was three sheets to the wind. He had a handful of single bills out and seemed to be enjoying Ruby's show just fine.

The groom, on the other hand? The look on his face said that he couldn't wait for the show to be over. And Nate was right there with him.

He'd been in and out of their room between groomsmen activities, and Ellie had been gone all day. The memory of her beneath him, her skin flushed from arousal, had given him more than one uncomfortable moment throughout the day.

And there was something more than that, something that he could admit to himself but wasn't quite ready to say out loud. He'd missed her, entirely apart from the sex. He liked spending time with her, talking to her. It wasn't news to him —he'd always liked her. But the woman who was so intent on this just being a fling was making him feel things he'd never felt before.

He was busy contemplating ways to make an early exit and to convince Ellie to do the same when the man who'd been hitting on Ellie the night before slid into the vacant seat next to him. What was his name again?

"Nathan. Nice to see you again." The man—Harry, that was it—nodded, his fancy imported beer dangling from his fingertips. He gestured toward Chase with it, grimacing. "I'm thinking our groom isn't too impressed with the evening's activities."

"Hmm." Nate hummed dismissively. His mind was still on Ellie, mentally composing a dirty text. Some kind of order that would have her wet and on edge by the time they were both back in their room that evening.

"So, I wanted to ask you something." Harry shifted in his chair, looking right at Nate. Nate knew what he was going to ask before he actually did, and couldn't hide his irritation, working his jaw hard.

"Last evening I got the impression that you and Ellie were together. But Holly says that that's not true." Harry arched an eyebrow.

Nate tried to suppress a growl.

"And why does that interest you?" He heard the deathly calm come into his own voice, knew it was a dead giveaway of his feelings, but he couldn't bring himself to refrain, not when faced with competition.

Harry seemed to pick up on his tone as well, and flushed. "I just wanted to make sure the field was clear before asking her out."

With every other woman that Nate had been with, he really wouldn't have blinked an eye at the thought of her dating someone else. Dating and sex were separate entities, to his way of thinking.

But the mere thought of another man with his hands on Ellie, talking to her, leaning in close? It made that inner beast of his rage.

He knew that Ellie would kill him for admitting that anything had happened between them, but at that moment he didn't care. He needed to be the alpha, needed to let Harry know without a doubt that Ellie was his.

He opened his mouth to reply, but a voice from across the table cut through.

"Guys, I'm sorry, but I'm just not comfortable with this." Chase was leaning back in his chair, discomfort evident on his features. His flushed cheeks and glassy eyes said that he'd had a few more drinks than Nate had taken notice of, and the alcohol only seemed to be contributing to his misery. "I want Meredith."

Gavin groaned a protest, holding out a bill for Ruby, but Nate saw his moment.

"Well, let's go get her then." Deliberately turning away from Harry, he closed the space between himself and Chase and heaved his old buddy out of his chair. "Come on, bud. Let's get your lady."

Chase blinked up at him. "I suppose you've seen so many naked ladies that leaving one isn't a big deal for you, huh?" He gestured blearily toward Ruby, who shrugged, clearly not offended.

Nate frowned. There it was again, that mention of his playboy past. Was that really how people thought of him?

"I know where they were headed." Lucas chimed in, holding out his phone. Nate wondered how exactly he knew, since the women had been pretty secretive about the location, but he supposed it didn't really matter.

Squinting at the phone, he saw a picture of Harper, one of the bridesmaids, pouting saucily at the camera. Behind her was a neon sign that he recognized only too well—it had been hanging over the pool table in the only bar in town since he'd been sixteen and had to come haul his stepdad's drunken ass home.

He didn't hold a grudge over the venue, however. The bar wasn't anyplace special—his stepdad would have done his drinking anywhere, this venue had simply been the closest.

Chase peered at the phone too, then let out a tipsy cheer. "To McKay's Pub! I'm coming, Meredith!"

He pushed back from the table, looking elated at the thought of seeing his bride. And then, in a movement comical enough to make Nate forget all about his angst for Ellie for a moment, fell over on his ass.

It felt really, really good to laugh.

CHAPTER 14

The neon hurt his eyes as the group of guys pushed into the dimly lit bar. A squeal rose up from the group of women when they noted the new arrivals. The men had braced themselves for irritation that they were crashing the bachelorette party, but the women—with bottles of wine scattered over their table—seemed, for the most part, happy to see them.

Nate ignored the sudden increase in volume in the room, his eyes scanning the party for Ellie. Like a magnet, he found his stare drawn straight to her.

Her hair was drawn into a loose ponytail tonight, and he liked the way some strands had escaped to frame her face. She was dressed simply, in snug jeans and a red v-neck T-shirt, but she'd brightened up the ensemble with a coat of scarlet on her lips.

She was, without a doubt, the sexiest thing he had ever seen. Images flooded his mind, pictures of Ellie naked and kneeling in front of him, those cherry red lips wrapped around his cock, and he found himself shifting uncomfortably against the sudden tightness in his pants.

Making his way through the crowd, he leaned over the back of her chair. He let his lips brush her ear as he spoke.

"You'd better come up with an excuse to leave, because I have plans for that mouth of yours." He pulled back just enough to gauge her reaction.

A stone settled in his gut when, rather than flushing prettily or gasping, as he'd expected, she shifted uneasily in her chair.

"I've been debating texting you all night." She bit into her lower lip, momentarily distracting him. "I don't know how to tell you this."

Ice formed in his veins. Ignoring the guy behind him who'd been about to sink into the closest empty chair, Nate pulled it right next to Ellie, seating himself close enough for them to speak over the din.

"Look, if I crossed any lines last night, I'm sorry." The very idea was terrifying, not a sensation he was accustomed to. "But don't pull away. Tell me what bothered you and we'll work through it."

Ellie looked perplexed, then shook her head vigorously as comprehension dawned. "No, no. Jesus, Nate, it's not all about sex."

Relief flooded him, then suspicion. "Then what has you so worked up?"

Ellie's gaze was pulled from his face to something above and behind him. She smiled weakly, then looked back at him.

"Um." She gestured with fingers that had a death grip on the dregs of what looked to be a vodka cranberry. Nate craned his neck to see what she was looking at.

When he did, his blood turned to icicles in his veins. The woman standing behind him, wearing a black apron and holding a tray, was one he hadn't seen in a very long time—years, in fact. And yet, she was as familiar to him as his own face.

"Hi, Nathan." The brunette smiled nervously, her pale gray eyes darting nervously from Nate to Ellie and back. "Um, can I get you anything?"

Pale gray eyes—just like his.

Ellie had been trying to tell him that his mother was here.

———

Watching the reunion between Nate and his mother was like watching really bad reality television—awkward to the extreme. Hannah Archer looked far older than she had the last time Ellie had seen her, which was at least five years earlier, before she'd left town with her husband—the stepfather who had caused Nate so much pain.

Apparently she was back. And no one had thought to tell Nate.

Ellie watched as a myriad of emotions passed over Nate's face in silence. Shock, pain, rage... and then nothing. Just an icy cold veneer that froze his expression in impassive lines, so vacant that it sent a shiver down her spine.

The silence stretched out until Ellie wanted to do something, anything—break into song, strip naked, whatever—just to break it.

"Um. Eleanor, would you like another vodka cranberry?" Hannah awkwardly gestured to Ellie's near-empty glass.

Nate said nothing.

Ellie nodded, probably with more enthusiasm than was strictly necessary. "That would be great. Thanks." At least if Hannah went to get her another drink, it would give Nate a chance to recover.

With a lingering look at her son, Hannah nodded, then headed back to the bar. Nate sat frozen for a long moment before pushing away from the table.

"I need some air." He didn't look at Ellie as he moved, just shoved away from the group, his long stride eating up the distance to the front door.

Ellie watched him go, her heart in her throat.

She remembered every single time that Nate had come to the Marshall house with bruises and cuts, distress hanging over him like a dark cloud. His pain had in turn hurt her, but he'd hidden so deeply behind his veneer of badass that she hadn't been able to reach him to help.

Now she ached to run after him. To soothe his hurt.

But... they were involved now. Kind of. And in the early stages.

Would he appreciate her poking her nose into his business? Questioning him about something that was clearly tender?

She hesitated for a long moment, torn. Finally she let her gut lead her and hurried away from the table herself. They'd known each other for a very long time, and she'd be damned if she'd watch someone she cared about in pain while she sat back and did nothing.

She didn't have to look very far. Nate was seated on the edge of the sidewalk just outside the bar, his arms looped loosely over his knees. His expression was still blank, but he didn't tell her to go away when she seated herself on the pavement beside him, so she decided to take that as a win.

Going with her gut yet again, she sat with him in silence, leaning against him lightly so that their shoulders just brushed. She squeaked with surprise when he wrapped his arm around her and pulled her in closer, squeezing tightly like he could draw on her strength.

"Do you know if she's still with him?" Nate's voice was tight, as though it had been stretched over a thousand razor blades. Ellie's own heart bled at the raw emotion that she heard in it.

"I don't." She shook her head to emphasize the point. "I didn't even know that she'd moved back to town."

Nate digested this in silence before surprising Ellie yet again by pulling her into his lap, right then and there. She stiffened for a moment—anyone who walked by would have the news of their embrace all over town by morning.

But Nate needed her. And that was more important that worrying about what her family would think of whatever this was between them.

"You know what always hurt the most? It wasn't the beatings, wasn't the harsh words, wasn't the pain." Nate brushed a hand absently through the long tail of Ellie's hair, and she wasn't sure he even knew he was doing it.

"It was the fact that she wouldn't leave him. She wouldn't leave the man who hurt her child. And I had no control over that, no way to make her love me more." Ellie half-turned in his arms to find Nate smirking at her darkly. "I bet you're going to have a field day with that tidbit, huh?"

It took her a moment to understand he was referring to his taste for control in the bedroom. Her heart ached at the same time that her spine stiffened.

"I hope you're not telling me that you believe your taste for kinky sex has anything to do with you being screwed up by your parents." Her tone was sharp, and Nate looked up in surprise.

"Well, where else would it have come from?" He arched an eyebrow at her, darkly amused. "I couldn't control my mother. Now I want to control every woman I'm with. Makes sense to me."

Ellie shook her head, noting the way his eyes darkened when she disagreed with him. "Or maybe you just like what you like and want what you want and it has nothing to do with any underlying issues with your parents."

Nate snorted, looking down at a crack in the concrete. "Well, that would be tidy."

"Nate." Ellie turned the rest of the way, shifting so that she was kneeling between his spread knees. She looked up at him with wide eyes, noting the fine lines around his eyes that his angst had brought out. She'd never noticed them before—but then, maybe he'd never let her see them before.

"We're all shaped by our parents." She wet her lips, wishing for a glass of water. "But I really hope that you don't think you're... wrong... because of it."

Nate stared into her eyes for a long moment, and Ellie's heart contracted under the intensity of the gaze. In that moment she forgot that he was a player, forgot that there were people waiting for them inside the bar, forgot everything but her, Nate, and the air they were breathing.

"No matter where I got it from, control is something I need." Nate dipped his head and, without warning, bit into the curve of Ellie's neck. She gasped, the touch completely unexpected, then tugged away to look at Nate questioningly.

"I'm feeling very out of control right now." He spoke quietly, his eyes again fixed on hers. He didn't ask, didn't demand, didn't order, but Ellie understood without words what he needed.

"Let me help." She placed her hands on his knees, then slid them up his thighs. He hissed at the touch, his stare darkening.

"Be sure, Ellie." He deliberately looked down her body, then back up. "I'm not in the mood to be gentle."

The words made her shiver, but it was with anticipation, not fear. Nate would never hurt her, of that she was certain.

"I don't need you to be gentle." Using her grip on his thighs for leverage, she slowly stood, then extended a hand back to him.

"Let me help. Control me. I want you to."

CHAPTER 15

Control me. I want you to.

A shiver worked through Nate as Ellie's words hit home. He'd heard something similar from the lips of countless women before, but never with such raw honesty riding beneath.

Never with the same reasoning behind it. Ellie was offering herself to him—all of herself—to ease his pain. She cared enough to give herself to him.

That, more than anything, was what made his pulse stutter. And in that moment he needed her far too badly to do anything but accept.

He took her offered hand, and he knew that doing so meant he accepted everything she was giving.

Using their linked fingers as a tether, he tugged her tightly against his chest. She stumbled a bit on her low heels, and he savoured her small gasp when her soft breasts pressed into her chest.

Wanting to hear the noise again, he tangled his fingers in the golden length of her ponytail and tugged. Sucking in a mouthful of air, Ellie lifted her gaze. He still half expected to see fear or trepidation in her eyes, the things that he'd imagined for so long to be what she'd truly feel.

Instead he found heat, blue fire that ignited an answering flame in his very soul. Thinking that she'd never accept what he wanted, who he was, had still not been enough to quench his desire for her. The years they'd known each other before, they were kids. The years since, when he thought of her, he'd convinced himself she'd run screaming. But now, with the discovery that she harboured the same dark cravings he did?

It was enough to bring him to his knees.

"This is what's going to happen." He released her hair, sliding his hand down to cup the back of her neck. "You're going to go to the ladies' washroom. You're going to go into the largest stall and close the door behind you. Then you're going to pull these tight little jeans that are taunting me down around your ankles. Panties, too. You're going to face the wall and put your palms flat against it. And then you're going to wait for me. Understand?"

Ellie nodded, wide-eyed, then stiffened and changed to a shake of no. "I—I can't. I'm sorry."

"What do you mean, you can't?" There it was again, that knee-jerk reaction that had him wondering if he'd pushed her too far, but she was quick to continue.

"No! It's not that I don't want to." Her face flamed crimson, and she looked down at her feet. "It's, ahh…"

"Tell me."

"I'm not wearing any underwear," Ellie whispered loudly, her fingers clenching on the front of his shirt. "So I can do everything else, but I can't do that."

Just when Nate had reached a point in his life where he thought he couldn't be surprised anymore, this woman set him back on his heels. Her confession, voiced in that whisper that was both ashamed and defiant, was almost enough to make him break his rigid control.

For a long, wild moment he thought about just opening the front of his jeans and hauling her astride him right then and there, never mind who might see. He wanted—no, he needed—to sink into the completion that only Ellie was able to give him.

He clung to his last shred of common sense and stepped back, putting a slender but vital sliver of space between them.

"Go into the bathroom. Do as I said. And then wait." With a light touch to her shoulder, he pushed her away.

She didn't even hesitate, though he noted that the pulse beating against the paper-thin skin at the line of her jaw throbbed. And though her eyes were wide, there was a definite extra sway to her hips as she walked away.

She wanted this—wanted him. She was offering him the keys to heaven, and he'd be a damned fool not to take them.

He watched two minutes pass by on his Philippe Patek watch before he followed Ellie back through the front doors of the bar. Ignoring the crowd, he wound his way to the small hallway to the left of the bar, where the washrooms had been located the last time he'd been there.

He saw his mother standing behind the bar, a bottle of beer in one hand, and a ruby colored highball in the other. She opened her mouth as if to speak to him, but he let his gaze just slide right off of her as if he didn't see her or, worse, as if she meant nothing to him anymore. And she didn't— that moment outside in which he'd spilled his soul to Ellie had been brought about by the sheer surprise of seeing Hannah Archer when he hadn't expected to.

Now? He was focused on Ellie. He needed her. Craved her with every fiber of his being.

Pushing through the door of the ladies' washroom, he found a woman he didn't know applying lipstick in the mirror.

"Um, hi?" She cocked her head at him, meeting his gaze in

the mirror before recapping the lipstick. He smiled at her but made no move to retreat, just rocking back on his heels with his hands in his pockets.

"Okay then." With a strained smile, the woman shoved her makeup back in her purse and pushed past Nate to leave the small washroom. He distinctly heard the words *hot but weird* as she went, and he couldn't help a small snort of laughter.

Oh, if she only knew.

Only one stall door was closed. The idea that they could be walked in on and discovered would heighten Ellie's arousal, but he found that he didn't actually like the idea of sharing their intimacy with anyone.

That, too, was a first for him.

"It's me." He knocked on the closed stall door, short and sharp. He heard the metallic cling of the flimsy lock, then slid into the small sliver of space when the door opened, insinuating himself into the cubicle and locking it behind him.

Ellie was there, just as he'd told her to be. She'd worked her jeans down to her ankles, and was facing the wall. Her hands were splayed on the white tile, the tips bloodless, as though she was holding on for her life.

The sweet curves of her ass were bared to his view, and he growled deep with satisfaction.

But first...

Drawing back his hand, he swatted her across one of those pale cheeks. Her shocked cry echoed throughout the small room, and he smiled darkly to himself.

"That's for not wearing panties." Sliding his fingers into the heat between her legs, he slid one deep inside, savoring the way her wetness clenched around him. "The next time I discover that you're trying to tempt me like that, I'll haul you across the nearest flat surface. Keep that in mind."

"Y-y-yes." Ellie's thighs clenched around his hand, trying

to hold him in place, but he laughed and withdrew his touch anyway. She moaned with disappointment.

"You're going to have to be quieter than that, or you'll have the entire bar coming in to see what's going on." Nate slid his damp fingers up through the crevice that divided the two globes of her ass, and Ellie sucked in a shaky moan. "I don't care, myself, but I suspect that you'll be a little upset if the entire wedding party comes in to find me buried inside of you while you scream out my name."

"Jesus, Nate!" Ellie arched her back as he took his free hand and worked her T-shirt up and over her breasts. Another tug and her bra was riding low, offering her plump breasts up to his touch like plums on a platter. He tweaked each nipple, rolling until they tightened into hard peaks. "We can't—oh—oh God—we can't do this here. Anyone could come in!"

"Are you saying red?" He slid his hands down the soft planes of her stomach, then once again buried it between her legs. His thumb found her clit, and she cried out as he began to circle the small bud hard and fast.

"No. No, of course not—I—" She sagged back against him, her knees giving out as he worked her clit, reading the signs in her body that told him she was fast approaching climax. "I just—I can't—"

She was almost there, her chest heaving, her skin sheened with sweat. Just before she could fly over the edge, he pulled away, savoring her startled cry.

"What? Why?" Sweet Ellie actually banged her fists against the wall with frustration, and he did his best to cover up a laugh. "That's so mean. Why would you do that?"

The desperation in her voice woke something dark deep inside of him, and again he had to bury the need to simply push himself inside of her and take what he needed. He held on to his control, but only just.

"When you tell me no, you'll find that you don't like the consequences." Deliberately, he dipped his head and sank his teeth into the nape of her neck. He bit hard enough to turn her skin red, deeply satisfied to see his mark on her body.

He expected her to apologize, to stammer, to blush prettily. Instead she stiffened, then pushed back against him, rubbing that delectable ass over the rigid erection that pressed against the front of his pants.

"You're going to have to do more than that to control me." She continued to rub, rocking back into him with movements designed to drive him insane. "I'm stronger than that."

"What are you saying, Ellie?" Roughly he grabbed her ponytail, tugging so that she was forced to turn to the side. She pressed her cheek to the cool tiles of the wall, and she laughed breathlessly when he got right in her face, forcing her to look at him.

"I'm saying, make me." Her eyes sparked, and she pushed back against him, and he understood. She hadn't really been protesting him having her here—she'd been playing a game. She wanted him—wanted him to take her as far as they could go.

"When you're screaming loud enough that the whole bar hears you, just remember that you asked for it." With another nip to her shoulder, Nate reached for the fastenings of his jeans. He undid the zipper, the sound harsh and metallic in the otherwise silent room. Their combined breaths echoed as well, a prelude as he shoved his pants and boxers down his hips and tore open the condom that he carried in his wallet.

Quickly sheathing himself, he positioned himself at her entrance, feeling her slippery heat even through the layer of latex. Grabbing his cock at the base, he rubbed himself up and down that crevice that divided her ass again, noting that she rocked back into him when he reached the pucker that lay hidden between.

No doubt about it, Ellie Marshall was his kind of girl—dirty to the core.

Her heels raised her up a bit, but she was still so small compared to him. Grabbing her hips, he adjusted her position so that she was bent over more deeply, her naked pussy an offering to his need.

Bending his knees, he positioned himself at her entrance, then drove in hard and fast and without warning.

"Nate!" Ellie arched back to meet him, then hissed when he encountered resistance inside of her. As he'd discovered the night before, she was tight and he was large, and with her legs anchored together by her jeans the fit was even more snug.

But she was going to take him all. He needed it, and she needed it too.

"Hold on tight, baby." Ellie's fingers scrabbled against the tiles as he continued his advance. He felt her flesh pulsing around his rigid length, squeezing, rippling, and his eyes rolled back in his head at the delicious sensations.

It wasn't enough. It would never be enough.

Growling, he grabbed her hips again and hoisted her higher, bending her over further. The angle opened her wider, and he worked his way home, seating himself to the hilt inside that decadent heat.

His groan rent the air; hers followed. They stayed still for a moment, absorbing the sensations of filling and being filled. Before long, the dark, relentless need started to again claw at his insides, demanding that he ride this woman and make her his.

He pulled out nearly all the way, gasping for air as if he'd been submerged in the sea. One more deep breath, and then he was plunging back in, searching for something he'd never before realized that he needed.

Inside her, fully seated inside of her, his demons flew away.

So he stayed there again for a long moment, letting his mind empty and then fill up again with everything that was Ellie.

Beneath him, Ellie was giving as much as she got, not content to be passive in this encounter, though she'd been the one to tell him to take control. With the lightning quick rolls of her hips, the way she reached for him, the breathy little pants that escaped those naughty lips of hers, she urged him higher and higher, demanded that he take more.

He had no choice but to do as she commanded.

Placing one hand flat on her spine, he tangled the other in her hair again, her messy ponytail falling free, the wheat colored strands lying in silken ropes on the creamy expanse of her bare back. Using his grip as an anchor, he quickened his pace, still seating himself with every thrust, but his movements coming faster and faster and again and again, until there wasn't enough air left in the cubicle for either of them to breathe.

Remembering her earlier reaction to the touch, he slid the hand on her back down through the cleft of her behind. Her groan was barely audible, an animal sound, and it spurred him on as he found her tight pucker and stroked his index finger over the ring of muscle.

He hadn't expected her to protest, and she didn't, instead pushing against him, as eager for more sensation as he was. Using her own slickness to aid him, he worked the tip of his finger inside, and the way her body shook as he worked the digit in and out of her entrance set him on fire.

"That's it, Blondie. Take me." He continued to slam his cock inside of her tight channel, faster and faster, savouring the sounds their flesh made as they joined. And at the same time he worked at her tight rosette, his other hand tugging lightly at her hair as he guided them both toward release.

"Nate." Ellie released the wall, reaching behind herself to grab at his hips and pull him closer. "I need—I need to—"

"I know, baby. Just hang on." He intended to release her hair, to again work at her clit until she came for him with those pretty cries, but he never got a chance. Her pussy tightened around him, clenching and releasing as she pressed her cheek to the wall and bit her lip to hold back a scream.

He ground out a curse when her rippling flesh tore his own last shreds of control from his grasp. The grip of her pussy on his erection, the heat of being inside of her had the pleasure gathering in his toes, his scalp, the base of his spine before shooting through his cock in an explosion that made his vision go white.

He lost track of time and place. Still inside of her, Nate wrapped his arms around Ellie and held her tightly to him, her back to his chest. The heat and sweat from their lovemaking sealed them together, and as he rested his cheek on the top of her head he thought that he'd never felt anything more right.

It was Ellie who finally turned, squiggling in his arms until she faced him. Those perceptive eyes of hers searched his face before she pressed a quick kiss to his lips, then began to straighten her clothing.

"I'll head back out first, okay?" Damn it, but when she looked at him like that, she could see right inside of him. And if she could in that moment, he'd be getting his heart stomped on, because she'd see how much she'd come to mean to him, and how much he didn't want her to dismiss him as what she thought he was—a playboy.

He nodded, not sure what else to say. And as she went, the noise increasing momentarily as she opened the door, he knew that he would do whatever it took to change her opinion of him... and to keep her for good.

CHAPTER 16

Without Nate inside of her, Ellie felt empty as she rejoined the now combined bachelor and bachelorette party.

Snagging a seat at the busy table, she signalled a waitress —not Hannah—for another drink, and watched as Kate let loose on the tiny stage with a karaoke rendition of Black Velvet.

"Thanks." Gulping at her drink when it arrived, she welcomed the buzz of the alcohol. After what had just happened between her Nate, she was more than empty—she felt as though she'd been hollowed out and put back together again.

Sitting there alone, without him, felt... wrong. The sex had been mind-blowing, but it wasn't enough. She wanted him here, beside her, his arm around her, showing the world that she belonged to him. And that was exactly why sleeping with him had been a stupid idea to begin with. She took another massive gulp of vodka cranberry, the alcohol at the bottom of the drink stinging her throat as she swallowed.

She wasn't stupid—what had just happened between them

was... big. There was a connection there that extended beyond sex. It had been there since they'd first met so many years ago.

But she also knew that in all probability, it wasn't enough to keep him around. They had great sex, absolutely. And they liked each other—they were friends.

But was Nathan Archer, the filthy rich bachelor, the darling of the tabloids, the arm candy of half the supermodels alive, going to give up everything to be with an optometrist from Seattle?

Not in her wildest dreams.

"Need a fresh drink?" A fuchsia colored beverage decorated with a lime wedge appeared in front of her nose. She followed the sight up until she found Harry grinning down at her, clearly pleased to be there.

Her heart sank, even as she forced a welcoming smile to her lips. "Harry. Hey. Thanks." She'd had quite enough, but it was a sweet gesture.

A sweet gesture that was going to get him absolutely nowhere. He was a nice guy. He was handsome. From the surprising thumbs up that a drunken Holly was shooting her from down the table, clearly her family approved.

But that connection just wasn't there. She was too tightly anchored to somebody else.

"So listen, I know this weekend is crazy with wedding activities." Harry grinned, not seeming to notice that she was just playing with her beverage instead of drinking it. "But Holly said you live in Seattle. I'm just outside, in Tacoma."

Oh, no. Here it came. Being nice was bred in Ellie's bones, so she smiled at him as he spoke, but everything inside of her shouted to flee.

"Once we're both back home, I'd love to take you for dinner." Harry offered a winning smile, revealing a row of even white teeth. He probably even flossed daily. Damn it. Why couldn't she drum up even a speck of interest in him?

"Do you mind if Holly gives me your number?" Harry reminded her of a puppy, begging for a scrap with hopeful eyes. "Or, um, you could give it to me yourself?"

Ellie opened her mouth to reply. In the past, she would have been sucked into a date she didn't want to go on just because she hated to say no and hurt someone's feelings. But this time something else entirely spilled from her lips.

"Look Harry, you seem like a great guy. And at any other time in my life, I probably would have jumped at this offer." The way his face immediately fell made her feel like she was crushing a bug beneath the heel of her pump, but she continued on anyway. "I'm just... well, I'm already involved with someone. It's not serious but, ah, my attention is kind of elsewhere. And that's not fair to you." And that was the truth. She couldn't agree to a date with Harry at all while her feelings were otherwise engaged. Even if she knew that it was foolish to entertain any hope in the direction of Nathan Archer.

"I see." Harry looked down at his hands, then surprised her by swigging from her drink. She couldn't help but laugh when he downed the contents of the glass in one swallow, then grinned up at her cheekily.

"Thank you for being honest with me." He winced a bit at the alcohol burn. "And I like you enough to say that if your timing changes, I hope you'll give me a call."

She nodded, though she couldn't imagine doing any such thing. Her thoughts and feelings were too full of Nate.

"I have to ask, though... is it that guy from yesterday? Nathan Archer?" Harry frowned a bit, scanning the room as if looking for the man in question. Ellie's gaze followed, but she didn't see those familiar, piercing eyes anywhere. "And I'm not saying this to further my case, but because you seem like a nice girl. I don't know if you read magazines or follow headlines at all, but he's always out with a different model or actress on his arm. He seems like he's a bit of a player."

Ellie couldn't hold back her wince, feeling as though Harry had punched her in the belly. This obviously wasn't news to her, but still, it hurt to hear the words coming out of someone else's mouth—as though someone else confirming what she already knew made it more real.

And admitting her feelings would make it more real still. Swallowing thickly, she forced a smile onto her face and shook her head slightly at Harry's inquisitive expression.

"No, no, not him." Her mouth was completely dry, and she suddenly wished for the drink that Harry had just consumed.

"He seemed awfully protective of you at the rehearsal dinner," Harry pressed, and Ellie felt an answering twinge of annoyance.

He might think he was just being nice, looking out for her, but her feelings for Nate were nobody else's business. And she didn't even want to admit them to herself, let alone to a virtual stranger.

"He's an old family friend." Ellie forced this out, then quickly pushed away from the table and stood. "Anyway, it was very nice to see you again, Harry, but tomorrow's the big day. And someone is going to have to wake up and drag the bride out of bed."

Ellie gestured to the stage, where Kate had made room for Meredith. A very tipsy bride—accompanied by her equally drunken groom—was wearing a cheap white tulle veil attached to a plastic tiara, and was singing an off-key rendition of Sonny and Cher.

Harry and Ellie both winced as the duo cackled into the microphone while staring dreamily into each other's eyes.

A tug in her belly had her turning her head in the direction of the bar. Nate was standing by it, his arms crossed over her chest, ice dripping from the glare he was shooting the woman he was speaking to—his mother. The hatred that radiated from his tense frame made it hard to believe that this was the man who had only minutes before caused the soreness that made the space between her thighs ache.

His gaze flicked to her, then returned to his mother. The lack of recognition she felt in that quick glance made her stomach roll with confusion.

He'd accepted the comfort that she'd offered him before. Now, though? He could have been looking at a stranger.

Ellie needed air.

Mumbling a quick goodbye to Harry, she pushed through the bar and out the front door, avoiding looking at the small patch of concrete where less than an hour earlier, Nate had set her nerves on fire. The sky overhead was velvety dark, clouds obscuring the stars, and if she held still she could hear the waves of the lake lapping at the shore.

This was where she was from, and no matter how much her family drove her crazy, this place was a part of her—in her blood.

Nate, though? Nate had run hard from here, and fast, and never looked back. She'd certainly never blamed him for that, but it only served to highlight the differences between them.

Blinking against the sudden flood of emotion, Ellie rolled her shoulders back to stretch them out, then started out in the direction of the motel. Cabs this late at night were unheard of in Ruby Lake, so she walked. And she hoped that by the time she returned to the room she shared with the man whose scent was still on her skin, she'd have her head on straight and her emotions in check.

Nate watched helplessly as Ellie walked out the front door of the bar. His entire being longed to go with her, to borrow from her strength, but first he had to deal with his mother.

"I'm not sure how to phrase this so that you stop asking. But no, I am not interested in having breakfast, lunch, dinner, coffee, or anything else with you."

As he looked at the woman who'd given him life, hatred and despair filled him, a potent cocktail, and he knew that he'd do anything to keep Ellie from being tainted by this part of his life.

"It's been a long time, Nathan." Hannah's eyes, so much like his, shimmered with unshed tears.

He couldn't find it in himself to care. He'd been hurt too much, and not just physically by Hannah Archer.

"It's time we caught up and made this right between us."

Was she kidding? Things between them would never be right. They couldn't possibly be.

He shook his head, not replying, but she pressed on.

"Look, son, I know you've made something of yourself. I want to hear about it. I want to know what's happened to you since you left." Hannah reached out and placed a gentle touch on his shoulder; he shrugged her away as understanding dawned.

Made something of himself. What an idiot he was. She wanted money.

He'd thought it wasn't possible to feel more hatred for this woman who hadn't protected him when he'd been young and vulnerable, but it seemed he'd been wrong. He could.

"Every fiber of my being wants to tell you to fuck off. You don't deserve a red cent of the money that I've broken my back to earn. But you know what, I'll give it to you. What will it take to get you to leave me alone forever? A hundred thousand? Two? Hell, you know what? I'll give you a quarter of a million in return for a promise that you'll go to hell and leave me alone."

"Nathan." Hannah reached out for him again, and again he shrugged away from her touch.

"You don't have the right to touch me." Man, he'd thought he was over all of this—thought he'd long since buried this hatred and grief. The fact that it still clung to him like oil to skin made him want to vomit. "You gave up that right every time you let him do just that."

She flinched, her eyes dropping in shame.

Turning, he swiped a hand over a suddenly sweaty brow. He wanted a drink. No, he wanted an entire bottle. More than that, he wanted Ellie here with him, holding him tightly, telling him that everything was going to be okay.

How could he hope for anything with her when *this* was the example he'd had of happily-ever-after? He started to take a step when the damn woman had her hand on his shoulder again. This time she spoke before he could push away.

"I left him, you know. Last year." There was a hint of steel in Hannah's voice, something he'd never heard before. "I wanted you to know, that's all."

Nathan paused for a moment, letting that sink in. Rational thought told him that he should be happy that his mother was finally free of the man who'd ruled over them both with an iron fist.

Instead, the taste of betrayal was bitter on his tongue.

"You've left him." There was no emotion in his voice. There couldn't have been, because he didn't *feel* anything. The simple words had emptied him out, leaving nothing but a shell behind. "Last year."

Hannah moved in front of him, nodding earnestly, her eyes shining with hope. "I thought that maybe this would mean that we could... maybe we could rebuild our relationship a bit. I've wanted to contact you so many times over the last year, I just haven't known how—"

"Don't," Nate almost yelled, all of his feelings rushing back inside of him in an overwhelming tsunami that almost brought him to his knees. "Just don't."

"Don't?" Hannah's slender brows arched in confusion. "Don't what?"

"Don't contact me." Nate infused his voice with ice. There were so many things whirling around inside of him, freezing them and shoving them back down seemed like the only thing he could do. "Don't contact me. Don't do anything. Just don't."

Hannah parted her lips as if to reply, but Nathan walked away before she could speak, his body as stiff as if he'd received one of the beatings that his stepfather had so loved to give out.

She'd left Tom last year. Well, that was fucking great. Nate was a man now, and strong enough to stand on his own. But when he'd needed her? When he'd been young and he'd needed his mother to *be his mother*, to step in front of him and keep him safe from the fists, the words, the never-ending anger?

She hadn't been able to do it then. She hadn't had the strength to be his mom.

Stepping out into the still air of Ruby Lake, he filled his lungs and let the rage disperse in the night. His past had helped to shape who he was, and at this point in his life he wouldn't change it.

But if Hannah Archer thought she could come trotting back in to play the role of mommy, she'd have to keep on walking. Because the one thing she'd taught him that had helped to be the success he was today?

He didn't forgive. And he certainly didn't forget.

CHAPTER 17

A whisper of Nate's cologne hung in the air of their shared room. The scent only served to enhance the soreness between Ellie's legs, the tender spots on her hips from where his fingers had dug into her flesh.

She did her best to ignore those little reminders as she stepped out of her heels, then stripped off her tight jeans and T-shirt. Tossing them aside, she made her way to the shower, shutting the door firmly behind her and locking it, even though Nate had seen everything there was to see not even an hour before.

She needed a minute alone to process everything that had happened in the last couple of days.

Hissing as the scalding spray hit her skin, Ellie tipped her head back to wet her hair. Inhaling the rapidly thickening steam, she tried to let go of the jumble of emotions rioting around inside of her.

Tomorrow was her brother's wedding, after all. She should be preparing to celebrate with him, not feeling torn apart by the very notion of attending.

She couldn't get the look in Nate's eyes out of her head. When he'd been standing talking to his mother, the blankness that she'd seen there had—well, it had terrified her. Logically, she figured that he was compartmentalizing. He'd been away from Ruby Beach for so long, and hadn't expected to see Hannah, so it only made sense that he was trying to keep his feelings about that away from everything else in his life.

But that only served as a reminder for her, an indication that when it came to whatever this was between them, there were things that he was probably not going to share with her. Ever.

And when it came to Nate, Ellie was selfish enough to want it all.

She washed and conditioned her hair, rinsing out the scents of beer and stale air that always seemed to accompany a trip to a bar. Stepping out of the shower, she wrapped herself in a towel that felt like cardboard, scrubbing it over her skin as if to wash away the feel of Nate's hands.

It didn't help—she could feel the imprint of every one of his fingertips, claiming her. Her throat thickened as tears that she didn't want started to rise.

She was falling for him. Hell, she'd fallen for him years ago. But right now she had no one to blame but herself for the fact that, come Monday, her heart would be an open wound.

"Shit." Ellie reached for her robe, only to discover that she hadn't brought it into the tiny bathroom with her. She eyed the puddle of clothing that she'd stripped off, but it was lying in a pool of water and besides, she was loathe to put dirty clothes against her clean skin.

She wrapped the towel tightly around her breasts. The party had still been raging when she'd left—chances were good that Nate was still there.

Of course, this meant that as she exited the bathroom on

a cloud of steam, clinging to the towel, she found Nate sitting on the edge of the bed. Her fingers clenched on the stiff terrycloth as he lifted his head to look at her, a part of her expecting the same blankness that she'd seen as he spoke with his mother.

Instead, the gray of his eyes showed a million different shades of feeling. Grief, rage, and heartache, all things she would have thought that the bad boy of Ruby Lake was impervious to—they were all there, calling out to her in the same way the damaged teenage boy had once done.

Now, like then, something about the way he looked at her told her that he needed her. And despite her reservations about protecting her heart, she couldn't help but give him what he seemed too proud to ask of anyone else.

"Nate." Cautiously Ellie closed the space between them, perching herself on the edge of the bed next to him. She opened her mouth, then closed it again, not sure what to say.

"I don't want to talk about it. Not right now." Nate stood, then started stripping off his shirt. Ellie couldn't stop the acceleration of her pulse as the solid planes of his chest, the ink, the glint of that ring in his nipple came into view.

Slowly, she released her grip on the towel. She was confused, she was overwhelmed, but one thought overcame it all. Her heart was already his. And if he needed her to ease his pain, he could have her, body and soul.

The damp towel fell to the floor, leaving her naked to his stare. His hands made quick work of his jeans, sliding them and his boxers down the muscled length of his legs, leaving his own nudity open to Ellie's avid stare.

She sucked in a deep breath, wondering what he was going to do, what he had in mind. Did he want her hard and fast again, did he need her to surrender? Or would he need something even more?

Her pulse stuttered when, rather than reaching for her

with the rough touch that she'd come to crave, he cupped her face in his palms and dipped his head to kiss her. The glide of his lips over hers was light, almost sweet, yet Ellie could still taste Nate's possession on her tongue.

She expected his hands to move to the usual places, to stroke and ignite the flames. She was wet already, something she seemed unable to help when it came to him. But rather than cupping her breasts, tugging her nipples, sliding his fingers inside of her, he pulled the covers of the bed back and eased her back on the pillows before lying down beside her.

"I just need to be with you." He wrapped an arm around her waist, pulled her back to his front, speaking into the tender skin at the nape of her neck. Ellie felt her heart trip, then take that final stumble as the warmth of his breath misted over her skin.

"Is that okay?"

She swallowed thickly, willing herself to relax into his embrace. But every nerve was a live wire, loaded with sensation and ready to snap. This wasn't just sex. It never had been. And now it was oh so much more. She was in love with Nathan Archer. Maybe she always had been.

But even as she offered Nate what he needed, the warmth of her embrace and her quiet understanding, she knew that it changed nothing. On Monday, he would still be gone.

———

Nate had slept better with Ellie in his arms that he had in recent memory. It was a strange sensation, waking up feeling relaxed and refreshed rather than irritable and in strong need of coffee.

With Ellie sprawled across the bed fast asleep, Nate pulled on some fresh jeans and headed to the nearby diner that they'd hit up two nights earlier. He didn't feel the clawing need for caffeine that he usually did, but he still got a cup of steaming brew and sipped at it, black, pretty sure that he'd need the fortification for the day ahead.

Ellie was sitting up in bed when he returned, paper cups in each hand and a brown bag tucked under his arm. He noted that she'd pulled on one of his T-shirts, and the sight of her in his clothing did funny things to his heart.

"Morning." He could tell just by looking at her that she was feeling guarded, and though it made his heart sink, he couldn't blame her.

He'd opened himself up to her last night. He hadn't known what else to do—he'd needed her. But he also knew that, to a woman as smart as Ellie, a woman who didn't care about things like his money or the parties he was invited to, he wasn't exactly a catch.

And didn't that just figure. He'd finally found a woman he wanted to keep, and he'd scared her off before they even got started.

Ellie's stare darted around the room before settling back on Nate, as though she felt trapped. He watched as her lips curved into a forced flirty smile.

"Snuggles *and* coffee?" She reached for the steaming cup that he held out toward her, her smile not quite reaching her eyes. "I must have been very good in a former life."

He knew what that flirtatious smile meant—she was deflecting, trying to take them back in time two days to when this had just been about sex.

Too bad that he was a million miles beyond that already. And he knew, he just *knew* that she was right there with him, she just didn't want to be. Whether it was his screwed up family or his reputation, he didn't know.

What he did know was that he had to prove to her that

he was so much more than what she thought—that they could be good together. And it wasn't enough to tell her—he had to show her.

He'd already started with sex. Next he'd show her they were compatible outside of the bedroom, too. Though looking at the way her rosy nipples pressed against the stretchy white fabric of his T-shirt, he realized that that particular resolution just might kill him.

"I thought we could both use the caffeine today." Seating himself cross-legged on the bed across from her, Nate opened the brown bag he carried and offered her a foil-wrapped breakfast sandwich.

"True enough." She took a long sip of her coffee, making a greedy noise deep in her throat that made him shift, hoping she didn't notice the fact that his cock was already swelling, just from being around her.

"God, this is good. How did you know that I like it with cream and sugar?"

"That's how you used to take it." He watched, riveted, as she ran her tongue over her rosy lips. "I took a gamble that your taste hadn't changed."

He grinned, glad he still knew her well.

He'd found something—someone—worth risking everything for. And risking everything was exactly what he planned to do.

"Some things never change," he said as he unwrapped his own breakfast sandwich, biting into the egg and bacon concoction, even though it tasted like sawdust with his mind otherwise occupied. "And other things change completely."

Ellie's spine stiffened as she set her breakfast down on the empty brown wrapper. "Nate—"

In his pocket his cell phone vibrated before starting to ring, a sharp, staccato blast he'd chosen to grab his attention no matter how deeply he was focused on work. He hesitated before answering, wondering if he should ignore it, then decided it would be good to let Ellie have a moment to think about what he'd just said.

"Archer." Nate turned away from Ellie, looping his legs over the side of the bed, but he kept an eye on her as he did. Her lips were pursed, and she was clearly thinking.

Good. Let her think about things that had changed. Let her think about *him*.

"Nate." On the other end of the line, Chase sounded more than a little worse for wear. "Wasn't sure you'd be up."

"I'm not the one who drank a dozen bottles of beer last night." Nate couldn't help but grin a bit at the groom's expense—what were friends for, after all?

"Shit!" A screech from behind him had him whirling, his heart in his throat. He found Ellie with coffee all down her front, hissing at the heat.

"Hold on!" he barked into the phone before tossing it onto the bed. With efficient movements he stripped the stained shirt off of Ellie, then probed at the abused skin with gentle fingers.

It was pink, but that would fade shortly—the coffee hadn't caused a serious burn. Still, he had half a mind to drag her into a cold shower, just in case.

Ellie's hands waving in the direction of the phone he'd forgotten about deterred him from that. "Is that Chase? Pick it up or he'll think that something is wrong!"

Rolling his eyes, he gestured toward the bathroom, indicating that she should rinse herself off. Instead she picked up her sandwich and settled herself back on the bed as he again picked up his phone.

"Sorry about that." Nate watched as Ellie finished her sandwich, then eyed his. He couldn't hold back the grin when she stole a piece of bacon out of it, smirking at him. "Did you need something, Chase? I'm just about to hop in the shower here."

"Why are you with Ellie right now?" Chase might have been hung over, but the edge of brotherly protection was plain and clear in his voice—a deadly blade. "Especially if you're about to hop in the shower?"

CHAPTER 18

Shit. Chase had heard Ellie's scream. And Nate had shot himself in the foot with the shower comment—he couldn't claim that he'd just run into Ellie somewhere in town.

More than that, he didn't *want* to. He wanted to tell Chase the truth—that he was in love with his little sister, and that he'd do anything to make her happy.

But a certain blonde spitfire would skin him alive if he did. And since he was trying to give her happy thoughts in his direction, it didn't make much sense to piss her off.

"We both got stuck staying at the motel, remember?" He actually couldn't remember if he'd told Chase that or not, but it didn't matter—what mattered was that he didn't know they were staying in the same *room*. "Ellie got pretty drunk last night. I thought she might need some coffee before today's events, so I brought one over."

"What? No, I didn't!" Ellie hissed at him as she crumpled her now-empty cup and threw it at him. "What are you talking—oh."

She clued into the fact that Nate was covering, but still

shot him an exasperated look, muttering as she stood and made her way to her duffel bag. Nate found himself more than a little distracted by the fact that she was naked and seemed to have forgotten than all important fact.

"Right." Chase didn't sound convinced, but he didn't press the matter either, and Nate exhaled on a sigh of relief. "Anyway. I just got a call from some trombone player, wanting to confirm details for today? He gave your name."

"Trombone player. Right," Nate repeated, though his attention was firmly on Ellie and the way that her breasts swayed as she bent over her bag. "What's the issue?"

"Dude, *what* trombone player?" Chase sounded aggrieved. "We don't have a trombone player."

"Huh?" Nate forced himself to pay attention to his friend. It was Chase's special day, after all. "Oh, right. Well, shit. I suppose the cat's out of the bag then."

"Explain." Chase's voice was full of suspicion, and Nate frowned. What did he think, that Nate had hired a herd of strippers to prance down the aisle behind Meredith?

"I heard Meredith say once that Love Actually is her favorite movie." Nate waited; Chase waited. With a sigh of exasperation, he continued. "Okay, at least let this be a surprise for her, okay?"

"Not getting any younger, Nate," Chase muttered to someone in the background, and Nate distinctly heard the word *aspirin*. It put him in a slightly more forgiving frame of mind.

"Well, if it's Meredith's favorite movie, I'm assuming she's made you sit through it a time or two."

Ellie took that moment to lift up her bag and upend its contents, and Nate had to stifle a groan as the flesh of her ass jiggled with the movement. Needing to focus, he turned away from her completely, facing the door.

"Remember that scene where Keira Knightley and the one dude get married?" he asked.

"Sort of."

"Work with me, Chase." Nate ran a hand through his hair. He felt the spikes of it sticking up in the wrong direction and snorted. A far cry from his usual groomed look, but he hadn't even thought to look in a mirror this morning. "The wedding. Keira Knightley. They're in the church, and their recessional music starts playing. Then one by one, different musicians stand up in the crowd and start playing along. By the end of the song, there's almost a freaking orchestra, a choir, and a gospel singer playing the couple out of the church."

There was silence on the other end of the line, and for the first time in a long time, Nate squirmed with uncertainty.

"I, ah. I thought it would be a nice wedding gift." He swallowed, wincing to himself. Maybe it wasn't—maybe it was just lame. "Aaah… surprise." The silence stretched out, and Nate started to feel like the world's biggest dumbass. "Look, if you hate it, I'll cancel it. No big deal." Man, but what a nightmare that would be. All of the musicians were coming in from Seattle.

Well, he'd get his assistant to do it. It would be her punishment for booking him into this motel in the first place.

"No. No, man. It's great." Chase's voice on the other end of the line sounded suspiciously thick, and it set Nate back on his heels. "Trust you to out-romance me at my own wedding."

"Uh." Nate wasn't sure what to say to that, so he settled for grunting. "Only if you're sure."

"Yeah, I'm sure. Meredith is going to love it." For the first time in the conversation, Nate could hear the smile in his friend's voice. "I have to say, I'm surprised it's coming from you. But thank you, man. Thank you so much."

Nate muttered a goodbye, then just stood for a moment as he contemplated Chase's final words.

I'm surprised it's coming from you.

Well, what the fuck was that supposed to mean? Did the entire world think of him as one big, self-centered asshole, a playboy who thought of nothing and nobody but himself?

Remembering that Ellie was in the room, he turned, his stomach clenching. She watched him with a curious gaze, and he felt the muscle around his heart tighten just looking at her.

If everyone thought the same thing about him, then he probably deserved it. But that shit was changing... today.

———

The phone call from Chase niggled at Ellie the entire drive to the Lodge.

She hadn't questioned Nate about it after he'd hung up the phone, she'd just continued getting ready, throwing on jeans and a sweater and piling her hair into a messy bun on the top of her head—she'd get hair and makeup done with the other bridesmaids later that afternoon. But she hadn't been able to stop herself from puzzling over it.

She knew that there was more to Nate than his reputation. A good chunk of her fear for her heart stemmed from the fact that *he* didn't seem to know it. But setting up a big, probably expensive, romantic send-off for his childhood best friend and that friend's new bride?

That wasn't exactly the action of a man who was clinging to his bachelor status. It didn't reflect the thoughts of a man who was still determined to eschew marriage at all costs. And she was way over-thinking all of this, probably because of the vulnerability that Nate had shown her last night. Which didn't mean anything beyond the fact that he'd needed someone and she'd been handy.

With a deep sigh, she thought longingly of the coffee that she'd spilled all over herself. She could really have used that caffeine pumping through her veins right about now.

"Hey." Chase was waiting in the lobby when Ellie finally pushed through the front doors. He captured the garment bag with her bridesmaid dress just before it fell to the floor—Ellie was also balancing a large shopping bag and her makeup kit.

"Thanks." She paused to readjust her load before reaching again for the dress, this time planning to throw it over her shoulder.

Chase held it back before she could take it. Having seen her brother after more than a few nights in which he'd had a bit too much to drink, Ellie could tell that he was feeling more than a little under the weather this morning, and when she took in the stern lines on his face she felt her stomach do a slow roll.

The men didn't have anything planned right now, in comparison to the spa treatments that the ladies were getting. Chase could still be sleeping—and from the looks of it, he needed it. So why was he here, lying in wait for her, *brotherly lecture incoming* flashing all over his face?

"Do you have time for some coffee?" Chase gestured to the small main dining room where the tinkle of cutlery and water glasses told Ellie that breakfast was currently being served to the majority of the Lodge's guests.

"Uh…" There was clearly something weighing on her brother's mind. Normally she would put off her plans to make time for him, but right now she was torn. As Meredith's bridesmaid, she had a responsibility to attend to the bride today.

And more than that, something told her that she didn't want to have the conversation that Chase wanted to. At all.

"I actually have to dump this stuff off in the bridal suite, and then meet the rest of the girls at the spa." Ellie smiled weakly as Chase narrowed his eyes at her. Damn it, did he know? How had he found out? "We're getting mani-pedis before hair and makeup. There was talk of waxing."

Chase winced, as she'd known he would. She took the chance to smile apologetically before turning back to the stairs.

"Hang on." Her brother's arm closed around her elbow.

Making a face, she turned back to him, this time not bothering to hide her annoyance. "You know that Meredith hates it when people are late," she reminded him, tugging her elbow free. "I've got three minutes to get my butt to that spa."

"I just wanted to know if you're still bringing a date tonight." Chase pinned her with that intense pale blue stare that had always made her squirm as a kid. "You replied yes on the card. Miles, wasn't it? But I haven't seen him anywhere. Is he driving in today?"

"Miles. Right." Two days earlier, the mention of her ex would have made depression and anger swirl through her in a storm of despair. Right this moment, though? She could barely remember what he looked like. "No, actually. Miles and I broke up right before I left Seattle. I'll be flying solo tonight. Sorry, I forgot to tell you that for your meal counts."

She held her brother's gaze, lifting her chin a bit in challenge, even though guilt swamped her, making it hard to breathe.

She'd spent the last two nights pressed skin-to-skin with her brother's best friend. When she thought of it like that, it seemed so... wrong.

And once again she found herself wanting to spill.

But what was there to tell? That she was indulging in a weekend of kinky sex with a man that her parents had never really approved of, and that tomorrow she'd return to her practice in Seattle alone?

The reminder left a bitter taste in her mouth. Her expression must have shown it, because concern etched itself in fine lines over Chase's face.

"Just... don't ever settle, okay, El?" Chase reached for his ring finger, searching for the band that wasn't there yet. "Don't ever settle for someone who doesn't give you everything you deserve."

Ellie stared at her brother for a long moment, her heart pounding. He knew. He had to know.

But how could she tell him that the one man capable of giving her everything she needed was also the one man who would break her heart tomorrow?

"Someone's sentimental today." To lighten the mood, she shifted her bags, then reached out to give Chase a small peck on the cheek. "Don't you worry about me, bro. I'm Ellie, remember? Everything's under control."

With that, she turned and headed up the stairs that would take her to the bridal suite and the spa. Her words echoed in the cavernous hall behind her, and to her ears the tone was mocking.

For the first time in her life, she'd handed the reins of her control over to someone else—to Nate. So why, when that made her so happy, did she feel so completely empty inside?

CHAPTER 19

"I don't care where you sit. Just... space yourselves out." Nate paced in the front lobby of the Lodge, his cell glued to his ear. Harper, one of the other bridesmaids, cast him a curious glance as she slipped by, already dressed in her bridesmaid gown, but Nate turned away, trying to focus on the call with... was this the violinist? One of the musicians he'd hired for today. He'd been fielding calls from them all day, and he felt a definite headache brewing at the base of his skull.

Normally he wouldn't have had a problem slipping into corporate mode and organizing everything, down to the most minute detail. Today, though? All he could focus on was Ellie.

To her way of thinking, this thing between them was over as soon as they went back to Seattle—which was tomorrow morning. He couldn't let the best thing in his life walk away. Since he suspected she'd have a few choice protests to being kidnapped, that meant that he had some work to do today.

As he hung up the phone, he noted that traffic in the lobby was picking up, caterers and wait staff and people in fancy dress crisscrossing the golden hardwood floors. He craned his neck, looking for Gavin and Lucas. They were supposed to be pouring whiskey down Chase's throat right now and delivering bracing *your life isn't over* speeches, but he'd had to duck out to deal with a herd of neurotic musicians.

A laugh as bright as sunshine cut through the din, and Nate stilled. He'd know Ellie's laughter anywhere. Drawn like a magnet to its other half, he followed the sound into the large hall where the ceremony was going to take place.

Ellie stood at the front of the room, doing something with a large swath of purple ribbons. Her hair was drawn up and away from her face in a neat style that made him want to pull out pins and mess it up. She was wearing far more makeup than usual, smoky shadows that made her eyes look even bluer, and something painted on her skin that made it smooth like ivory. She had her contacts in again, and as always, he missed the thick plastic frames that usually sat on the bridge of her nose.

The amethyst colored silk clung to her ample curves as she moved, and Nate stood, transfixed. She didn't look quite like his Ellie, all glammed up like this, but she still looked lovely.

"If you're good with doing the ribbons, I'll go get the rest of the bouquets." A man's voice cut through Nate's trance. His hands clenched into fists as Harry stepped into his line of sight, sleeves rolled up to his elbows as he hauled a large cardboard box.

"Sounds good." Ellie smiled up at the other man, and they exchanged words that Nate couldn't make out, though he could hear the rise and fall of voices. When Harry threw back his head and laughed, then touched Ellie flirtatiously on the shoulder, jealousy was an electric green flood that threatened to pull him under.

Before he could think it through, he'd entered the hall,

loosening his tie. He must have made some sound, because both Harry and Ellie looked up at his approach.

"Right." Harry looked from Ellie to Nate, then back to Ellie again, disapproval written in his slight frown. "I guess I'll be going, then. If you're sure you're all right, Ellie?"

"I'll be fine." It should have felt good, the fact that all of Ellie's attention had snapped straight to him the second he'd entered the room, but even at this distance he could detect a hint of wariness in her eyes.

She still wasn't fully on board with this—with them. It crushed him even as it sent steel resolve into his spine.

He hadn't become rich and successful by backing down when the going got rough. No, he always got what he wanted, and this time what he wanted was more important than anything else in the world.

"You look beautiful." He closed the space between them, barely noticing when Harry banged through a side exit. Ellie shuddered, a deep breath that drew his attention to the exposed flesh of her breasts. He wanted to reach out and touch, but reminded himself of his mission for the day.

He had to prove to her that she meant something to him besides sex. Which, looking at her in that dress, just might be the death of him.

"Nuh-uh." Ellie cast him that flirtatious grin, the one he'd realized she brought out when she wanted to distance herself from him, to bring things back to a simply sexual state. "No touching before the ceremony. I just paid a fortune to get my hair and makeup done. You're not getting it all messed up."

"Wasn't planning on it." Nate savoured the uncertainty that crept into her eyes at his words.

"What?" Ellie's spine straightened, her fingers twisting nervously in the skirt of the dress. "I—don't I—I mean, don't you like the dress?"

"I've told you before, Ellie. I don't care about the dress. I care about getting you out of it." He moved a little bit closer, close enough that she could hear the words that he'd pitched low. She sucked in a breath when he dipped his head to whisper into her ear. "What I don't like is the way other men are going to look at you tonight."

Ellie trembled, turning her head to look over his shoulder. "That's not fair. You can't say things like that to me unless..."

Her voice trailed off, and Nate wanted to shout with frustration. Why couldn't she just say it? Damn it, why couldn't *he?*

"You're the one who wanted this to be what it is," he reminded her, shifting so that their bodies just barely brushed. He ground his teeth together when his suddenly solid cock brushed against the soft warmth of her belly. "But you also know that I'll be stripping you out of this dress tonight. You know that I'm going to have you stretched across the bed, my mouth between your legs. And until that happens, I get to be protective of what's mine."

"*Nate.*"

Against him, Ellie stiffened, but the heat radiating from her skin told him that she was loving every minute of his dirty talk.

"How the hell am I supposed to go walk down the aisle now?" she asked on soft whisper.

"Not my problem, Blondie." He grinned down at her, smirking at the sparks of temper flickering over her face. "Just know that with every step you take, I'll be picturing you naked, on your knees and screaming my name."

"You're an asshole." He'd pushed her, that was easy to see, but she was also aroused as hell. Her skin was flushed the pink of a seashell, and her chest trembled as she inhaled.

Well, in for a penny.

"You've got a dirty mouth for such a sweet looking girl." He smiled again, slow, deliberate. Even a bit cruel. A sadistic streak inside of him enjoyed the fact that his expression sent her a step back. "Later tonight, I'll find a better use for that mouth than swearing at me. But right now I think you need a lesson. You need to remember who you belong to."

"Who I *belong* to?" The words came out on an indignant squeak. "Oh, I don't think so—"

"You're the one who assured me that this is what you want." He felt his heart thump as he spoke. In that moment, with their eyes locked solely on each other, he craved nothing more than to bend her over the nearest chair, to take her hard and fast so that when she walked down that aisle she *felt* him with every step.

But this wasn't all about sex. He needed to throw her off of her game. Even if that meant throwing him off of his own, in the process.

"Lift your skirt." Ellie gaped at him, and he merely arched a brow. "Unless you have other plans for tonight, lift your skirt. I want to see what's mine."

Her mouth opened and closed like a fish out of water. He expected her to protest, even to storm out. If she had, it might have made things easier for them both.

Instead, she inhaled deeply, tangling her fingers in the skirt of her dress. Under his stare, he could almost see the submission soften her flesh, making her melt into his command.

He watched, transfixed, as she slowly inched the silk up, up the creamy expanse of her thighs. Finally the skirt was at her waist, revealing her centre, the place he wanted to *live* in.

A small triangle of lavender lace teased more than it covered. Thin ribbons ran from the cloth, over the creases that divided her legs from her stomach, to her hips where they were tied in neat little bows. A pretty present, just waiting for him to unwrap.

The thong was so skimpy that he became very painfully

aware of the fact that sometime between this morning and now she'd been waxed. The smooth pink skin beckoned, made his fingers itch to touch.

"Mine." He had so much he wanted to say, *needed* to say, but the words kept getting stuck inside. His gaze raked her face, praying that he would see some of the same intensity that he felt reflected there. "You're mine."

A shadow fell over her delicate features, and she let her skirt drop, hiding her centre once again. Her breath rasped in and out, or maybe that was his—standing this close to her, so wrapped up in her, he wanted to grab her and kiss her and never let her go.

He knew her well enough to read her expression, though, and the panic he saw there was a giant fist squeezing his heart. But she didn't run, she didn't cry, she simply looked him in the eye and inclined her chin—a princess acknowledging her power for the first time.

CHAPTER 20

A final glance in the mirror before the ceremony told Ellie that her mask was in place—she looked completely composed, calm and ready to celebrate the happiest moment of her brother's life.

Inside, though? That was a completely different story. Inside, a hollow ache had settled in the place where her heart usually resided.

Neither of them had said the words, but she wasn't an idiot. This thing between her and Nate, she wasn't the only one who didn't want it to end. And while part of her wanted to go running straight into his arms, the rest of her—the sane, rational part—kept reminding her that was a very bad idea.

No matter his feelings for her *now*, Nate lived the lifestyle of the rich and the famous. They might have a connection. But would those feelings last once they were away from the intimacy of this weekend? Once they'd left the nostalgia of their pasts behind and entered the real world? His world?

She'd deliberately avoided him before the ceremony,

knowing he'd try to pin her down and get inside her head, and she just... she needed some time to think.

Ellie tried to push Nate from her mind as she watched her brother and Meredith exchange vows in front of family and friends. Her brother, who had once been completely against everything that marriage stood for, had happiness radiating from every cell of his body.

Ellie was so delighted for them that it hurt. At least, that was what she told herself the pain was. It certainly couldn't have been because she wanted the same thing—and wanted it with the one man who would never be able to give it to her.

As Chase and Meredith were pronounced husband and wife, and Chase dipped the redhead low for a kiss, Ellie dared to sneak a peek at Nate. To her dismay, he wasn't looking at her, but rather scanning the crowd, and her heart quickly thudded to the floor.

The loud honk of an instrument jolted her from her mood. Startled, she looked out over the crowd to find a young man in a tuxedo standing, a... was that a trombone? Yes, a trombone to his mouth. Ellie had forgotten all about Nate's gift for the bride and groom. She hadn't really processed what he'd been explaining to Chase earlier.

Eyes wide, Ellie glanced at Meredith. The event planner was no bridezilla, but she was a bit of a control freak, and this was definitely *not* what the schedule had pencilled in for recessional music.

A woman with long curly red hair and a saxophone joined the trombone player. Then another woman with a flute. Ellie couldn't hold back her gasp when the electric guitar kicked in and she realized that they were playing a Beatles song—recreating a scene from the movie Love Actually, which was one of Meredith's favorites. A full band, a vocalist, a choir, recreated the movie scene in every detail.

All this, just for his best friend and bride. Ellie knew that the money wouldn't even factor into the notion, but the whole idea—it was so awesomely *Nate*. The man he rarely let anyone see.

Tearing her stare away from Meredith, who was gasping delightedly in the middle of the aisle, Ellie dared take a look at Nate. This time he *was* looking right back at her, and the expression on his face made her heart swell.

He mouthed something to her, and she squinted to make it out—she'd never been able to see as well with her contacts as with her glasses. When she finally understood, she felt that strange flip in her belly again.

"Tell me what you want."

His stare held hers until the moment they had to walk back down the aisle, Harper with Nate, Ellie with Gavin and Kate with Lucas. But as she pasted a smile on her face for photos, she knew, with complete clarity, *what* she wanted, or rather who.

She wanted more than just this weekend with Nate. The question was, was she brave enough to reach out with both hands? And, if she did, would she get what she wanted?

Or would she end the weekend picking up the pieces of her broken heart?

———

Nate knew that he hadn't misunderstood the longing that crossed Ellie's face just before the bridal party was shepherded back down the aisle. He also knew just what the nerves that quickly followed meant.

They'd had a magical couple of days, but even though she trusted him with her body, she was still leery of him with her heart. The fact that she was nowhere to be found by the time he and Harper finished their walk had him clenching his jaw in frustration.

Damn it. His past, how he'd been raised, and the dating life he'd chosen up until now, was not the sum total of who he was. Why couldn't she see that?

"Not that I'm in the habit of insulting a pretty face, but you might want to try smiling." Kate, the bridesmaid with the blue streak in her hair, took a place against the wall beside him, straightening the strap of her dress, which was the same amethyst as Ellie's. "You're going to scare the guests."

"Aren't you a sweet talker." He eyed the woman beside him warily. She hadn't made a move on him all weekend, but since he'd acquired his fortune, well, he'd learned that women could be sneaky.

"Relax, cowboy. I'm not after whatever it is you've got in those pants of yours." Her fingers tucked a stray strand of blue behind her ear. "Though I'm sure that it's mighty fine. At least, Ellie thinks so, doesn't she?"

Nate grunted, automatically looking around for Chase. Truth be told, he would have been happy to shout his feelings for Ellie to the world. She, however, would have been less than pleased to have her brother informed of the down and dirty sex that she'd been having with Nate. Especially on his wedding day.

"Don't worry, your secret's safe with me." Kate grinned, then reached for Nate's hand. She slapped a key card into it. "But you might be interested in knowing that your little blonde is currently upstairs decorating the honeymoon suite. The bride and groom won't be up there for hours."

"Why are you doing this?" Nate eyed the card suspiciously. In his world, people didn't do favors for nothing.

"Well, she seemed like she was in an awful hurry to get away from you. And I like to stir the pot." Kate smirked, shrugging a shoulder covered with dancing swirls of bright ink. "I also really don't want to decorate the honeymoon suite." Nate couldn't help it; he barked out a laugh. For just once, he decided to take a gift at face value.

"Thank you." But Kate was already gone, winding through the crowd on her way to... Gavin. And the ex-soldier was watching her approach with a curious mixture of terror and delight on his face.

Well, that would be interesting. Almost interesting enough to make Nate want to stick around and watch the fireworks.

But then he thought of Ellie, her shoulders bared in that pretty silk dress, her eyes shadowed with something smoky, making them look even more passionate than usual as he brought her to climax.

His no-sex promise to himself was clearly giving her way too much time to think. Overthink, in fact. So for his next plan of attack?

He couldn't make her say all she wanted was him. But he wouldn't go down without a good fight. And even if it was all for nothing, he'd make damn sure that when Ellie looked back on this weekend, she'd never forget Nate Archer.

———

Red rose petals were scattered over the soft duvet. Long-stemmed roses in the same shade were artfully arranged in a modern blown glass vase on one of the artisan wooden bedside tables. A bottle of sparkling wine was chilling in a silver bucket of ice, and beside it on the small dining table, also on ice, was a platter of chocolate-covered strawberries.

Ellie had just put the finishing touches on a gift basket that she and the other bridesmaids had put together, all little things that the happy couple might want or need on their wedding night or the morning after—coconut water, aspirin, even a small bottle of massage oil, though she didn't much care to think of Chase using *that*.

The honeymoon suite was all set for a big night of romance. And looking around, Ellie could do nothing but feel her heart ache.

She didn't want to get married right this second or anything. Hell, before this weekend, she hadn't been certain that she wanted to get married at all. But it just went to show that when the right person was involved, all previous notions went right out the window.

Ellie had first felt that spark between her and Nate when they were little more than children, and now...

While this weekend had started with him helping her prove a point, that she was a desirable woman, she'd broken the rules. Hell, had she ever had a chance? A man who would arrange such a sweet romantic gesture for his friends—it melted the steely reserves that she'd so desperately tried to shore up.

She'd be lying to herself if she said that she wanted anything other than Nate to tell her that he wanted her forever. But even if he did, no matter how hot the flame between them burned, she knew, she just *knew*, that out in the real world, away from their home town, it would be extinguished with one small gust of a supermodel.

It wasn't low self-esteem saying that, nor was it pessimism. It was just a fact. His dates were featured in the tabloids. He was one of America's most eligible bachelors.

And she? She was an optometrist from his childhood. Pretty on good days, but still lacking that sparkle he couldn't resist. The math wasn't hard.

So all that was left was to decide how to handle their final encounter—and she knew there would be one. She'd never make it hard for him to walk away. But that didn't mean she wouldn't gorge herself on every last drop of him before he left.

She wasn't even surprised to hear the electronic beep that signalled someone using their key card to enter the room. She'd seen the determination in Nate's eyes before she slipped upstairs. He hadn't gotten where he was in life by giving up.

And ninety per cent of her was thrilled to have that kind of drive focused on her. The other ten percent, though? It was absolutely, completely terrified.

"You're hiding from me." Nate slipped into the room and closed the door behind him with his heel, then latched the security chain. She expected him to stalk toward her, to run his hands over her body, to do the things that already felt familiar.

Instead he stood just inside the room, hands stuffed in the pockets of his suit jacket. And unless she was very much mistaken, he was pissed.

"I'm not hiding." His irritation teased out her own, and she turned away from him, pretending to fuss with the contents of the gift basket. "Someone had to decorate the room for the newlyweds. I was elected."

"Don't lie to me." Nate's voice was sharp, sharper than she'd ever heard it before, and she whipped her gaze to where he stood, his lean frame set in tense lines. "Whatever else happens here, Ellie, we'll be honest with each other."

"I—" Why did this suddenly feel like the end? And why did it feel like her fault? Panic rushed through her, turning her fingers to ice and clogging her throat.

"Ellie." Cursing beneath his breath, Nate closed the space between them. Ellie reached for him, wrapping her arms around his shoulders. He pulled her in close against his chest, and she drew in a deep breath, savoring his scent.

His next words stopped her cold.

"Don't you see, Ellie?" He spoke into her hair, still arranged so carefully in the neat blonde coils from the salon. "The ball is in your court. I need you to tell me what you want. I can't give it to you unless you do."

Ellie felt her pulse stutter. Nate brought out a side of her that she hadn't known existed, and with him she could push herself... but he was asking her for the one thing she couldn't do.

"Nate." She knew what she wanted to tell him—that she wanted more than just this weekend. But she couldn't be one of those women who threw herself at him. How could he want her in return if she did? They all threw themselves at him.

And though he waited, watching her with his face set in impassive lines, she wanted to be more to him than just another woman. She wanted to be different. And if he wanted more than a weekend, he was going to have to say so.

"Kiss me." Okay, maybe she *wasn't* so different from all of those other women, because as he tightened his arms around her, desperation reared up, slamming against her ribcage, demanding to be heard.

Still, the words that mattered stuck in her throat.

No, she couldn't tell him, but maybe she could show him —could show him even just the merest sliver of what she felt.

"Ellie." Nate's voice was raw as he allowed her to drag his face down to meet hers. And when his lips crashed into hers, she could taste the same desperation fuelling her, and to her mortification, a single scalding tear slipped down her cheek as emotion wracked her body.

"Just tell me. Please." Nate spoke the words with his lips still pressed to her own, one hand reaching up to tug at the smooth coils of her hair.

The words remained lodged in her throat. She pressed her lips to his again. She needed the fire. He gave it to her, but banked the bright flame with tenderness, leaving her trembling and unsure even as she gave him everything she had.

The sound of a key card fumbling at the lock had Nate freezing where he stood, his arms full of Ellie. He blinked, everything fuzzy, all of his senses saturated with Ellie, as he tried to blink his way out of the haze she had him in.

"Nate!" Ellie's wide blue eyes were full of panic as she shoved him away. Her hands worked frantically through the mess he'd made of her sleek hairstyle, then traced over the lipstick that no longer glossed her mouth. "Someone's coming!"

And that—that was all it took to snap him out of his trance. Taking one stride forward, closing the space between them again, he tangled his hand in her hair, tilting her head up until she was forced to look him in the eye.

"Let them see." Ellie tried to tug away; he held firm. He watched as something that looked to him like hope fluttered across her face, mirroring what he felt in his heart.

He wanted so badly to tell her what he felt, what he wanted. There were a million reasons why he needed her to make that move, to prove that she really wanted him—issues with his mother, all of the women who had only wanted his money, needing to know for certain that, with her submissive nature, she hadn't been pushed into agreeing with what he wanted, just to please him.

All of that fell by the wayside when confronted with the thought of losing her. He'd shove aside his pride, his dominance, everything that made him a man, if only it meant that he could keep her in his life.

"Let them see, Ellie." The electronic beep of the card in the actual lock sounded; they only had seconds.

The door opened, and there was a curse as it caught on the security chain that Nate had slid into place when he entered the room. "Open the damn door, you two. I know you're in there."

It was Chase.

He knew.

Ellie's eyes were wide with terror.

"We're not doing anything wrong. Let him see that we're together."

"You've taken this too far, Nate!" she whispered fiercely as she pulled again at his grip on her hair.

He let her go, his heart shattering loudly enough that he was sure he could hear the shards of it crashing to the floor.

"This will never work. You know that. And I'm not telling Chase something that will hurt him and ruin his wedding day for no reason."

I'm not telling Chase something that will hurt him and ruin his wedding day for no reason.

Even after all of their shared history, even after everything that had happened between them this weekend, she still thought he wouldn't stay. The realization was like a blow straight to his gut.

Wordless, he stared down at her, trying to read the expression in those summer sky eyes.

The fact that she looked away told him everything he needed to know.

"Open the fucking door." Chase pounded on it with his fist. "Meredith saw you both head up here. We need to talk. Now."

CHAPTER 21

Turning resolutely away from Ellie, Nate undid the security chain. Chase shoved forward into the room, and Nate simply stepped out of the way, impassively watching his best friend face off with the love of his life , as though it was happening to someone else.

"Ellie." Chase looked his baby sister up and down, then groaned. Nate watched as Ellie's hands fisted at her sides, catching in the silky fabric of her dress.

She said nothing, but as Chase looked from Ellie over to Nate, there was no denying the mess of his sister's hair, the swollen lips, the tension that filled the room.

Chase glared at Nate. Nate stared back impassively until his friend pointed a finger at him sharply.

"I'm not surprised by this, coming from you. You've always wanted her, though I thought that maybe, just maybe you could hold yourself back, given that she is my little sister."

Chase looked ready to punch him, and Nate...Well, before Chase had rushed through that door, Nate would have been ready to fight back, just to prove that his feelings for Ellie were real. Now, though... now that he truly understood how she thought of him?

There was no point. He'd stand here and let Chase beat the shit out of him, because without Ellie, what did it matter, after all?

"And you, Ellie." Chase turned back to his sister, disappointment etched in the lines of his face. "I thought you were smarter than this."

"What the hell is that supposed to mean?" Ellie's spine straightened, and Nate felt a quick flicker of hope. Had she changed her mind? Was she going to own up to what they had between them?

"I mean that Nate is my friend," Chase started, casting a sidelong glance at Nate. The judgment he saw there...

It transported Nate right back to his teen years, back to the days when most of the town looked at him and saw nothing but trash.

"He's my friend," Chase repeated slowly, stuffing his hands in the pockets of his suit trousers. "But you know what he's like, El. You *know*. No matter what rainbows and unicorns you've dreamt up in your head about the two of you... they're not going to happen. Nate's a player. Hell, he'll tell you that himself. And you deserve more."

Chase gestured to Nate, as if asking him to support his point.

And in that moment Nate wondered if the biggest fool of all here was him.

He'd thought that when it came down to it, at least his friends would have his back. But maybe, even to them, he'd always been just low class Nathan Archer.

The silence was deafening as Nate swallowed thickly and looked at Ellie. She met his eyes, and her lips parted. He felt hope rise—here, finally, was someone who would defend him. Someone who saw him as he was.

But she said nothing, nothing more than a choked little cry that escaped her lips. And then Nate had to face the truth. Ellie cared for him. He knew that. What they had between them was real.

But she saw him the way the rest of the world did—as a playboy who would break her heart.

And as he shook his head and slammed out of the silent room, he knew that he had no one to blame but himself.

———

"What the hell were you thinking?"

Ellie blinked as Chase took her by the shoulder and gave her a little shake. She wanted to swat him away like a fly, every cell of her body screaming at her to run after Nate.

She'd made the right decision, hadn't she? She and Nate would never work. They couldn't. Even her own brother didn't believe in them.

But the pain that had flashed through Nate's eyes before he'd slammed through the door told a different story. Had she just thrown away the best thing that had ever happened to her because she was scared? Scared of being out of control? Of being just another woman who passed through his life, when he, of all people, had always made her feel special?

Wasn't that her answer right there?

"Ellie!" This time Chase did shake her a bit, and she rounded on him. He blinked at the ferocity of her expression, holding up his free hand in surrender.

"Whoa. Settle down." He took a cautious step back, clearly not having forgotten the warning signs of his sister about to fly into a rage. "I'm just looking out for you."

"You know, I'm getting damn sick of living my life according to how other people think I should." Ellie shoved away from her brother, stooping to pick up the hair pins that

Nate had scattered on the floor. Turning so that she didn't have to look at Chase, she jammed them back into her hair at random, not caring about the end result.

"What do you mean?" This time, when she looked at her brother, she found him rocking back on his heels, studying her, but with the traces of judgment gone.

He just looked puzzled, and Ellie wanted to smack him upside his thick skull.

"I mean that everyone in this family, in this *town*, has always expected me to act a certain way. To be the smart one, the well-behaved one. The one who never makes a fuss." Ellie jabbed the last pin into her hair, wincing as it scraped along the tender skin of her scalp. With nothing else for her hands to do, she clasped her skirt in damp palms again. "Did it ever occur to you that maybe that's not who I really am?"

"And you think that Nate sees you the way you really are?" Chase asked incredulously. "I suppose you see the real him? That you're the only one who understands him? El, if you knew half of what he was into—"

"Maybe he and I aren't quite as different as you think." Ellie spoke quietly, waiting a moment for the words to soak in. When Chase flinched, she knew she'd hit her bullseye. "And I'm going to tell you right now, what is or isn't between myself and Nate is none of your damn business. It's not Mom's business, it's not anyone in this town's business. Mom never understood about Nate, but I thought you did. He was your best friend and you let him down too." She shook her head sadly. "Nathan Archer is so much more than any of you have ever given him credit for."

Tossing the key card at her brother, Ellie slammed out of the room that she'd so neatly decorated, and as soon as she passed through the doors, urgency overtook her. It might have taken her dumbass of a brother to make her see the truth, but the words she'd just spoken?

They were absolutely on point. Nate was the best man she knew, and he'd been so, so right. Who cared who knew about them? Sure, she'd be embarrassed if in the end, he ditched her like he had so many other women. But would he? If she truly believed he was more than what others thought of him—didn't she owe it to him, to herself, to give *them* a chance?

Her phone chimed, signalling an incoming text. Her heart leapt into her throat—maybe it was Nate.

It was Meredith.

TEXT:

To: Ellie

From: Meredith

I didn't mean to sic Chase on you. Don't be too mad at him.

Ellie narrowed her eyes. She'd be as mad as she wanted. But the second message thawed the ice, just a bit.

If you're interested, I think Nate is getting ready to leave. I don't think you'll be surprised to hear this, since it's my wedding day, but love is worth fighting for. Go get him. I'll cover for you.

Urgency spurring her onward, Ellie quickened her pace, and then again until she was running.

Forgoing the elevator, she sprinted down the stairs.

She had to catch up to him, had to apologize for doubting him. She had to make this right.

Downstairs, she skidded to a stop just inside the doors of the hall where the reception was being held. Heart in her throat, she looked around frantically, her gaze seeking out every dark haired man that she could find.

"Are you all right, Ellie?" She looked up at the voice, finding Harry at her side, concern etched on his face. She saw him take in her wild hair, her messy makeup, and winced. "You seem... distressed."

It was hard to come right out and ask, since asking seemed to be confirmation of her relationship with Nate, but hell. Wasn't that why she was looking for him? "Have you seen Nate anywhere in the last few minutes? Nathan Archer?"

Harry's mouth pinched together in a thin, judgmental line that made him look far less attractive than he had earlier. Yes, he seemed like a nice enough guy, but she was damn sick of being judged.

"Spare me the lecture, please." She smiled politely, but didn't bother to sugar coat her words. "I know you don't approve. But if you could just tell me if he's passed through here, that would be great."

Harry sipped at his wine, seeming to mull over his choice of words. When he finally spoke, what he said had Ellie's heart crashing to the floor.

"I'm sorry to upset you." He set his glass on the table and reached for Ellie's shoulder in a gesture that was likely meant to be comforting, but instead made Ellie's skin crawl. "He did pass through here. But then he left. And, ah... how do I put this delicately? He wasn't alone."

"What?" That didn't make sense. At all. It hadn't been more than fifteen minutes since they'd been together in the honeymoon suite, and Ellie knew, she *knew* that those feelings he'd shown her there had been real. "Who was he with?"

"I'm sorry, Ellie." To his credit, Harry squirmed. "It was one of the other bridesmaids."

Ellie nearly doubled over as the impact of those words hit her. She had seen Nate chatting with Kate, the bridesmaid with the blue hair, earlier, but hadn't thought much about it. But...

She, Ellie, had just stomped all over the feelings that Nate had offered her. Was it really so strange to think that he'd jump right back into his old ways? That he'd soothe the ache with another woman? And Kate was nowhere to be found, just like Nate. But ... her heart just couldn't bring herself to believe it.

"Excuse me for a second." Holding up a finger, Ellie pulled out her cell phone. With trembling fingers, she pulled up Nate's contact information.

It went straight to voicemail. Slowly, she set her phone back on the table, blinking helplessly up at Harry.

He patted her awkwardly on the shoulder. As one might a puppy. "I take it that things in that department are over?" He gestured to Ellie's cell phone. "With Nate?"

She let a strangled noise escape her throat, not trusting any other words to come out.

"Right." Harry picked up her phone, Ellie staring after him dumbly as his fingers slid over the screen. After a few seconds, he handed it back to her. "Well, like I said. Now that things have changed, I'd love to take you out sometime. I just added my number to your contacts."

What?

CHAPTER 22

"You just added your number to my contacts? While I'm sitting here with an obviously broken heart?" Slamming her phone down onto the table, Ellie stood, letting fury guide her actions.

Shock emanated from Harry as she rose to her full height, bristling under his gaze.

Was this really how people saw her? A woman so sweet that she'd put up with something like this—a man making a pass at her while she was feeling low and vulnerable?

Never. Again.

"You need to go, Harry. And don't ever contact me again."

"I think you're overreacting just a bit. You're upset." Again, he patted her shoulder, and Ellie almost screamed. "When you calm down, you'll see I'm just interested in you. Genuinely. And I'll treat you right."

Unlike some other men, were the words left unspoken.

And with that, Ellie had had it. She reached for the half full glass of wine that Harry had set on the table, and with one quick flick of her wrist, emptied the contents into his face.

He sputtered, and she gasped as he stared down at her in sheer disbelief.

She was pretty shocked herself, even as grim satisfaction swept through her for having finally, for once, stood up for herself. Even if she had overreacted. Sort of.

Then she heard applause. Turning, she found her cousin Holly standing beside the table, delight written across her face as she observed the scene in front of her.

"Why, you—" Harry grabbed a cloth napkin and started scrubbing at his shirt.

Ellie could have told him that he'd be just fine, since it was only white wine, but truly? In that moment she didn't care.

"Oh, Harry. Get over yourself," Holly said. Then, to Ellie's shock, Holly handed Ellie her nearly full martini glass, as she made shooing motions at her ex-boyfriend. "She told you she was hurting and asked you to leave, and you were a prick. Just go."

Harry made another series of unintelligible noises before doing just that, spinning on his heel and stomping away.

Ellie watched him go with her mouth hanging open, not quite able to believe what she'd done.

"I have to say, it's nice to see you standing up for yourself for a change." Holly shook her head when Ellie tried to hand back her drink, gesturing for Ellie to drink it herself. Not sure what else to do, Ellie did, slipping into one of the chairs at the empty table.

She opened her mouth to speak, then closed it again, eyeing her cousin as she did.

Holly smirked as she slid into a seat across the table from Ellie, straightening the top of the dress that her ample bosom was threatening to spill out of.

Finally, Holly's words penetrated the shock of her own behaviour. "What do you mean, it's nice to see me standing up for myself?" Ellie narrowed her eyes at Holly suspiciously. A lifetime of barbs from the woman had taught her to be wary.

"Oh, relax. I'm not trying to be a bitch. Well, not any more than usual." Holly waved a hand at Ellie. "I mean it. You've always let people push you around. Me included. It's nice to see you get some backbone."

"Are you drunk?" Ellie narrowed her eyes.

Holly laughed.

"Just a tiny bit tipsy. Just enough to say something I should have said a long time ago."

Ellie was caught by surprise when Holly reached across the table for her hand. It was... well, it was freaking weird.

"I know I've always given you a hard time. You made it so easy, always being the good girl. I knew you'd never fight back and I'm just enough of a bitch to enjoy watching you squirm." Holly made a face, and Ellie felt the irritation of a lifetime ripple over her skin. "But you've always had it all figured out. You knew what you wanted out of life, and you went and got it."

What? Holly was envious of her?

"Trust me, I am so far from having it all figured out." Ellie snorted indelicately, looking down at the last inch of liquid in her glass. Shrugging, she decided to be in for a penny, and drained it.

Holly barked out a harsh laugh. "You do too. You have a *career*."

"I thought you said I was a purveyor of nerdware."

"You live in the city."

"Moving away isn't exactly hard."

"You have someone in your life who cares for you. Actually cares for you." With this, Holly pierced Ellie with a stare. "Why haven't you told anyone that you and Nate are together? Apart from Harry, of course."

Ellie looked at Holly, and as Harry's face, dripping with wine, played across her memory, she felt her lips twitch. Holly's expression mirrored her own, and within seconds they were both giggling, picturing Harry's expression as the nice girl he'd expected to spend the weekend with upended her drink in his face.

Once the laughter had died down, Ellie saw that Holly was still waiting for an answer to her question. And she wasn't entirely sure that she had one.

"I..." It was a combination of things, and therefore not an easy one to answer. God, had it really been just a couple of days ago that she'd thought she wanted just a fling with Nate? That she'd been so sure she could protect her heart?

"Look." Holly reached across the table again, catching her cousin's fingers in hers and squeezing. Ellie stared down at their entwined hands, still puzzled by this newfound side of her relative. Had the queen bitch of Ruby Lake really changed? Probably not. That would be too much to ask. But she obviously had a side to her she'd never let Ellie see.

Just as Nate had a side he'd only let Ellie view.

Regret for her hasty behaviour wrapped around her and she sighed.

Releasing her, Holly gestured to the waiter for another drink. Ellie arched an eyebrow, noting the alcohol flush already spreading over the other woman's skin. Holly was just tipsy enough for this conversation to happen, but she wasn't so drunk that this wasn't real.

"Do you love him?" Holly asked.

Ellie reeled, startled. She hadn't been expecting that question. She hadn't even let herself entertain the notion.

She had feelings for Nate, sure. She'd had them for a long time. And he'd awakened a sexual force inside of her that she hadn't even known existed.

But love? Falling in love with him was just stupid.

Wasn't it?

Or was she so far gone, she didn't even have to think to answer the question? If she didn't love him, she wouldn't have pushed him away earlier.

"You know, some of us spend every waking moment searching for someone to love." Sitting up straight as the waiter brought her fresh drink, Holly downed it in one swallow, then picked up her small clutch purse, clearly finished with the conversation. "If you've found it and you walk away from it for some stupid reason, then you deserve all the hell that I gave you over the years."

And then she was gone, the strange conversation a mere echo, as though it might never even have happened.

Ellie sat still for a moment, turning it over in her mind.

Love. Could she admit that she loved Nate?

She was on her feet before she could even finish the thought. Hell yes, she loved Nate... she'd loved him for as long as she could remember.

And she'd do whatever it took to prove it to him.

––––––––

"Thanks for the ride." Nate shifted uncomfortably on the velvety seat of Kate's ancient Toyota Corolla. The upholstery was scratchy enough to irritate his skin right through the fabric of his suit pants.

And that made him feel and sound like a complete wuss. But he was man enough to admit it—he'd grown accustomed to the perks that wealth afforded him.

"No prob." Kate adjusted her rear view mirror, pulling out a lipstick and retouching the shimmering purple color on her lips at the same time as she signalled her turn into the parking lot of the motel.

Nate winced at her split concentration driving.

"You sure you're good from here?" she asked, shifting to park so he could exit the car.

"Yeah." After the scene with Chase and Ellie, Nate had needed to get the hell out of there... out of the room, out of the lodge, out of the entire damn wedding. He was certain his former best friend no longer wanted him there, anyway.

Kate had offered to give him a ride.

"Actually, no. I'm not good."

She looked at him quizzically; hell, he wondered himself if he was crazy. But suddenly the thought of going into that damn motel room, where the scent of Ellie's strawberry shampoo would be hanging heavily in the air, was the last thing he wanted to do.

"Can you take me to McKay's?" Before this weekend, Nate had never operated on instinct. He was the first to admit that he liked to plan, that he liked control.

Then he'd walked into that motel room, and back into Ellie's life. The little blonde had pried loose his iron-clad restraint, leaving him open to impulses that he normally would have ignored.

Like the impulse that was riding him right now—the one that nagged at him to go confront his mother.

"Sure thing, cowboy." Tossing her lipstick into the unused ashtray, Kate swerved back onto the road and continued until the neon lights of McKay's were visible in the blueberry twilight. She skidded to a stop in front of the main doors, and Nate dug his fingers into the seat at the recklessness of her driving.

"Thanks for the lift." Eager to get out of the cramped car, he undid his seatbelt and slid out. Kate smirked before peeling backward in a cloud of dust and gravel and reeled out of the small lot, which was mostly empty.

Mostly empty... but Nate recognized one vehicle there, the ancient Impala that his mom had driven, even back when he'd been a teenager. He was shocked that it was still running, then shrugged the concern away. Not his problem.

Straightening his spine, he made his way through the front doors of the bar, reminding himself that he was in control here. He wanted some answers, but he could leave at any time. He was here by choice.

None of this stopped him from feeling just the slightest bit like a little boy again when he stepped into the bar and immediately locked eyes with his mother.

Hannah Archer's mouth formed a small "o" of surprise at the sight of her son.

CHAPTER 23

He nodded once in reply, affirming that he was there to see her, before seating himself at a table in a back corner. It had a perfect view of the door of the ladies washroom, and remembering what he and Ellie had done in there made a shard of glass twist in his gut.

He pushed that thought away. She'd made her choice. And more than just man to woman, as dominant to submissive lover, he had to honor it.

As his mother crossed the bar toward him, he tried to shake away thoughts of Ellie and the friends he'd left behind at the wedding. But he couldn't—Ellie, Chase, Gavin and Lucas, even his mother, his stepfather—all had a hand in making him the man he was today.

Before he could fully accept that after years of denial, he needed some answers.

"Nathan." Hannah had taken off her apron and left it behind the bar—he figured she was taking a break.

When she handed him a glass with two inches of amber liquid over ice, he took it warily, cocking his head.

"Jack on ice. That's your drink, right?" She twitched,

fingers working themselves nervously against the thighs of her jeans, as she seemed to have some internal debate before finally seating herself across the small square table.

"It's one of them," Nate finally acknowledged before taking a cautious sip. He shouldn't have cared that this woman knew that one small detail about him, but for some reason, he really did.

They sat in silence for a long moment, the heaviness of it broken only by the clink of glass behind the bar. Nate shifted uncomfortably in his chair.

He wasn't used to so many of the sensations he'd been feeling this weekend. He was used to be in command, which meant that finding himself at a loss for words was doubly frustrating.

"You said you left Tom." Finally, he let a thought spill out of his mouth.

Hannah drew in a shaky breath.

Nate noticed that her hand kept sliding down to pat at the right front pocket of her jeans—the place she'd always kept her pack of cigarettes. He wondered if she'd quit.

He wondered why he cared.

She drummed her fingers on the tabletop, then surprised Nate by gesturing to his glass. "May I?"

"Sure." Nate slid the glass of whiskey across the table to Hannah, who lifted it, inhaled the heady fumes, then took a big gulp.

"Better." She huffed out a breath, staring down at the table before finally looking Nate in the eye. As he'd always been, he was startled by how similar his own eyes were to hers—like looking in a mirror.

"Yes, I left Tom." She took another, smaller sip of the whiskey before sliding the glass back across the table to Nate. "I suppose you want to know why."

"That's one way of putting it." Nate snorted out a

sarcastic laugh. When Hannah regarded him quizzically, he shook his head. "The question is more... why now?"

"Ah." Hannah bit her lip, then twined her fingers on the table in front of her. "Why now, and not back then, you mean?"

"Bingo." Rage surged anew as he watched the woman who was supposed to be his mother ponder the question. Jesus, didn't she understand, even now, what it would have meant to him as a kid if she'd chosen her son over her husband, just once?

"I know that I can't ever make it right." Swallowing thickly, Hannah blinked in the dim light. "And I certainly don't expect you to understand."

"Try me."

"Sometimes in life you're lucky enough to meet someone special. The one, I guess you could say."

"Don't, do *not* tell me you thought Tom was *the one*." Nate slammed a fist down on the table, making the ice cubes in his drink rattle. "That's bullshit and you know it."

"I wasn't done." Hannah arched an eyebrow. "For me, that man was your father. On paper, we seemed completely wrong for one another. Nothing fit. And yet somehow everything did."

Ellie's face flashed through Nate's mind. He shoved it away as his heart started to ache.

"When he died, I was—well, I was sick. Mentally. I'm sure you remember." He did, oh he did. His loving mother had turned into a weeping zombie, unable to do more than cry or rock herself in a corner. "Then I met Tom. And for a while, he was the reason that I could be myself again."

Nate felt a sliver of pity for the woman his mother had once been—but only a sliver. She'd been his *mother*, damn it, and her job had been to protect him.

"I won't go into the psychology of abuse with you. I suspect you're long past the point of caring, anyway." Hannah smiled wryly, but there wasn't any merriment in the expression. "Just know that somehow, some way, my entire being, my sense of worth, became wrapped up in Tom. I couldn't function without him, not even to give you what you needed. He was certainly not the one for me, and I know it wasn't healthy. But that's the way it was. And I'm glad that you finally know."

Nate had been sitting stiffly throughout Hannah's entire explanation, and now, as she regarded him warily, he found himself sinking back in his chair. Curiously, cautiously, he poked at the feelings rioting around inside of him.

He wasn't ready to forgive her. He'd had one too many of Tom's fists in his face for that to ever happen. But now that he'd experienced what he had with Ellie, now that he knew firsthand the gut wrenching pain of losing her...

He had a bit more insight into how someone's world could fall apart in the blink of an eye.

Hannah looked at him hopefully as he shoved his chair back from the table. A momentary flicker of something inside of his chest had him reaching for her hand, but he snatched it away before he made contact.

"Thank you for telling me." Solemnly, he stood. What did this moment call for? A hug? A handshake? He couldn't bring himself to do either.

Hannah opened her mouth to speak, then seemed to think better of it, only to change her mind again.

"I wish you well, Nathan." There was a sad finality in her voice.

Nate thought he'd steeled himself against any feelings for her years ago, but her words were a thorn prickling at the delicate skin of his side. "I... I wish you well, too." He nodded before finally turning away.

He didn't know if he'd ever see her again, but he'd gotten what he'd come for, and that was enough.

Hannah called his name before he'd gotten two steps away, and he turned back, looking over his shoulder, his defences instantly rising. What now? Was she going to ask for money? Tell him this had all been a joke?

"Is it true that you're dating Eleanor Marshall?"

Nate almost laughed. Dating wasn't exactly the right word, since she was embarrassed to let anyone know that they were together.

But then again, it was none of Hannah's business, so he settled for a non-committal shrug. "Why?"

"I always liked her." Hannah smiled, and Nate felt all of the hurt that Ellie had dumped on him in the last few hours sucker punch him in the gut again. Yeah, he'd always liked her too. Too bad she didn't feel the same way.

"And if Eleanor Marshall is the one for you, then I can't have screwed you up too badly."

The metal key almost slipped from Ellie's hand as she jammed it into the lock of the motel room door.

Please be here, please be here. Pulse pounding, she slammed into the room that she and Nate had shared for the last few nights, then moaned with frustration when a quick glance around told her she was too late.

Everything of Nate's was gone. The only trace that he'd been here at all was the lingering scent of his cologne in the air, something musky that made her mouth water, a reminder of everything they'd done together in this very room.

"Shit." Ellie sank down onto the bed. She'd been banking on his being here in the room, on being able to apologize and explain, since he still wasn't answering his phone, and he hadn't returned any of her texts.

She was too late. What should she do now?

Do you love him?

Unbidden, Holly's voice echoed in her head. She'd never have imagined that Holly would be the one to give her solid love advice, but the way that her cousin had laid it out, well, there weren't many other ways to look at it.

Yes, she loved Nate. Maybe she always had. And in the face of those feelings, how could she care what she looked like to the rest of the world?

She'd pursue him until he told her to stop. After the way she'd acted in front of Chase, she at least owed him that.

Picking up the corded phone that sat on the bedside table, Ellie pressed zero for the front desk and at the same time started shoving things into her duffel bag. He couldn't have gotten very far.

And as for Harry's tale of Nate leaving with Kate? She owed it to Nate to hear his side.

"Yeah?" Ellie immediately recognized the voice that answered as Stephanie, the front desk clerk who'd batted her very underage eyelashes at Nate on Friday.

"Yes. This is Eleanor Marshall in room forty-two." She thought the girl might have snorted on the other end of the line; she didn't really care. "Can you please tell me if Nathan Archer has checked out, and if so, when?"

There was a moment of silence, followed by a long, drawn-out sigh and the clicking of nails on a keyboard, though Ellie would have bet her yearly salary that Stephanie already knew what she was painstakingly taking the time to look up.

"He checked out half an hour ago." The words were followed by a protracted sigh. "The room is paid in full."

"Great, thanks." Ellie slammed the phone back down in

its cradle, then turned to zip up her bag. Lugging it to the door of the room, she tossed the key back on the bed where the maid could find it later.

Half an hour. Assuming he was heading home, that meant she wasn't far behind him. She could get to him before any more damage was done.

Pulling her cell from her purse as she crossed the parking lot to her car, Ellie jabbed in a contact as she dumped her bag in the back. Climbing into the driver's seat, she looked down at her uncomfortable high heels before kicking them off. She'd drive barefoot.

The din on the other end of the line when the call was answered made her wince, but she hadn't expected anything else—her brother was at his own wedding, after all. And Meredith had told her to go ahead and chase after her man.

"I'm sorry, El." Chase sounded like he'd had a few drinks since she'd seen him last. "I'm just trying to look out for you. But I'm sorry I pissed you off."

"You can make it up to me right now." Ellie jammed her car keys into the ignition, then put Chase on speaker. "And I don't want to hear any grumbling about it. I need Nate's home address. And I need it now."

CHAPTER 24

He shouldn't have just left.

As Nate rode the elevator from the underground garage where security guards watched over the handful of expensive vehicles he owned, he scowled, knowing that it had been a dick move to leave without telling Ellie, never mind how much she'd hurt him.

After talking to Hannah, he'd needed some space. Some time to think. He'd call Ellie in the morning, even though just thinking her name had his fingers itching to trace themselves over her skin.

Rather than carrying him straight to his penthouse, the elevator slowed and smoothly stopped on the lobby floor. Nate felt his hackles rise, and then again when the sleek metal doors opened to reveal a cluster of people clutching tablets and cameras, some of which started going off in his face the second that the elevator doors opened.

"Samuel, what the hell is going on?" Slapping a hand against the side of the elevator door to stop it from closing again, Nate stuck his head out of the elevator and glared at his bellman.

The elderly man in the smart maroon uniform looked as bewildered as Nate felt, shaking his head and holding out his hands. "I don't know, Mr. Archer. But they say they were invited and they won't leave." Samuel gestured helplessly, and Nate's stare followed the gesture.

And then there she was. Ellie was standing barefoot in his lobby, still wearing the silky bridesmaid dress, her hair still tangled from his fingers. His heart thudded in his chest, having her so close.

Looking at her, knowing that she was there for him?

Any remaining doubts he had that she was his *one* slowly started to melt away.

"Hi." Slowly, Ellie crossed the lobby, closing the space between them. She didn't touch him, her blue eyes full of uncertainty as she looked up at him where he stood, half in and half out of the elevator.

"Hi." For the second time in as many hours, Nate found himself at a loss for words—and this time, he knew that he really needed to find the right ones.

"I'll go first." Nate had no idea what he was going to say, but Ellie cut him off, rising on her toes to press her fingers to his lips.

"No. Let me." He arched an eyebrow, then nodded at her to continue.

"It kills me that you think I'm ashamed of you. I'm not. I never could be." Ellie let her hand slid from his lips down to tug gently on his tie before continuing. "Not wanting to tell anyone had nothing to do with you. It was me. I... keeping it a secret kept it just about sex. Or at least that's what I told myself. I couldn't bear the thought of being just another woman to you."

"You've *never* been just another woman." Unable to refrain from touching her any longer, Nate cupped his palm around the back of her neck, savoring the little sigh she gave as he did. "And I understand... well, I understand not telling anyone this weekend. *You* might not be ashamed of me, but I've never been your family's favorite person."

Hell, he'd never been his own family's favorite person. But after his talk with Hannah, he knew that he could start shedding the weight that had been hanging around his neck for most of his life.

"Don't." Ellie's voice cut through the air, a wickedly sharp blade. "Just don't. Where you come from isn't who you are, and I don't ever want to hear you say it again."

"Haven't you gotten bossy?" He smirked, but it was a cover for the hummingbird wings of hope that had taken flight in his chest. Where was she going with this?

"I've always been bossy." Ellie scowled, then gestured at the crowd of people clustered in the lobby, watching their every move. "But I haven't always stood up for what I wanted. That's changing right now."

Ellie stepped back from him; Nate watched her, puzzled. These people were paparazzi—he even recognized some of them. They liked to snap his picture and chronicle his love life in the gossip section of the Seattle paper, or in the brightly colored tabloids that lined the supermarket checkouts.

What the hell were they doing here now?

"You think I'm embarrassed to admit to anyone that I'm with you. And I was worried about other people seeing me as just another woman chasing Nathan Archer, the hotel tycoon." Lights began to flash as the reporters turned on their devices, recording Ellie's speech. And Nate felt that wild hope continue to grow inside of him.

Was this wild, wonderful woman really doing what he thought she might be?

"I called a few news outlets on my way home. Don't lecture me about talking on the phone while driving. I used speaker phone." She narrowed her eyes at him, and he stifled a chuckle. No, he wouldn't bring that up later, but they'd be having a chat about how fast she must have driven. Maybe even a lesson to prove the point.

That is, if this was going where he thought it might be going.

"I knew that I could come here and tell you how I felt, and you'd understand." Ellie swallowed audibly, looking up at him, searching his face with her eyes. "But I wanted to do something bigger. Something that would prove to you that I really mean it."

Tentatively, she reached out, reaching for his hand. He gave it to her, lacing his fingers through hers, savoring the feel of her pulse pounding against his.

"That's why I called these reporters here tonight." Ellie turned away from the crowd, and when she met his gaze he felt his heart skip a beat. "I'm standing here to say in the most public way possible that... that I love you, Nate Archer. I think I always have. And I don't care who knows."

The gesture hit him like a blow to the solar plexus, even as the reporters crowded inward, firing questions about their relationship and snapping pictures. He couldn't have cared less what they were doing—his attention was entirely consumed with Ellie.

"This is going to be splashed all over the papers by morning." He tilted his head to the side, tugging her gently in his direction. When her soft warmth collided against him, he couldn't hold back his moan of satisfaction.

This was where this woman belonged—right here, with him.

"Let it splash." Ellie smiled up at him, her expression quizzical. "Though I did just bare my soul in front of witnesses. You could give a girl a break and maybe reciprocate."

"Hmm. That sounds like a reward." Without warning, Nate slid his arms beneath Ellie and hoisted her off of her feet. She squeaked as he cradled her against his chest and retreated to the elevator. "And I'm thinking you have several punishments to get through before we get to the reward."

Against him, Ellie shivered, then without warning, sank her teeth into the muscle of his pec, right above his nipple piercing. He hissed, then smirked down at her, expression full of wicked intent.

"That first night, I told you that if you walked through that door, there was no turning back." Dipping his head as the elevator doors slowly closed, he brushed his lips ever so softly over her own. "Now that you've said you love me? I don't think you know what you've gotten yourself into."

"Nate!" Impatient and clearly irritated at not getting the response she was searching for, Ellie slapped a hand against his chest. "Don't tease me."

"I intend to do far more than tease you." He moved the hand cradled behind her knees to the sweet gap between her thighs, and when she gasped he took advantage of the moment and kissed her soundly, his tongue dipping between her lips to claim.

"Do tell." Ellie was breathless when he pulled back, her skin flushed. Having reached the top of the building, the elevator doors swished open to reveal the entryway to his penthouse. He carried her in, right across the threshold, and nothing had ever felt so right.

"Teasing is just the beginning of it." Backing her against a wall, he let her slide down his body, groaning at the sweet heat of her body working against his. He punctuated every movement with a kiss, until they were both flushed and panting, and she was whispering his name.

Fisting a hand in her hair, Nate tilted her head so that she looked right up at him. So that she saw him, the real him, the way that he saw her.

The way that he always had.

"For the woman I love? Teasing is just the start." Emotion swamped him as pulled her even more tightly against him. Never again... never again was he letting her go.

"For the woman I love? She gets it all."

ABOUT CATHRYN FOX

About Cathryn Fox

New York Times and *USA today* Bestselling author, Cathryn is a wife, mom, sister, daughter, and friend. She loves dogs, sunny weather, anything chocolate (she never says no to a brownie) pizza and red wine. She has two teenagers who keep her busy with their never ending activities, and a husband who is convinced he can turn her into a mixed martial arts fan. Cathryn can never find balance in her life, is always trying to find time to go to the gym, can never keep up with emails, Facebook or Twitter and tries to write page-turning books that her readers will love.

Connect with Cathryn:
Newsletter
https://app.mailerlite.com/webforms/landing/c1f8n1
Twitter: https://twitter.com/writercatfox
Facebook:
https://www.facebook.com/AuthorCathrynFox?ref=hl

Blog: http://cathrynfox.com/blog/
Goodreads:
https://www.goodreads.com/author/show/91799.Cathryn_Fox

Pinterest http://www.pinterest.com/catkalen/

ALSO BY LAUREN HAWKEYE

Harlequin:

Wet (Spice Briefs)

Take Me Down (Spice Briefs)

Tie Me Up (Spice Briefs)

Lead Me On (Spice Briefs)

Let Me In (Spice Briefs)

Taking the Heat (Spice Briefs)

Vampire Island (Darkest Desire of the Vampire) (Nocturne)

The Darkling's Surrender (Nocturne Bites)

The Darkling's Desire (Nocturne Bites)

Seduced by the Darkling (Nocturne Bites)

Some Like It Wicked (Nocturne Bites)

Awaken to Pleasure (Nocturne Bites)

Playing Dirty (Dare)

Crossing Lines (Dare) *(coming soon)*

Sweet Temptation (Dare) *(coming soon)*

James Patterson BookShots:

Christmas Sanctuary

Entangled:

Claiming the Enemy (Brazen)

Kiss of the Irish (Brazen)

Uninhibited (Scorched)

Spring Fling

Other Titles:

Love Me for Me

Love Me If You Dare

One Night with the Billionaire

A Bride for a Billionaire

The Island of Eden

Unspoken

Untouched

The Chase

The Billionaire's Dare

Mr. Hot Stuff

Three Little Words

www.ingramcontent.com/pod-product-compliance
Lightning Source LLC
Chambersburg PA
CBHW051641180726
48284CB00006B/1817